***"What did you think you were doing just now?"* Mike asked.**

"Helping to improve your relationship with your daughter."

"That's not your job."

Brenna smirked at him. "I wouldn't even consider it my job if you were doing yours."

The blatant criticism was too much. When he couldn't think of a comeback, he said, "This is so not your business, lady!"

A snort burst from her mouth or her nose, or somewhere, and Mike knew he'd gone too far. But so had she.

"Lady?" Coming from her lips, the word sounded like the worst sort of insult. "Did you just call me *lady?* The calendar says we're in the twenty-first century, Mike."

He rubbed his face. He wasn't a chauvinist. Never had been. "Listen, check us out all you want. The bottom line is I don't want my daughter in your house or anyone else's without my knowledge. I hope I'm making myself clear."

"Crystal." Brenna managed a smile and a wave at Carrie in the truck. When Brenna turned back to Mike, she made sure her features displayed the seriousness of her intent.

Dear Reader,

We hear a lot today about soldiers coming home from battle zones. Joblessness, uncertainty and post-traumatic stress syndrome have become our working vocabulary to understand the men and women we are so indebted to.

In *A Soldier's Promise*, I have isolated the story of one such brave man who returned home only to find the life he'd counted on no longer existed. But he forged ahead because of a promise he'd made to his dying wife and, with the help of friends, and one very special teacher, he learned that life isn't over until you give up.

I hope you'll enjoy the story of Mike and Brenna, one a soldier, one a teacher, both American heroes.

Cynthia Thomason

HARLEQUIN HEARTWARMING

Cynthia Thomason

A Soldier's Promise

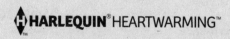

Recycling programs
for this product may
not exist in your area.

ISBN-13: 978-0-373-36678-1

A SOLDIER'S PROMISE

Copyright © 2014 by Cynthia Thomason

Printed in U.S.A.

www.Harlequin.com

CYNTHIA THOMASON

inherited her love of writing from her ancestors. Her father and grandmother both loved to write, and she aspired to continue the legacy. Cynthia studied English and journalism in college, and after a career as a high school English teacher, she began writing novels. She discovered ideas for stories while searching through antique stores and flea markets and as an auctioneer and estate buyer. Cynthia says every cast-off item from someone's life can ignite the idea for a plot. She writes about small towns, big hearts and happy endings that are earned and not taken for granted. And as far as the legacy is concerned, just ask her son, the magazine journalist, if he believes.

Books by Cynthia Thomason

HARLEQUIN HEARTWARMING

BLUE RIDGE AUTUMN
MARRIAGE FOR KEEPS
DILEMMA AT BAYBERRY COVE

HARLEQUIN SPECIAL EDITION

2172–HIS MOST IMPORTANT WIN

HARLEQUIN SUPERROMANCE

1120–THE MEN OF THORNE ISLAND
1268–YOUR HOUSE OR MINE?
1312–AN UNLIKELY MATCH
1345–AN UNLIKELY FATHER
1393–AN UNLIKELY FAMILY
1464–DEAL ME IN
1483–RETURN OF THE WILD SON

Having been a teacher, I know what a difficult, rewarding and inspiring job it can be. This book is dedicated to the great teachers I've worked with over the years, among them Darby, Tila, Linda, Bill and Rosemary. There are many students who owe their success to your guidance.

CHAPTER ONE

BRENNA SULLIVAN SCRATCHED around the bottom of her large purse until she found the raggedy fan she'd been given as a wedding favor three years ago. She fanned her face vigorously while trying to squeeze under the shade of a scraggly oak tree in front of her car. Her fellow staff member and best friend in Mount Union, Georgia, approached from across the shimmering parking lot, causing Brenna to check her watch for what seemed like the hundredth time.

"Have I been standing out here in the ninety-degree sun long enough for even Super Teacher Diana Montgomery to be leaving the building?" she asked herself. "No matter. Another few minutes and I'll be dead from heatstroke."

"What are you still doing here?" Diana asked when she reached Brenna's car. "It's Friday afternoon. The students left over an hour ago. I expected you to have already begun celebrating the end of a successful first week of school."

Brenna blew her bangs off her forehead with an impatient breath and leaned on the hood of her seven-year-old Mazda. "I wish I were."

Diana looked confused. "What are you waiting for?"

"A mechanic. I called Alvin's Garage forty-five minutes ago. And as usual, Alvin's 'We're on our way' is a gross exaggeration."

"What's wrong with your car?"

"Won't start."

Diana stared at the shiny silver sedan, which Brenna kept immaculate and in good running order. "Do you know why it won't start?"

"Do I look like a mechanic?"

"You look like a wilted redheaded sunflower. Maybe it's time to consider that mechanic a no-show. I'll give you a lift home."

"I can't leave," Brenna said. "I'll give the guy another few minutes. I have plans for tonight. I need my car."

Diana set her cumbersome briefcase, probably stuffed with papers to grade, on the pavement. She and Brenna both worked at Mount Union High School; Diana taught English and Brenna taught home ec. Just about everything in Brenna's classes was accomplished during school hours, leaving very little work to take home, which suited her just fine. She liked devoting her off-hours to her own pleasures.

"I'll just keep you company until the mechanic arrives," Diana said. "Both the men in my life will be occupied with football practice until at least six."

"Don't be silly. Go home and wait for your husband and son. Why should both of us melt out here?"

"Maybe this is your guy," Diana said as a blue pickup truck sped into the lot. A magnetic sign on the door indicated it had come from Alvin's. The driver jolted to a stop a few feet from Brenna's car.

"The cavalry has definitely arrived," Diana said. "I might as well stay until we know he can get your car started."

"Thanks."

"By the way, where are you going tonight?"

"The Riverview Tavern," Brenna said. "You're welcome to come…"

She never finished her invitation because

the driver of the truck stepped out and walked over to them. Brenna did a double take. She couldn't remember this man working at Alvin's. He was tall with a muscular build that was obvious even under his beige mechanic's uniform. What hair Brenna could see peeking out of a ball cap was dark and wavy. He wasn't smiling. Not surprising in this heat.

"I hope you're looking for me," Brenna said.

He pulled a work order out of a breast pocket embroidered with the name *Mike* and *Alvin's Garage* in blue letters. "I am if you're Brenna Sullivan."

"Yep. And what took you so…"

"This is your silver Mazda?"

Enough small talk apparently. "Yes, it is."

He stuffed the work order back in his pocket. "You said it wouldn't start?"

"That's right. I hope it's something minor and you don't have to have it towed."

"'Scuse me."

She stepped aside. He sat in the driver's seat and turned her key in the ignition. Nothing. Not even the clicks she had heard earlier.

Brenna cringed. She was thankful Diana hadn't left yet. She might need a ride after all.

Diana spoke in Brenna's ear. "Have you ever seen this guy before?"

"No." Even if this man were just an Alvin's employee, she would have remembered him. "Why do you ask?"

"I don't know. It's just interesting. He could be our first new man in town in a long time. Maybe he's single and you and he…"

Brenna frowned at her friend's blatantly coy grin. "Don't get any ideas. I'm not looking and you know it. And if I were, I wouldn't be scouring Alvin's Garage for a date."

The man got out of the car and opened the hood. He next opened the hood on his truck and finally removed some battery cables from a box in the cargo area.

"What are you doing?" she asked him.

"Charging your battery."

"Oh." She watched his practiced, abbreviated movements. He didn't waste time or effort. He appeared to know what he was doing.

Diana nudged her. "He's good-looking, don't you think?" she whispered.

"Stop it." But the comment did make her study his face again.

Though he remained basically expressionless, his features demanded her attention. Serious to a fault. Yet fine lines around his eyes and mouth indicated he'd done his share of smiling, or maybe frowning. And his eyes. Now that she really looked, she found herself staring into them. Very dark, intense. And much too thoughtful for a guy who spent his time staring at spark plugs. Or did cars even have spark plugs these days? Brenna recalled reading that everything in cars was digital now.

After a few minutes, he disconnected the cables, got back in her car, fiddled around with knobs on the dashboard and started the engine. The Mazda purred like the sleek kitten it was. He got out, took the work order from his pocket again and wrote some numbers down.

"That'll be thirty-five dollars," he said.

"What did you do?" she asked. "I didn't see you fix anything."

"Nothing needed fixing." He covered his mouth with his hand.

Brenna stared at Diana. She mouthed the words *I think he's laughing at me.*

Diana shrugged. "Appears so."

"What's so funny—" she pointed to his pocket embroidery "—Mike?"

"Women, I guess."

"What? That's just demeaning…."

He readjusted the seriousness to his face. "The problem with your car was what we call a parasitic drain."

"And what exactly would I call it?" Brenna asked.

"Probably a dead battery."

"And why did it die?"

"It was raining this morning. Did you have your lights on?"

"Of course. It's the law. Why do you…" She realized where he was going with the discussion. "I must've left them on when I got to school," she admitted.

"Not only that, you left your satellite radio running all day. Between the two the battery was drained."

Diana snickered. Brenna ignored her.

"I know I should have turned the lights off," she said. "But I wasn't aware that the radio could drain the battery."

"It wouldn't by itself." He pushed his cap up, releasing strands of dark hair onto his forehead. "Did you ever read the owner's manual on this car? It would tell you stuff like that."

"Of course I did." She paused as he narrowed his eyes at her.

Diana grinned. "She read the part about how to operate the moonroof."

Brenna glared at her.

"Even though you only needed a jump, I have to bill you for a service call." His lips twitched as he handed her the bill. "A check will be fine. Alvin knows you."

That last part sounded like another dig, as if she was so inept she handed out thirty-five dollars on a daily basis. For heaven's sake. She wasn't the only woman who depended on a mechanic.

She scrounged through her purse a second time and pulled out her wallet. "I assume you'll take paper money," she said, handing him three tens and a five.

"Never had a problem with cash," he said, tucking the bills into his pocket. He nodded at both women. "I'll be going, then."

He started to get in his truck, but Diana stopped him. "Excuse me, Mike, but are you new to this part of Georgia?"

Brenna turned to give her friend another pointed stare.

"Been here a couple of months," he said, one foot in the truck.

"Oh. How do you like it?"

"Okay."

"Do you live in town?"

"About three miles out."

He got in the truck, but apparently Diana wasn't done grilling him. "Do you have family, Mike?" she asked.

He squinted into her face. Was he offended at the question?

"I don't mean to be nosy," Diana said.

Brenna huffed. *Yeah, right.*

"We're a friendly town," Diana added. "Perhaps your wife would like to join us girls some afternoon…"

"I'm not married."

Brenna had had enough, and she was certain the mechanic had, too. "I'm sure this man has to get back to the garage, Diana," Brenna said.

"I do," he said. And as quickly as he'd come into the lot, he left it.

"What was all that?" Brenna said. "You made that man uncomfortable. I can't imagine that he enjoys being treated like Mount Union's catch of the day."

"Well, he could be a catch…for you."

"I already told you—don't get any ideas."

"You didn't find him the least bit attractive?"

"I didn't find him anything but rude and condescending." That wasn't exactly true. Brenna usually drew conclusions about every man she met, and she'd done so with this guy. Mike had a sort of earthy appeal that some women might find attractive. But earthy appeal wasn't at the top of Brenna's priorities. Not even close. "Parasitic drain," she muttered.

"Well, I think he's very good-looking," Diana said. "He's rugged and well built. And I could practically smell the woodsmoke coming from those eyes of his."

So Diana had noticed that feature, too. Still, Brenna wasn't going to get into this discussion. "Shouldn't you go home and fix supper or something?"

Diana smiled. "Don't be mad at me, Bren. I just want you to be as happy as I am."

Brenna stared at the angelic face that was so typical of Diana. "How do you know I'm not? What makes you happy isn't the same for all women."

Diana considered the statement. "Point taken."

"You go home to your son and your husband, and I'll put on my cowgirl boots and kick up my heels at the Riverview. I'll bet we both go to sleep happy."

"Maybe so. But one person won't be so happy tonight."

"Who's that?"

"Mike. He didn't get a tip and he didn't get your phone number."

"You're impossible," Brenna said. "He obviously didn't want my phone number, and he didn't deserve a tip."

WHEN SHE PULLED into her driveway, Brenna was thinking about which pair of jeans she'd wear out that night. She parked her car and walked to the front porch of the 1930s-era three-bedroom Craftsman-style cottage she'd bought four years ago and renovated with light earth-toned paint and sage-green trim. Her friends called the place "darling" and "charming." Brenna was just grateful every day that she called it home.

She'd only taken a few steps along the brick walkway leading to her front door when she noticed a girl sitting on her wicker love seat. Brenna stopped, stared at the girl and realized she was familiar.

The girl raised her hand. "Hi, Miss Sullivan."

Oh, no. The girl called her *Miss Sullivan.* Had to be a student. "Ah…hello."

"Do you know who I am?"

Brenna searched the crannies of a mind that had already mutated from school to weekend mode. "I think you're in one of my classes. Is that right?"

"Yeah. I'm in your third-period cooking class. My name's Carrie Langston."

Brenna remembered calling the name off her roster, but she hadn't yet had time to put a face to each student's name. "Sure," she said. "Carrie." She walked the rest of the way to the porch. "What are you doing here, Carrie? How do you know where I live?"

"It wasn't hard to find out. I just said I'll bet you have a nice house, and one of the other kids in class told me you lived here on the river." She looked at the colorful stained-glass panel centered in Brenna's front door. "I was right. This is a cool place."

Mount Union was a small town. Brenna

figured lots of her students knew where she lived. But none of them had ever come calling before. Brenna made a point to avoid sending that kind of welcoming attitude. To keep her school life separate from her personal one, she didn't go to games or chat with students in the hallways about their problems. There were counselors for that job—and teachers like Diana Montgomery. If her past had taught Brenna one thing, it was that she should maintain a noninvolvement policy.

"I don't know why you're here, Carrie, but if you came to talk to me about school, you could have waited until Monday…"

The girl's voice dropped to a chastised tone. "I didn't come to talk about school."

"Oh." That was even worse. "I can't imagine anything else that couldn't wait. This is the weekend, and…"

"I'm sorry, Miss Sullivan. I just needed someplace to go, and, well, you seem so nice in class."

Intrigued in spite of herself, Brenna leaned against a porch column. "Why do you need a place to go? What's wrong with your home?"

"It's not nice like this is."

Since Brenna hadn't seen this girl before

this year, she assumed she was new to the school system. "So where *do* you live exactly?"

"Outside of town."

"How far outside?" Brenna wondered if she would have to drive the girl home. If so, there was a liability issue with having a student in her car. And she'd be late meeting her friends. Precisely why she didn't get involved.

"I live beyond that old mill, the one on White Deer Trail. Do you know where it is?"

Brenna did know. Diana and her family lived close to that location. So did other families who preferred the rustic, remote neighborhood. But Brenna hadn't known another house existed beyond the long-defunct gristmill.

"Why aren't you there now?" she asked. "Do you need a ride? I'm sure you missed the bus."

"I did, but I can call someone. I thought I could just hang out here for a while."

"That's not really such a good idea." In desperation Brenna quoted school board policy. "We have a strict nonfraternization policy here. The school board frowns upon high school students visiting teachers' homes."

The girl hung her head. Long, dark waves of hair hid her face, but Brenna thought she heard a sniffle. Oh, dear. What would she do if this girl suddenly burst into tears? What was she so upset about? She was obviously clean and well cared for, like just about all the kids in Mount Union. Her clothes were stylish. She wasn't anything like the students Brenna had had her first two years of teaching.

Carrie scrubbed her face with both hands and looked up. She seemed in control. "It was dumb of me to come here. I was just hoping you'd let me stay awhile. But I can go somewhere else."

"Where?"

"Someplace. You don't have to worry about me."

Brenna sat on the wicker chair next to the love seat. Something was going on with this girl, something Brenna might not be equipped to deal with. Remembering the hard-learned instincts to remain distant— the ones that had stayed with her since her first teaching position—she put her hand on the girl's arm. Even that slight bit of familiarity made Brenna uncomfortable.

"What aren't you telling me, Carrie?" She studied the girl's face, her bare arms, looking for bruises and hoping she wouldn't see any. All she saw was clear, pale skin. Yet something wasn't right.

"Do you have problems at home?" Brenna asked.

The girl didn't say anything. She just twisted her fingers in her lap.

"Carrie? Do your parents know where you are?"

"It's just my dad, and I don't know. Probably not."

"Give me his phone number. I'm going to call him."

"No!" She brushed bangs from her forehead, revealing red eyes. "I said I'd go. You don't have to take care of me. I get it."

"I'm not telling you what to do," Brenna said. "But you can't stay here. I've got plans tonight."

Why did that suddenly sound shallow?

"Sure, I understand," Carrie said. "I guess I was wrong. I thought you'd be easy to talk to."

Me? I seem easy to talk to?

Carrie continued, "I don't have any friends

here. Where I used to live, one of my teachers talked to me a lot. She even came to my mother's…"

"Your mother's what?"

"Never mind. It's not important. I shouldn't have come here. I'll go."

"I don't mean to sound short with you," Brenna said, "but you should be home. And you sound like a girl who just needs to make some friends her own age. There are lots of ways to make friends. On Monday we can discuss it. You can join a club…or something."

"Sure, I'll do that." Carrie stood and walked slowly to the steps leading from the porch. With each footfall, Brenna felt the sting of her conscience. But she didn't want to be this kind of teacher again, the Diana kind. She'd tried it once and still suffered from her decisions. Besides, Diana was used to Mount Union kids being in her house 24/7. She had a son in high school and a husband who worked at the school. And she hadn't been through what Brenna had been through at her last job. Brenna had only herself, and she just couldn't risk getting involved like that again.

Why hadn't Carrie gone to Diana's? Brenna

watched her walking away and sighed deeply. When Carrie reached the sidewalk, Brenna called to her. She almost didn't recognize her own voice. "Are you hungry?"

Carrie turned. "A little."

Brenna managed a quick mental survey of her refrigerator. "I could probably rustle up some mac and cheese and a couple hot dogs."

"I could eat that."

"Okay, then. Come on back." Brenna stood. "We can talk a bit if you want. And then you'll go home, okay?"

"Sure. Okay."

Brenna unlocked her door. "I'll get out of my teacher clothes and fix us that mac and cheese."

She changed into worn cutoffs and a T-shirt and gathered her humidity-frizzed red curls into a ponytail. So much for getting to the Riverview on time.

During dinner preparations she and Carrie talked about Mount Union High School. Brenna gave her some tips on what kids in town did, where the closest movie theater was, things she thought would interest a sophomore. She also told Carrie about the Cultural Arts Center that was being planned for the community. Brenna was chairing the committee for the center and hoped it would be beneficial in a town that offered little in the way of teen activities.

"Besides the center being a meeting place for teens, we're going to offer special classes," Brenna said. "Drama, music, other courses that have been eliminated due to budget cuts."

"Classes?" the girl asked. "Over and above having classes in school?"

Okay, maybe that sounded lame, but Brenna knew several students who would take advantage of enrichment courses. "There will be activities, too," she explained to Carrie. "Movies, dances, games, a whole range of choices."

Carrie didn't comment on the center, but halfway through the cheesy casserole, Brenna saw the girl smile for the first time.

"This is really good," the girl said. "Thanks for fixing it."

"You're welcome. We make this in class, you know. About midway through the semester."

"That'll be cool."

Brenna carried her plate to the sink and looked over her backyard. The sun was setting, turning the trees on the other side of the river to gold. "It's late," she said. "Maybe you'd better call your father and tell him to pick you up."

"He's not worried about me."

"Well, regardless, you can't walk home in the dark. It's a long way to the mill."

"I'll be okay. I take care of myself."

Brenna took her seat on the other side of the table and stared at Carrie for a moment. The girl looked down and forked her leftover noodles around the plate. "Is there something you'd like to tell me, Carrie?" Brenna asked, hoping the girl wasn't harboring a big secret, the kind that had led to heartbreaking decisions once before. She swallowed, knowing she could have opened the door to something she didn't really want to hear. "Is everything all right at home?"

Brenna held her breath. *Please just let this be a case of a new kid in town who's experiencing some loneliness.*

Carrie mumbled into her lap. "It's that obvious?"

Oh, boy. "Is someone treating you badly?" Brenna asked.

Carrie swallowed hard. She didn't answer the question.

Brenna leaned over the table but resisted the instinct to place her hand over the girl's. "Has someone hurt you, Carrie?"

Still no answer. Carrie didn't look up.

"Because if so, there are people who can help. But you need to tell someone…"

She never finished giving advice because movement in front of her house caught her eye. Through her open door she saw a police cruiser pull to the curb. Carrie gasped and stood up.

"This is about you, isn't it?" Brenna said.

"Maybe. I don't know. I didn't mean to be any trouble. I'll just go out the back…"

"No, you won't. You're coming with me."

Like a prisoner being led to the gallows, Carrie walked ahead of Brenna to the living room. She sat in a chair out of sight of the front door. Brenna opened the screen to police officers she knew well. "Hi, Boone, Lila. What's going on?"

"We've had a missing-kid report, Bren," Boone said. "She's one of your students and we're following every lead." He took out a photo and showed it to Brenna. "This is the girl."

A sweet face surrounded by a tumble of black curls smiled at Brenna from a typical school photo.

"Her name's Carolyn Langston," Lila Menendez said. "Her father's about ready to tear the town apart."

Brenna opened the door wider. "Come on in."

The officers walked to the middle of the room and stared at Carrie. "You're her, all right," Boone said. He pressed a button on a device on his shoulder. "Located the girl. She's at…" He waited for Brenna to give him her exact address and repeated it.

"How'd she end up here, Brenna?" he asked.

She briefly explained how she'd found Carrie on her porch. "Can we talk outside?" she asked the officer.

"Sure." Boone spoke to his partner. "Lila, you stay here with the kid. Make sure she doesn't go anywhere."

The young police officer crouched beside Carrie. In a soft voice she said, "Are you okay, honey?"

Carrie nodded and Brenna led Boone to the end of the porch, where their voices wouldn't carry to the interior of the house. "I think this kid's in trouble," Brenna said. "I'm suspecting some kind of abuse."

"Did you see any injuries?"

"No, but she's very unhappy. She doesn't want to go home."

"Well, Brenna, that describes a bunch of teenagers. Even me a few years ago."

"That may be, but this girl's reaching out for help. I think you need to notify someone in authority."

"I'll talk to the chief about it. But right now I've just got to return this kid to her father. He's probably on his way over here to pick her up. He seemed plenty worried to me."

Yeah, and I wonder why. Was the father afraid the kid would tell on him? "You won't let her go if you think something's not right, will you, Boone?"

"I'll check it out, Brenna." He pointed to the street, where a blue pickup was screeching to a halt behind the cruiser. "There's the dad now. I'll explain things to him, tell him the kid came here of her own accord. We don't want him holding you responsible."

"I don't care about that," Brenna said. "I'm just concerned about Carrie."

The driver's door swung open and a man in a beige jumpsuit stepped to the asphalt.

"Hey, I know that guy," Brenna said. She stared at the man of few words, Mike the mechanic, as he strode purposely up the walk to her door.

CHAPTER TWO

"WHERE'S MY DAUGHTER?" The words shot from Mike's mouth like blasts from a pistol. He headed straight for the front porch, looking neither right nor left.

Boone stepped in front of him and put his hand on Mike's chest. "Hold on a minute, buddy. Let's all calm down."

Mike evaded the officer with a defiant maneuver. "Calm down? Are you kidding? Is Carrie in this house or not?"

"Yes, she's in there. And she's fine."

He released a pent-up breath, and his shoulders relaxed slightly. "Okay." Then he glanced around, seeming to take in the darkness that had settled over Brenna's shrubs, the unfamiliarity of his surroundings and, finally, Brenna. "I know you," he said. "You're the silver Mazda."

She crossed her arms over her chest. "Actually, the silver Mazda is my car. *I'm* your daughter's home ec teacher."

Confusion battled with panic in Mike's face. "What's Carrie doing here? Did you bring her?"

"Brenna had nothing to do with Carrie showing up at her house," Boone said. "That was your daughter's decision. Brenna has just been talking to her. She didn't know until we got here that a missing-child report had been filed."

Mike glared at her. "And it didn't occur to you to call me?"

Struggling to control her temper, Brenna said, "First of all, I don't even really know you. Second of all, a teenage girl is capable of calling her parents herself—if she feels confident doing so."

His mouth opened and then closed again. Apparently he hadn't come up with a way to respond to the implied criticism. "All right," he said after a moment. "I'll just get my daughter and leave."

Brenna kept her features blank, though inside she was seething.

Mike took another step toward the porch. "I'll talk to her about what happened. She won't bother you again."

"That's not the point."

Ignoring her, he marched up the steps to her door. His work boots sounded heavy on the polished wood planks of her porch floor. It was as if this man had come to claim property. She glared at Boone and gave him a do-something look. Mike and Boone were about the same age with similar builds. Boone was a good cop who wouldn't be intimidated by Mike's aggressive behavior. And besides, Brenna had always suspected that Boone had a thing for her, and she knew he would intercede because she'd asked him to.

Boone grabbed Mike's elbow. "Not so fast. I'd like to talk to you before you go in to get your daughter."

Mike turned sharply. "What do you mean?"

He nodded to the front lawn. "Come on down here so we can speak privately. I'd like to clear up a few things in this investigation."

"What things? And how did this suddenly become an *investigation?*"

Though obviously not pleased with the delay, Mike did follow Boone's orders. The two men ended up under Brenna's ornamental cherry tree. Boone spoke in a calming manner but gestured dramatically with his hands.

At first Mike's features remained stoic.

Then his eyes widened. His jaw dropped. His expression took on the veiled semblance of disbelief. His mouth formed the words *no* and *never*.

Boone eventually put his hand on Mike's upper arm. The two had seemed to reach an accord or perhaps a stalemate. Brenna could only hope that Boone had made his point clearly and with the full power of his badge.

They both came back to the porch. "I should tell you that I'm going to leave this case open for a while," Boone said. "Just until things settle down."

Mike turned around to stare at him but said nothing.

"We take our kids' safety seriously in Mount Union. As a father, you can understand that," Boone added.

Mike went to the screened door. "Carrie, come on out now. It's okay. We're going home."

Carrie walked onto the porch. Lila was with her and had her hand on Carrie's shoulder. When she saw her father, Carrie hooked her thumb in the waistband of her jeans and gave him a little wave. "Hi, Dad."

He shook his head once and looked down at her. "Are you all right?"

"Sure. I'm sorry if I worried you. I just thought I could talk to Miss Sullivan for a while. I didn't realize how late it was getting or that you'd be wondering where I was...."

"You didn't think I'd be wondering?" Mike looked at Brenna. The anger in his eyes had dimmed just enough so she felt Boone had accomplished something with his talk.

"We'll discuss this when we get home," he said to his daughter. He started down the sidewalk with Carrie by his side. As he passed Brenna and Boone, he said, "Thanks for your help. My daughter and I will be fine."

Brenna watched him open the passenger door for Carrie. The girl looked back once and then climbed inside. Through the window, Brenna saw Carrie's shoulders slump. She stared into her lap and seemed so very small in the large truck cab. Mike started around to the other side of the vehicle.

"Mr. Langston," Brenna called out.

He stopped under a streetlight and looked back.

She hurried down the walkway to meet him in front of his truck.

"What is it, Miss Sullivan? I thought we were done here."

"I know," she said, looking into those seriously dark eyes again. Only now they seemed even more mysterious in the shadows of night. What was going on behind those eyes? She stammered, something she hadn't done since she was ten years old, "I…ah…I like your daughter, Mr. Langston. She's a sweet kid. And I'm sorry for any distress this situation caused you."

His brow furrowed. "I'll get over it."

"Yes, I'm sure you will. Carrie and I had a nice talk. I think she might be a bit lonely, being new to the area and all. I don't think she meant to worry you. She was just reaching out…"

Mike leaned on his truck hood and gave Brenna a top-to-bottom scrutiny. "Miss Sullivan, I'm sure your intentions were good, but a fourteen-year-old girl doesn't need to be out on her own at night. If she wants to reach out, she can darn well tell me she's doing it before she goes off to the house of someone I don't even know."

Brenna bit her bottom lip as her temper flared once more, heating her face. She couldn't argue that a child shouldn't be going places without telling the parent, but the last time she looked at her clock, it had said 8:30 p.m. Hardly a dangerous hour for people to be out, especially in Mount Union, Georgia. But maybe Mike didn't realize how safe his new town was.

"I think we know each other better now, Mr. Langston," she said. "And I'm starting to know Carrie. I'm going to make myself available to her whenever she needs to talk."

Brenna shuddered. Had she actually stated outright that she intended to become involved with a student?

No doubt about it. She had.

"I'll be checking in with her," Brenna added. "Just so Carrie knows she has someone older to talk to, a woman. It can't be easy living with a father only."

"Nothing's easy about this, Miss Sullivan." Mike scrubbed his hand down his face. He suddenly looked tired. "You check to your heart's content, but I don't want my daughter in your house or anyone else's without my knowledge. I hope I'm making myself clear."

"Crystal." Brenna managed a smile and a wave at Carrie in the truck. When she turned back to Mike, she made sure her features displayed the seriousness of her intent. "You have a good night now," she said.

He strode around to the driver's side and got behind the wheel. When he turned the ignition, Brenna felt the rumble of his truck engine through the soles of her sandals. Carrie stared out the window while the truck pulled away. Brenna stepped onto the curb and watched them until the vehicle had rounded a curve in the road and the taillights had disappeared.

THEY HAD ALMOST reached the town boundaries when Mike spotted the Golden Arches ahead. He turned to his daughter and spoke the first words he'd uttered since they'd gotten into the truck. "You want something from the drive-through?"

"No. I ate at Miss Sullivan's."

He continued past the McDonald's. "You like her, this teacher?"

"She's okay. She seemed real nice in class. Made it sound like we'd have fun trying different things this semester. I thought she might be like Mrs. Grant, my history teacher at home."

Mike gripped the steering wheel. He wished

Carrie would start thinking of Georgia as "home." But no, she kept referring to the small California town near Camp Pendleton that way. Mike couldn't blame her. After thirteen years in the military, he was having a hard time adjusting to civilian life in quiet, tradition-bound Mount Union. But they both had to try. Mike didn't want to go back, and in his heart, he believed a break with the old life was best for his daughter, too.

"You know why I was so upset about what you did, don't you?" he asked.

"Not really. I mean jeez, Dad, this town must be, like, the safest place in the universe."

Was she kidding? Did all kids assume they were invincible? "I'm figuring you had your cell phone with you."

"I always have it."

"Then why didn't you call?"

"Come on, Dad. I'll be fifteen in a couple of weeks. I shouldn't have to call you every time I decide to take a walk."

"Sorry, but yes, you should. I want to know where you are all the time. It's my job to know." That sounded harsh. "I mean, it's my responsibility."

"I would have called eventually, when I

needed a ride. I didn't call right away because I knew you'd come get me immediately." She twisted her hands in her lap. "I thought I might get lucky and you'd work late. Sometimes you do."

She felt *lucky* when he worked late? He could only shake his head. For his part, he always worried about Carrie when he was at the garage late. "My work hours have no bearing on what happened tonight," he said, getting back on topic. "I need to know about you all the time."

She gave him a look that had to have been followed by an eye roll. Thank goodness he couldn't see her expression in the dark truck cab.

"What you need, Dad, is to back off once in a while," she muttered.

"What's that?"

"Never mind."

"You are not old enough to be out on your own. And we haven't lived here very long. It's all new. So when you're not in school, I have to know exactly where you are."

"Yeah, like I'm ever anywhere but that stupid cabin."

That stupid cabin was Mike's attempt to

start over. It was small but cozy, and he considered it perfect for the two of them. "We go places," he said. "We're not always in the cabin."

"Places little kids go with their dads."

He thought back over the past three months. He'd taken Carrie fishing and boating. They'd gone into Savannah for an overnight and seen the sights. They had a trip planned for Atlanta soon, where they'd visit the capitol building and see historic homes. Okay, maybe he hadn't exactly asked his daughter what she'd like to do, but Mike had thought he was managing pretty well.

He drove silently until he reached the narrow path to his grandmother's cabin. The lane was rutted and dark. He still had numerous holes to fill in with new gravel; he'd get to it soon. He'd eventually make all the improvements on his list. It was the least he could do to thank his grandmother for suggesting that he and Carrie move here, far from the painful memories.

He parked in front of their house, but didn't get out of the truck right away.

Carrie looked over at him. "What?"

"I just bought you that new smartphone,"

he said. "The one with all the gadgets you just had to have."

She took the phone from her pocket. "And I love it, and I said thank you."

"Yes, you did. You also promised to use it to stay in touch. You don't have any excuse for me not knowing where you are and what you're doing."

"Fine. I get it. It's either your rules for the cell phone or handcuffs. Those are my options."

So much drama. Even after being in a war zone for years, Mike didn't know how to handle basic family dynamics.

They got out of the truck. As Mike walked to the house, his mind buzzed with the changes he'd been facing recently. When had teenagers become complete cyber citizens? Every kid in town seemed to have a fancy phone or a tablet or some other techie instrument that kept them occupied in their homes and on the streets. Carrie had moved to Georgia with her own state-of-the-art laptop, which she kept fired up all day, every day. Getting her away from the computer was like coaxing an otter out of the river.

He'd given in to the new phone, but he'd

made a mental note to keep tabs on whom she was talking to.

And teachers? What the heck? Mike didn't remember having a teacher who looked even remotely like Miss Sullivan. He'd taken notice of her in the parking lot earlier and had liked what he saw. Not that he was looking. But a few minutes ago, despite his anxiety over Carrie, he'd gotten an even better view of the teacher. Her reddish hair, which had been bound in some type of bun thing at school, hung to her shoulder blades in a wavy ponytail, looking touchably soft in the streetlight.

He'd caught a scent of something nice and citrusy, too.

He put his key in the lock and opened the old plank door. *What's gotten into you, Mike Langston?* His wife hadn't been dead a full year yet and here he was thinking of his daughter's teacher as if he was starved for learning. Well, it had been a long time. A full year in Afghanistan without visiting home and then the loss.

Carrie followed him in the door. She wrinkled her nose. "It stinks in here."

He sniffed. "I don't smell anything. What does it smell like?"

"Like mold and dust because everything in here is a thousand years old."

"These are your great-grandmother's things. Of course they're old."

"Right," Carrie said, passing by him and heading to her room. "I'm going to check my email."

He had to quit thinking of his own needs. No sacrifice was too great when a man found himself trying to be a full-time father for the first time in his life and apparently messing up on a daily basis.

THAT EVENING MIKE had the same dream he'd suffered from night after night just after his wife had died. He was running along a nearly abandoned tarmac, trying to reach one lone plane. The whine of the jet's engines punished his ears. The passenger door closed. He was going to miss the flight so he ran harder, shouting for the pilot to stop. Sweat poured down his face and chest so that when he woke, panting and feeling his heart pounding against his ribs, he had to grab a towel and dry off.

He had the dream only occasionally these days, when he had a problem with Carrie or the familiar crushing guilt weighed heavily upon him. A chaplain had told him Lori's illness was God's will. The camp psychologist had told him it wasn't his fault. He hadn't believed either one of them. If he'd only known about it. If he'd been there for her…maybe things would have turned out differently.

He got up, pulled a pair of sweatpants over his boxers, went into the kitchen and filled a glass with water. Sometimes he smiled at his grandmother's choice of glassware. This one was an old jelly jar featuring Yogi Bear. Mike didn't smile tonight. He simply reached for the pill bottle, dropped one white tablet into his mouth and swallowed. First anxiety-busting drug he'd taken in four weeks. He was doing better. He'd commit himself to a hospital before he'd allow his system to become addicted to the things.

His hand over his chest, he sat at the table and took several deep breaths. "It's okay," he said aloud, careful to keep his voice low so he wouldn't awaken Carrie.

The men in charge of the army's elite rangers corps were good men. Dedicated professionals. They treated their special-force soldiers with respect. Still, what happened to Mike a year ago was unforgivable, the ultimate betrayal by both his commanding officers and his wife. The message from the general had come in the early-morning hours. Mike had still been at mess in the tent the army had erected outside of Kunduz. The instructions from the general had been simple and direct: *effective immediately, you are hereby relieved of duty to attend to a personal matter.*

The "personal matter" had been his wife's terminal illness. He'd made it home two days before she passed. He was able to say goodbye, make the promises she needed to hear and forgive her for her decision not to tell him about her health problems. But he hadn't forgiven her and maybe never would.

He still grappled every day with her reasons for not telling him she was sick. The army had known. His daughter had known. He hadn't until it was way too late. How can a wife not tell her husband she's dying just to avoid interrupting his life, his goals?

His breathing normal now, Mike stood, carried the glass to the sink and left the kitchen.

He had to be at work in a few hours, though not to advise how to keep his division vehicles running in the fight against terrorism, but to see why someone's 1998 Chevy or Honda or…whatever was stalling out. He could tell them why, though being a mechanic was not the job he'd always envisioned for himself. Not the position he could have achieved by taking advantage of G.I. college money. But Alvin's Garage was just another stall in his life right now, and fixing cars was a lot easier than fixing his life.

"WHAT ARE YOU DOING?" Diana asked when she saw Brenna thumbing through the attendance record. "Let's go to the cafeteria and get lunch."

"Yeah, I will," Brenna said. "Just a minute." She found what she was looking for and took a student punch card from the homeroom reports of absences for the day. "Great."

"Who are you looking up?"

Brenna hadn't talked to Diana since Friday afternoon. Diana didn't know that Carrie Langston had shown up on Brenna's doorstep. Or that she'd had words with the girl's father. She waved the card in Diana's general direction. "One of my third-hour students reported sick today."

Diana took a step back. "And you're making that sound like a national disaster because…?"

Brenna tucked the card back in the pack and walked around the counter. She took Diana's arm and led her into the hall. "It's a long story, but if you want to hear it…"

"Can you tell me over a sloppy joe and iced tea?"

"No. I don't want anyone to hear." As briefly as she could, she explained about the happenings of Friday evening.

"Wow," Diana said. "This girl is the daughter of Mr. Tall, Dark and Mechanically Inclined?"

"Yes, she is. And she's a troubled kid, just the kind you like to bring home."

"And yet…" Diana paused. "Apparently she didn't have a map to get to the right place and ended up with you instead."

"This isn't funny," Brenna said. "I think her father, the guy you obviously regard as Mr. Wonderful, is keeping her home so she won't have contact with me or anyone else. Or worse."

"I don't regard Mike the mechanic as anything in particular," Diana said. "I just pointed out that he was a hunk and available." She waited before adding, "But for the record, I didn't see anything in his quiet nature that would suggest he's holding family members captive."

"Come on, Diana," Brenna said. "You barely spoke to the guy the other day. And besides, it's the quiet ones you have to watch. Don't you ever see the news?"

"Look, if your instincts are telling you that something is wrong in this case, why don't you have BethAnn call the house and talk to the girl?"

"Get the guidance counselor involved? No, I don't think that's a good idea." Brenna learned five years ago that getting officials involved could be devastating.

"Brenna, you tell me all the time that you don't want personal relationships with your students, and if you really feel that way, referring your concern to a guidance counselor is the thing to do."

"But Carrie indicated a trust in me. I have to handle this." *Whether I think it's the best thing to do or not.*

"Fine. You call the house, then."

"I'll do better than that. After school I'm going to Alvin's Garage." A few seconds passed before she smiled at Diana. "Coming in this morning I noticed a clunk coming from under the hood of my car. I should probably get it looked at by a professional."

Diana studied Brenna's face.

"Why are you looking at me like that?" Brenna asked.

"I'm just trying to figure out if you're a pod person who managed to inhabit my best friend's body."

Brenna smirked. "Granted, this is unusual behavior from me."

"Sure is. As I recall, the only life you like to interfere in is mine," Diana added.

Brenna smiled. "But I'm all done with yours, and this is a special case. This kid came to me seeking help or advice or maybe even compassion. I don't know."

"But you're determined to find out."

"I guess I am."

"Then go get that junker of a car you own checked out. You can't be driving around in an unsafe vehicle."

Brenna nodded. "Exactly. Who knows how many lives I could be putting in jeopardy?"

"Now can we go to lunch? I'm starved."

Within minutes of the dismissal bell that afternoon, Brenna pulled out of the parking lot and headed to Alvin's Garage.

CHAPTER THREE

"LANGSTON, YOU GOT COMPANY!"

When he heard his boss holler, Mike poked his head out from under the hood of a '92 Ford SUV and stared across the garage to the office door. How could he have company? He hardly knew anybody outside of his work buddies. Except...

Yeah, he knew that redhead talking to Alvin.

Mel Francher, who'd worked at the garage for more than ten years, came up and nudged Mike in his ribs. "You got the good-looking teacher coming to see you," he said. "What'd you do? Poke a hole in her transmission fluid when she wasn't looking?"

Mike scowled at him. "Never. I wouldn't do anything to encourage her to come to the garage."

Mike wiped his hands on a clean rag and slowly approached his boss and Miss Sullivan. In pale denim slacks and a loose-fitting white shirt, she looked more like a "Miss Sullivan" today and less like the woman who wore shorts and a T-shirt and lived in the neat little bungalow. She still looked good, but he missed the legs.

"You remember our schoolteacher, Mike?" Alvin said. "You worked on her car Friday."

"Sure, I remember. What can I do for you, Miss Sullivan?"

"Call me Brenna," she said. It was a simple gesture, but it came out more schoolteacher and less friend.

"Brenna said she heard a strange sound coming from under the hood this morning," Alvin said. "She asked for you to take a look since you're familiar with the car."

"I'm familiar with the battery," Mike said. "But sure, I'll look."

"I appreciate that, Mr.… Can I call you Mike?"

"I've got no objection to that," he said. "Is your car in the lot?"

"Yes, right out here." She led the way outside.

Mike got behind the wheel of the Mazda and turned on the engine. He leaned out the door and listened. "What did it sound like?" he asked Brenna.

"Oh, sort of a ding or a ping."

He got out, walked to the front and angled his head close to the hood. "I don't hear anything out of the ordinary," he said.

"That's odd. It was quite noticeable this morning."

Mike suspected that *something* was noticeable, but he doubted it was a sound from Brenna's engine. He was pretty sure that what Miss Teacher noticed was Carrie's absence. Leaving the car purring gently, he said, "According to the sticker on your driver's-side door, this automobile has been serviced regularly. I noticed the odometer reads just sixty-five thousand miles. This car is a honey for a seven-year-old vehicle. So the only problem you have is possibly its owner. I myself only buy American-made vehicles."

She gave him an exasperated look.

He smiled to himself. "As I mentioned, a ping or a pong or a clink would be pretty rare on a car that has been maintained like yours has."

"That's why I was concerned," she said.

"I meant to ask Carrie if you were working today, but…"

"Miss Sullivan…"

"Brenna."

"Brenna." He turned off her engine. "Let's go into the office. Let me buy you a drink."

"A drink? I don't think so…"

He pointed through the picture window into the customer waiting room. "See that machine? I was offering you a Mountain Dew or a 7-Up."

"Oh, of course."

They settled at a small table. Mike took Brenna's order for a Diet Coke and brought the can to the table. He popped the top on his Mountain Dew and sat across from her. "Why are you really here, Brenna?"

"I told you. I heard a ping…"

"Or a ding, right?"

She didn't respond, and he figured it was time to eliminate *pings* and *dings* from their vocabulary. "I'm thinking this visit has everything to do with my daughter's absence from school today."

She sighed, turned the can in her hands without opening it. "Okay, fine. I realize I'm transparent, but I don't really care. I *am* wondering why Carrie was absent."

He purposefully didn't answer for as long as he could stretch out the silence. If that made her nervous, so be it.

"Let's be totally up front with each other," she said after a moment.

"Usually the best way to be."

"I'm concerned about Carrie."

"So you said Friday night."

Brenna folded her arms on top of the table and leaned slightly forward. "I want to know why she missed school today."

"Is the school board having teachers double as truant officers now, Brenna?"

"There's no need to be sarcastic," she said in a teacher voice that made Mike remember all the knuckle raps he'd gotten in Catholic school.

"You should be thankful someone cares enough to ask about Carrie," she added.

He would be if he wasn't so certain that Miss Sullivan had her own devious theory about why Carrie was absent, and he was looking like the Evil Mr. Langston. He glanced at his watch, knowing he was still on the clock. How much more time was he going to devote to this witch hunt? Despite the view across the table, which was pretty darned attractive, he knew he'd be better off cutting it short. "She's not feeling well," he said.

"What's wrong?"

"You really want me to tell you?"

She sat stone-still and waited.

Should he reveal a private detail of his daughter's life to this stranger? Oh, well, at least she was a woman, which made the delicate subject easier to broach. He released a long breath. "Okay, here's the story. About one day every month Carrie misses school and stays in bed with a heating pad on her stomach. This started when she was about eleven. If you can't figure out why that is, I suggest you go to the local library and take out a book on the subject of puberty."

Her face flushed. She cleared her throat. Mike got a perverse sort of pleasure out of seeing her discomfort.

"I see," she said. "That is an acceptable reason." She straightened her spine and said, "Was telling me that so hard?"

Well, yeah, it was. He'd only recently learned about this part of Carrie's life, and the day she'd talked about it with him he'd felt about as capable of handling the discussion as he would have been teaching a quilting class. To answer Brenna's question, he merely shrugged.

"I don't think we need to be on opposing sides here," she said.

"I'm on my daughter's side," he snapped. "Whose side are you on?"

"I'd like to help Carrie," she continued as if he hadn't spoken. "She seems lost and lonely. I'm sure you've noticed that."

"We're doing fine." Maybe if he kept saying that, it would eventually be true.

"I'm glad to hear that, but I'd still like to make myself available to Carrie if she needs to talk."

They were going down this road again. Why did every woman he'd ever met think they had to repeat everything? Did they believe all men were born with poor hearing?

"I already told you that talking to Carrie is okay with me. Just don't push. Let her initiate these conversations. I don't want anyone pressuring her."

She honestly appeared shocked. "I would never. We have rules in the school system that we have to follow."

"And I have rules as a father that I intend to follow. No taking my kid to places I don't know about. No digging for information, and no making her uncomfortable." He should have stopped there, but something inside him made him blurt out the very thing he shouldn't have said. "And no trying to be a substitute mother."

She stood, her can of soda still unopened. "I assure you, Mike, I have no interest in being anyone's mother. I've said what I came to say…"

"And found out what you came to find out?"

"Yes. I'm going to take your word for the reason for Carrie's absence."

"Swell."

She walked out the door and got into her perfectly running silver Mazda. As she pulled out of the parking lot, he was still thinking about how she looked marching to that car. Determined, offended and, he smiled, cute.

"You know better, Brenna. This is your own stupid fault."

She consciously eased off the accelerator. She didn't need to get a ticket on top of everything else. But she didn't stop scolding herself.

"This is why, since Jefferson Middle School, you've kept a strict nonintervention policy with regard to your students. You learned the hard way to let the Dianas of the world provide their shoulders to cry on while you just did your job and concentrated on your own problems." She grimaced. "Of which there are enough, I might remind you."

She drummed her fingers on the steering wheel and tried to think of anything but the past fifteen minutes with Mike Langston. No use. "What is going on with that family, anyway?" she said. "Did Carrie's mother die? Did she leave them? Is she still in their lives but only on a temporary basis?" Brenna was familiar with divorcing parents who used their children as pawns in a power struggle. She hoped that wasn't the case with the Langstons.

Truly that scenario didn't seem likely. Mike had said on Friday that he wasn't married. And Mike and Carrie had recently moved to Mount Union and definitely seemed to be struggling to adjust to each other and their new home. And another thing…why would

Mike choose a place so far out of town to live in? Was he hiding something? Was he purposely trying to keep his daughter out of the mainstream? She was just a kid. She needed contacts, friends.

"That's easy enough to figure out," Brenna said. "Diana knows the history of every person and building in this town. She'll know about property by the old mill."

An image of Mike's face appeared in the back of Brenna's mind and provided some details of his character. Strong lines curved around his mouth and eyes. Eyes like his had usually seen life at its most basic levels and experienced tragedy. And Mike's was an obstinate face. Ruddy from weather and wind and so serious that the man almost appeared as if he was afraid to laugh. His features weren't classically handsome, but Diana was right. He was interesting in a bold, daring way that made a person want to delve deeper, to learn more.

Brenna nodded to herself. Strange. A tall, fit man like Mike afraid to laugh. Why? Well, maybe because in her dealings with him, she'd given him precious little to smile about.

"Why should you care so much?" she asked

aloud. A few minutes ago she'd been so angry she'd walked out on him. Now she was wondering if she might be the one who could crack that granite exterior and get to the man underneath. For the sake of his daughter, of course. "But, girl, you have enough to deal with without having these two—"

Brenna's cell phone vibrated on the seat beside her. She glanced down. Great. Speaking of dealing… She pushed the button to her car speaker. "Hi, Mom. What's up?"

"Hello, darlin'. I was just thinking about you."

Her mother's thick Southern drawl seemed to permeate the air-conditioned cool of Brenna's car like warm maple syrup. Brenna took in a deep breath. She wasn't particularly fond of maple syrup.

"How are you, sweetie?" Alma Sullivan asked.

"I'm fine, Mom." Brenna's pat response. She never answered any other way. "Is everything all right at home?" She knew it wouldn't be.

"Your daddy and I are doing good, honey. My ironing jobs have dwindled down some, but that's okay. I don't much like ironing in the heat of the summer anyway."

"Mom, don't you have the air conditioner on in the trailer?"

"Not right now. It's not too bad. Tonight if your dad can't sleep, I'll turn it on."

Brenna wanted to ask what her parents were doing with the two hundred dollars a month she sent them in the summers so they could run the AC in their single-wide trailer, but she refrained. Her mother would just list the other necessities the money had gone toward, and Brenna would only feel worse than she did now.

She clutched the steering wheel until her knuckles went white and said, "So any news?"

"Well, yes. There's good news."

Brenna held her breath.

"Your dad got a few hours of work with that fella who moved into the unit next door. The man got hired to paint the inside of the Waffle House and he asked your father to help him. It was a godsend, really."

"Daddy's back wasn't hurting him?" Brenna asked.

"He took some of that twelve-hour pain medication and did okay."

Her mother paused, and Brenna waited for what was to come.

"But it's not all rosy here, Brenna May," Alma said, "and that's partly why I called today."

She tried to keep the edge of impatience out of her voice. "What's wrong?"

"The brakes on the truck went out. Wayne at the shop wants almost five hundred to fix them. We gotta do it, of course." Her mother emitted a nervous chuckle. "Can't be driving around with no brakes."

"Do you think it's a fair price?" Brenna asked. Mike's face popped into her mind again. She almost said, "I know a good mechanic."

"Oh, yeah. Wayne would never cheat us."

Cut to the chase. "How much do you need?"

"We'll pay you back. You know that."

"Yeah, I know."

"We've got two hundred and forty left over from the paint job, so…"

Brenna did the math. "You need two hundred sixty." She had that much in her checking account. At least she wouldn't have to raid her savings. "I'll send a check out tomorrow.

You'll get it Wednesday. Tell Wayne to go ahead and fix the car."

"I'd use your dad's Social Security check, but we need…"

"It's okay, Mom."

She disconnected as soon as possible and continued toward home. As she approached her comfortable cottage, she breathed a sigh of relief. Thank goodness she wasn't still living in that nine-by-nine trailer bedroom with its leak-stained ceilings, built-in drawers and tiny closet with a plastic shower curtain for a door. She'd grown up in that room. She'd worked her way through college living in that room.

She got out of her car, walked to the front porch that greeted her with planters of geraniums and pansies and delicate wicker furniture. When she opened her door, a blast of cool air welcomed her as she stepped inside.

She'd escaped that room in that single-wide trailer. She'd never told anyone about that room, not even Diana. And she'd never go back.

DIANA FROWNED DOWN at her plate of watery spaghetti. "There's just something not quite right about cafeteria pasta," she said, spreading her napkin on her lap.

Brenna smiled at her and added dressing to her salad. "I have to ask you something, Di."

"Shoot."

"What do you know about a house beyond the gristmill?"

Diana stopped twirling spaghetti around her fork and looked up at Brenna. "Did you say *beyond* the mill?"

"Yes."

Diana thought a moment. "There's only one house out there that I know of. A cabin, really. Not very fancy. In fact, almost primitive. It hasn't been occupied in a long time."

Bingo. "Who owns it?"

"Let me think. The last person to stay out there was a part-time resident, an older lady who used to come for the winters. But she hasn't been there in, I don't know, maybe ten years."

"And the cabin belonged to her?"

"I think so. It's one of those older places that some people say should be on the historic registry. It's what we used to call a pioneer cabin and was home to some of Mount Union's original citizens."

"Interesting."

"I know it's been modernized. The old lady had plumbing and power. You can see the wires running out that way from Con Electric. And phone cables, too."

"What was the lady's name?"

"Oh, jeez, Bren, I don't remember. I think it was Emily or Amy. Something old-fashioned like that. Her last name started with an *L,* I think."

"Could it have been Langston?" Brenna suggested.

"Could have been." Diana lifted her spaghetti to her mouth. Her eyes widened as she chewed. "Wait a minute." She swallowed, took a drink of water. "Langston? Isn't that the name of your new student, the one who came to your house?"

"Exactly. This family, the mysterious mechanic and his daughter, must be related to old Mrs. Langston somehow."

"And they're living in her place."

"Away from town, out of sight," Brenna said.

"Do you still suspect the worst about the father?" Diana asked.

"No, not the worst. He's not hurting his

daughter, at least in the way I thought when he picked her up at my house on Friday. But something is going on. That girl is unhappy. She's lonely. She needs..." Brenna couldn't say the words. They were still alien to her vocabulary.

Diana grinned. "You, Brenna? The girl needs you?"

Brenna sighed. "Yeah, she needs me."

"Well, holy cow. Look who's suddenly getting involved. I thought your volunteering to chair the renovation of the Cultural Arts Center for teens was the only extracurricular activity we'd get out of you this year."

Brenna smirked. "Yes, and it's a monumental activity, you must admit. I have you to thank for matching me up with that little job."

What Diana said was true. Maybe Brenna had seen too much of herself in Carrie Langston. Maybe she'd seen just enough of the girl's reticent, brooding father. Maybe she was ready to move on from her past. Whatever the reason, she was becoming emotionally involved with a student again.

"I'm thinking I need to go to the farm stand on White Deer Trail," Brenna said.

"I don't suppose your longing for fresh,

local vegetables has anything to do with the fact that the old mill is on White Deer?"

Brenna pretended surprise. "It is? What a coincidence."

Diana smiled. "You should know, Bren, it's a little hard to do a drive-by of Mrs. Langston's cabin. As I recall, once you drive in, the only way out is to turn around and leave the same way."

Brenna smiled. "I'll figure something out. I just have to go. I'm developing quite an interest in one of Mount Union's pioneer cabins."

CHAPTER FOUR

ON THURSDAY AFTERNOON, seven days after Brenna first met Mike Langston, she called the garage and asked to speak to him. One of the other mechanics told her to hold on, and he shouted Mike's name. At that point Brenna said, "Oh, I'm sorry. Someone's at the door. I'll call back." She had gotten the info she needed. Mike wasn't at his cabin.

She checked her watch. School had been dismissed an hour ago. The buses had all left within ten minutes. Carrie would be home, but if Brenna were careful, she wouldn't run into her. And now she knew Mike was at work, so there was no chance of running into him. She'd see old Mrs. Langston's cabin and draw her own conclusions about its livability.

She drove into the country, past the Montgomerys' house, the farm stand and the old mill, one of Mount Union's most historic buildings and a favorite field trip for elementary students.

Slowing her car just after the mill, she noticed a narrow drive winding into a stand of live oak and magnolia trees. The rutted path was overgrown. Brenna debated the wisdom of navigating it in her Mazda but decided her trusty little car could make it.

She progressed slowly, holding her breath at each bump in the drive. She'd gone about three hundred yards when she saw the roof of a house and a brick chimney covered with ivy and moss. There being no place to pull over, she stopped in the middle of the path and got out of her car. She hadn't gone too far into the trees that she couldn't back out safely and return to White Deer Trail.

Since she'd known she was going to make this trek after work today, Brenna had chosen to wear black jeans, a black-and-white sleeveless knit shirt and sensible sneakers. Her hair was caught up on her head with a tortoiseshell comb. She trudged ahead, keeping watch for tree roots that could trip her.

Hiding behind low branches, she approached the cabin. Getting her first look at Mrs. Langston's "pioneer homestead," Brenna was pleasantly surprised that the first settlers of Mount Union lived so well. The simple log structure was far from luxurious, but it appeared sturdy. The logs showed signs of wear, some splitting in places that glistened with some sort of patching material. At least someone had maintained the place. The porch had a substantial roof that extended across the front of the house. Two rocking chairs and an assortment of folksy implements sat on the wooden floor.

Brenna crouched down so she couldn't be seen from either of two windows on each side of the centered front door. A patch of gravel served as a parking area. The cabin's solid front door was open and a steady hum came through the screen door, indicating an air conditioner was working hard to keep up with the heat coming inside. She smiled, thinking the thoughtless gesture typical of a teenager who didn't have to pay the bills.

Carrie suddenly appeared in front of one window. Cords hung from her ears as she waved her arms over her head and danced to a tune only she could hear. The girl didn't appear nearly as miserable as she'd sounded the other night, and Brenna imagined Justin Bieber or Katy Perry blasting from those earbuds.

A slight stinging sensation on her arm drew Brenna's attention from the cabin. A mosquito the size of a Chihuahua hovered near her shoulder, and Brenna swatted it away. It returned with two or three of its buddies, who flew away with an ample supply of Brenna snack.

"Enough of this," she said. "I've stalked this child sufficiently to know she's not living in squalor."

Waving her hand in front of her face, Brenna returned to her car, got in and closed the door after swatting furiously to make sure none of the winged invaders had made it inside. She started her engine, slid the gearshift into Reverse and stepped on the accelerator.

And stopped with a jolt and a resounding thud.

She cringed. Had she hit a rock? A tree? An animal?

No. Unfortunately, she'd crunched into a blue pickup truck she'd seen most recently in front of her house.

Oh, no. Brenna thrust the shift into Park and slid down in her seat. She closed her eyes briefly. The primary rule of backing up an automobile punched into her brain with the force of her driver's ed teacher's gravelly voice. "Always look over your shoulder to make sure..."

She was still struggling to calm her pounding heart when a knock on her driver's-side window made her jerk upright. She stared into Mike Langston's aviator sunglasses before her gaze slid down to the thin line his lips made.

She mouthed the word *Hello* through the glass.

He made a twirling motion with his hand, and she rolled her window down a couple of inches. He continued to twirl.

She shook her head. "Mosquitoes," she said, pointing to her arm, where itchy pink welts had formed in the past few minutes.

"That's a shame," he responded. He lifted his glasses long enough to stare into her eyes before performing a cursory check of the items on her car seats. What did he expect to find? A half-empty bottle of wine? There was nothing incriminating there. Her phone, her purse, a Diet Coke.

The glasses dropped back to his nose. "You just ran into me," he said needlessly.

Common sense should have made her hold her tongue. But apparently common sense had just flown out that two inches of window space. "You're not even supposed to be here," she said. *Stupid, stupid, stupid.*

He frowned. "That's funny. Since I *live* here, I thought *I* had every right to *be* here."

"What I meant was…" There was no way out of this. "*I'm* not supposed to be here."

He nodded once. "That makes more sense. But seeing as you obviously are here, you might want to pull up a little. Right now my front bumper is close to riding the trunk of your dandy little foreign automobile. I'm thinking that's not good—especially since you seem to have so much trouble with this car anyway."

Well, that comment wasn't at all necessary.

"I expect we ought to exchange insurance cards," he added. "Though I doubt you need mine."

She definitely wasn't going to roll her window down more and invite blood suckers inside. She'd be a mass of swollen spots within minutes. "Can't you reverse?" she suggested.

"We can both back onto White Deer from here and discuss the situation away from these insect-infested woods."

"I'm not going to let you back your vehicle up anywhere in the vicinity of mine," he said. "Go forward to the house."

To his house? She didn't think so. She rubbed her hand over a bite, hoping to illicit his sympathy.

"I have a bug zapper on the porch," he said. "You'll be fine." He leaned on the side of her car. Only a thin layer of glass separated her from those honey-brown eyes she could imagine staring at her through the dark shades.

His nose practically touched the window when he said, "And since your whole purpose for being on this drive had to be to snoop on my property, this invitation should make you very happy."

She sensed his mind still churning, as if he weren't finished proving to her he'd figured out her scheme. She wouldn't have been surprised if he'd said, "And you'll never be invited back so you'd better take advantage of this offer right now."

For some reason, she decided if he did say that, she'd feel the loss, much more than she would have expected. Maybe it was the way he looked in those aviator sunglasses. He had a movie-star quality that she quite inappropriately noticed at this particular moment. Sort of a Gerard Butler cocky masculinity. She had a long way to go before forming a lasting impression of Mike Langston, but she really liked Gerard Butler.

Besides, what choice did she have? If he wouldn't move his car, she couldn't go anywhere. The only direction open to her was forward. She could pull in front of the house, wait until he pulled in as well and then maneuver quickly around and head down the drive. If Carrie was still wearing the earbuds, she might not even look out the window. And perhaps Mike wouldn't tell his daughter about the spy mission.

Brenna spoke out the two inches open at the top of her window. "Fine. But don't think for a minute that I'm interpreting this as a social invitation."

He almost smiled. "I know you're smarter than that. Actually, this is more an intimidation tactic. I'm much better in that arena than I am the social one."

I'll bet you are. She eased her car into

Drive and gently pressed the accelerator. The Mazda made a mournful screech and cleared a foot or so between it and the truck. Brenna didn't want to look at her trunk lid. She'd check it out when she was back in her own drive and could cry in private.

A moment later she pulled in front of Mike's cabin. She waited for him to park and then shifted into Reverse. Her ploy to execute a quick escape was working. Until the front door opened and Carrie stepped out.

"Miss Sullivan, hi!"

Darn it. She stopped, rolled her window down all the way and looked for mosquitoes. The zapper appeared to be doing its job, so she stepped out of the car. Leaving now would look much more suspicious than following through with a good ol' North Georgia howdy. "Hi, Carrie."

"What are you doing here?"

She glanced at Mike, who had an elbow on the top of his truck and was watching her through those sunglasses. His full mouth quirked up in a smirk that made the teacher in her want to threaten him with a visit to the assistant principal. And made the woman in her want to—

Stop it, Brenna. Not helpful.

She had to answer Carrie, not let her thoughts careen in another inappropriate direction. "Well, I...I was..."

"Miss Sullivan got lost, Carrie," Mike said. "I encountered her trying to back out of our driveway and suggested she come up to the house and turn around."

Carrie gave Brenna an incredulous stare. "But you've lived in this stupid town for, like, forever. How could you get lost?"

Brenna shot a quick look at Mike. "I've only lived here four years," she said. "And I... ah, I've never ventured beyond the gristmill."

Mike threw his keys on a rough-hewn table next to the front door. "You must have been daydreaming today, then," he said. "There aren't any houses but this one past the mill."

"We live in the booniest of the boondocks," Carrie said. "No one ever comes out this far."

"Why don't you offer Miss Sullivan some iced tea?" Mike said.

"I r-really shouldn't stay...." Brenna stammered.

Carrie clasped her hands together. "Oh, please. Other than repair guys, you're our first visitor. Can't you come inside and talk for a while?" As an added incentive, she said, "We have air-conditioning." She swept her arm around the porch, indicating the objects her great-grandmother had probably left behind. "You wouldn't think so because of all this old stuff, but I swear we do."

Brenna recognized an old wooden butter churn, handmade baskets, a few primitive iron tools on the wall. "These things are interesting," she said.

"If you like all these old things, you'll *love* the inside." A hopeful look on her face, Carrie held the door open.

"But your father..." Brenna said. "I'm sure he doesn't want company after working all day."

"I suggested the tea, didn't I?" Mike said. "Besides, after you have a look around, this place will have left a permanent impression on you." He lowered his voice. "And that should be well worth the trouble of the minor car damage you're taking home as a souvenir."

With no way to decline, Brenna preceded him inside and into one large room with a door and a hallway leading from it.

The inside of the cabin was basically Spartan, with a few well-used furnishings that Brenna decided must have been favorites of Mrs. Langston. An antique oak sideboard stood against one wall. A matching washstand and primitive chair occupied another. Facing a rugged stone fireplace was an early-twentieth-century sofa with wood arms and cushions that had been flattened by years of sitting. Only a floppy-eared coonhound lying on the braided rug in front of the hearth would have made the scene a perfect blend of countrified necessity and simplicity. But there was no dog, just the three of them.

Carrie called from the kitchen. "Dad, why are you home? Isn't it early?"

He glanced at Brenna before answering. "I came to check on things here. I got a call from an unidentified female at the shop, and when I went to answer, no one was there."

His glance mutated into a hard stare. Feeling her face flush, Brenna began concentrating on native animal prints on the walls.

"It wasn't me," Carrie said.

"I didn't know that," he answered. "I called here, but no one answered. I was worried."

Brenna remembered the earbud cords dangling from Carrie's head. No wonder she didn't hear the phone ring.

"Sheesh, Dad, you don't have to check up on me every minute," Carrie said from the kitchen.

"I'll try to remember that," he said, settling on the plaid sofa. "How's that tea coming?"

Carrie came into the living room with a tray holding three glasses. She set the tray on a scarred but clean pine coffee table and handed a tumbler to Brenna. Brenna sat on the other end of the sofa and smiled at the faded images of deer frolicking around the frosty outside of the glass.

"It's instant," Carrie said, looking down at Brenna. "Dad said I should learn to make it from real tea bags, but I don't see why."

Mike picked up a glass and took a sip. "I just thought you might like to do things the way your great-grandmother did."

Carrie gave him an incredulous look. "Why would I want to do that? Everything was such work back then."

He crossed and uncrossed his legs, cleared his throat, took another sip of tea and finally stood. "I'm going to change out of this uniform."

"Good idea, Dad," Carrie said. "You have grease on your shirt."

"Goes with the job," he said and headed toward the hallway off the living room. "I'll just be in there. You ladies talk all you want."

A few seconds later, Brenna heard a door close. Carrie sat in the spot vacated by her father and leaned close. "Do you see how awful it is out here, Miss Sullivan?" she said, keeping her voice low.

Brenna didn't want to put herself in the middle of any family dispute. Besides, she truly didn't find Carrie's living conditions to be "awful." Remote, yes, especially for a teen who was still more than a year away from getting her driver's license.

"I know it's hard to believe," Carrie said, "but my father really likes it out here. He keeps talking about nature and fresh air until I just want to scream. Spiders and mice are nature, too, you know."

Brenna smiled. "Your cabin is really only about three or four miles out of town," she said. "I'll bet some of the people in town have spiders, too."

"I suppose, but we might as well be a hundred miles away for all the times I get to go to the stores and do fun stuff."

"Your dad never takes you shopping?"

"Oh, sure, to the grocery and the hardware store." She grimaced. "I guess that's his idea of fun. And any time I complain he just tells me that we have all we need."

Brenna doubted that statement. "Other than some specialty stores, gift shops and local antique dealers, we don't have much. But there are malls in Libertyville, Athens and Augusta."

"Dad has taken me to those a couple of times," Carrie admitted.

Poor deprived child...

"But this dumb town is nothing like California, where I used to live. Out there we had tons of cool places to go, outlets and twenty-four-screen movie theaters."

Brenna understood that moves required periods of adjustments. Some people needed a lot of time to get used to a new environment, whereas others just seemed to fit in almost instantly. Brenna had been like that when she moved to Mount Union. The people who lived here, the town itself, offered much of what she wanted, the closeness of a community along with the privacy she needed, and especially a job she appreciated for many reasons. The students came from good, mostly two-parent families and didn't arrive at class with heartbreaking baggage every day. Brenna had had too much experience trying to deal with students' sad home lives, and she appreciated Mount Union's solid family values immediately.

For four years now she had done an admirable job in the classroom while maintaining the independence and separation she expected in a town like Mount Union. Okay, maybe she'd never been voted teacher of the year like Diana, but no one had ever complained about the job she did. Now here she was sitting in a backwoods cabin listening to a morose, lonely girl complain about the place Brenna had come to love. And she didn't know how she was going to handle it.

So she took a stab at counseling even though she knew it wasn't her strong suit. "You know, Carrie, maybe you should give Mount Union a chance. You've only been here a few months, right?"

The girl slumped down in her seat. "Three

long, miserable months. It feels like ten years."

"Once you make some friends…"

She sat upright. "Friends? How can I make friends when I'm not allowed to leave this—" she stared around the room as if she were watching a horror movie "—this *prison*." She grabbed Brenna's hand. "Talk to my dad, will you, Miss Sullivan? Tell him to cut me some slack. He doesn't know anything about being a father."

"I'm sure that's not true. He seems like a nice—"

"You don't understand. Not only does my dad not know anything about being a dad, he doesn't even know me. You ask him any question about me—what music I like, what movies I've seen. Heck, ask him my favorite color—he won't know. He never tried to know me. Not when I was growing up and especially not now."

The girl was close to tears. Brenna patted her hand. "What are you talking about? Why wouldn't your dad know you?"

"He was in the army the whole time I was a kid. He hardly ever came home, and if he did, he stayed a couple of weeks and left again. He was always in Afghanistan or Iraq or someplace." Her eyes grew moist. "That's not the way a family's supposed to be, is it, Miss Sullivan?"

Brenna had no idea how to answer. Her own family situation had been very different from Carrie's. Brenna's father never kept a job for more than a few weeks at a time, so he was home too much. Because of her dad's inability to find steady work, Brenna hadn't experienced stability in her life, either, for reasons very unlike Carrie's.

"He didn't *have* to be in the army all that time," Carrie continued. "He *wanted* to be. It's like he forgot he had a family."

Agreeing with Carrie would mean betraying Mike, a man Brenna suspected was trying in his own way to make up for lost time. To disagree with Carrie would only alienate a young girl who was opening up about her feelings. After a moment Brenna said, "You know times of war are hard on everyone, the soldiers and their families."

"Yeah, well, maybe. My mom just told me to appreciate the times Dad was home. But truthfully, the two of us learned to get along

without him just fine. We didn't need him."
She stared down at her lap. "At least until…"

"Until what?" Brenna asked.

She remained silent for several seconds, and then a voice, soft and low, came from the hallway. "Until her mother died," Mike said.

CHAPTER FIVE

MIKE'S GUT FELT as if it had just been slammed with a cinder block. Why had he said that? Five minutes ago, he'd gone into his bedroom to shed his dirty uniform and put on shorts and a T-shirt. He'd intended to walk Miss Busybody out the door to her car and wave goodbye. Yet, he just blurted out the one fact that Brenna could use to explain the dysfunction in his relationship with his daughter. No wonder Carrie was sitting on the sofa slack-jawed and wide-eyed.

"Dad, I can't believe you told Miss Sullivan about that," his confused daughter said. "I thought we weren't supposed to talk about Mom."

"I said until we knew people better." His defense sounded weak, but he had advised his daughter that the tragedy they'd suffered was best kept secret until they'd settled into their new town and started over. He didn't think his daughter needed the well-intended sympathies of people who were practically strangers. And he knew he didn't.

Well, he couldn't take the revelation back now. And in a way, he was relieved Brenna knew. This nosy home ec teacher had worked pretty hard the past few days to find out what was going on with him and Carrie—lying and snooping and telling him what *she* intended to do about *his* daughter—maybe she had earned the right to know. If Carrie seemed sad, there was good cause. And her depression wasn't his fault. Well, not entirely.

In the quiet shock that had settled over the women, Mike's sandals flapped loudly against his heels as he crossed the room. He supposed it was his responsibility to break the awkward silence and offer some sort of explanation. He started to, but Carrie stood and reminded him again of his mistake.

"You always say we shouldn't bring this up."

"I know. Before, when I said that, I was concerned that people would ask questions about your mom and upset you," Mike said. "Remember all the questions you got in California, all the forms we filled out? It wasn't easy for you."

"No, it wasn't, but now you just told my teacher!"

"Yeah, well, all the secrecy doesn't seem so important now."

Brenna stood and moved close to Carrie, making him feel seriously outnumbered. "Excuse me, Mike," Brenna said, "but why wouldn't you tell people about your wi… Carrie's mother? It would seem to me—"

Here she goes again. He held up his hand. "We didn't move here to draw that kind of attention to ourselves. We don't need anybody's pity."

"Again, maybe I'm overstepping…"

Since when did that stop you?

"…but sincere sympathy is different from pity. And the people in this town—"

"I know. You all have hearts of gold." He regretted the sarcasm the minute he said it, but he didn't want folks patting him on the back, offering artificial condolences and advising him how to raise his daughter. He'd figure it out on his own, even if it took him until she went off to college.

"I wasn't going to say that," Brenna insisted. "I just wanted to point out that people can be very understanding."

Yeah, sure. They'd tell him they *understood* how he must be feeling. They'd say they could *relate* to his grief. But all the platitudes would mean nothing. Because nobody could understand what it was like to be kept in the dark about your wife's three-month illness until just days before her death. Nobody in middle-American Mount Union, a town where family ties couldn't be broken with a machete, could know how ineffectual a man became when the only support he could offer the woman he married was a few meaningless words at the end of her life.

Brenna looked at Carrie with one of those predictable, pitying, doe-eyed looks he'd left California to get away from. "Now that I know, maybe I can help Carrie."

His daughter glared at him. "Thanks anyway, Miss Sullivan, but he doesn't care about helping me. If he did he wouldn't have brought me here in the first place."

The muscles in Mike's chest tightened, the first sign of an anxiety attack. He took a deep breath, managing to at least gain partial control. "I think maybe you should go, Brenna," he said. "I'll walk you out."

She didn't argue. She simply told Carrie she'd see her in school tomorrow, thanked her for the tea and walked to the door. Mike followed her to her car.

Before she got in, she did the strangest thing. She stood outside the safety of her car as if there weren't a mosquito within five miles of them and just stared at him. And she gave him a reserved sort of smile. It wasn't even close to a big ol' country-girl grin. It was subtle and understated, but it was genuine, and it made him feel better, calmer. His chest muscles relaxed. His anxiety began to fade. It had been too long since he'd interpreted anyone's smile as the real thing.

He cleared his throat. "Thanks for not overreacting to what Carrie said in there. This is a process for her and me."

"Of course it is."

She reached her hand out as if she would grasp his arm, but instead paused and then rubbed her palm along the side of her jeans. His own palm itched in response. He felt deprived, thinking that it might have been nice if she'd reached across those extra few inches and actually touched him.

"Do you mind if I ask you something, Mike?" she said after a moment.

"Go ahead."

"How long ago did your wife die?"

"Almost a year now."

"It's still very fresh."

"You could say that."

She looked into his eyes. He'd averted his gaze so many times when people gave him that sorrowful stare that he was surprised when he didn't automatically do so again. But what he saw in her green eyes was real, not manufactured to convey some sort of practiced sympathy. And a little uncomfortable, as if she usually tried to hide that part of herself. Well, heck, nobody could be as good at hiding their emotions as he was.

"I'm sorry," she said. "And I'm not saying that because I have a heart of gold." Her lips trembled as her smile widened and seemed to cut through the melancholy of the past minutes. "Some people would say my heart is more pot metal—not worth a whole heck of a lot."

He swallowed a chuckle. "Carrie would say

that's a step up. She'd tell you my heart is made of scrap metal."

"No, I don't believe that's true." She lifted her hand and touched his T-shirt just above his heart. His breath caught. It was a feather-light connection—her manicured fingernail just brushing the part of him that he'd thought had died. A muscle in his chest rippled with a pleasurable jolt of energy.

"I believe that under that shirt beats a real flesh-and-blood well of emotion," she said as she withdrew her hand and opened her car door. "Maybe you just don't show it often enough."

That's the safest way to be, Teach.

She slid into her car, but before she started the engine, Carrie came onto the porch. "Hey, Miss Sullivan, don't leave yet. I've just had the greatest idea."

Mike and Brenna both waited as Carrie bounded down to the parking area. "What's going on, Carrie?" Mike asked, confused by her rare burst of enthusiasm.

"Tomorrow is Friday," she said. "The first football game is tomorrow night. It's a home game."

"Okay. Do you want to go?"

"I *definitely* want to go."

He couldn't have been more surprised if she'd told him she wanted to wade into the river outside of Mount Union and catch trout with her bare hands. The idea that she wanted to go to a game with him warmed a spot deep in his belly. "Great. I'll take you."

She frowned.

"What's the matter?"

"I didn't think you'd want to go."

"Why wouldn't I? You know I like football." He looked at Brenna. "Can I get tickets at the gate?"

She shrugged. "I think you can, but I don't really know for sure. I don't go to the games."

"You don't?" He didn't know why he was surprised. Maybe because when he was on his high school football team, the stands were always filled with parents and students and every teacher he'd ever had. The whole community supported the team.

"I don't have an interest in sports."

"Oh." He turned back to Carrie. "We'll go, watch the game together. Maybe grab some dinner out. Would you like that?"

"Ah, Dad..."

"What?"

"I was kind of thinking you could just drop me off and I could go by myself...." She stared hard at Brenna. "Actually, I was going to ask if I could sit with you, Miss Sullivan. Maybe you could introduce me to some kids."

When she looked back at him, Mike tried to keep his expression neutral. Once again, Carrie's rejection hurt him, though he should be used to it. He'd thought maybe they'd found some common ground.

"I see. Well, Miss Sullivan just said she doesn't go to the games, and I'm not going to let you go by yourself."

"Dad, come on!"

Brenna's mouth moved, and Mike anticipated that she was going to point out that the activity was perfectly safe. She didn't follow through, however, and it was just as well. Mike wasn't letting Carrie go unless he went with her. They were still new in town. School had just started. The game was an after-dark activity. She didn't know anybody. There were all sorts of reasons he wouldn't consider dropping her off at the game and leaving her there, not the least of which was his own insecurity about fatherhood. "Sorry, Carrie, but..."

Carrie's mouth pinched in displeasure. "I can't believe you!" she said. "It's not fair!"

He took a deep breath and did a quick mental ten-count. "Take it or leave it. You don't want me to go. I won't let you go by yourself. That's the way…"

Brenna held up one slender finger. "Ah, if I may…"

It was coming now. Whatever she'd been about to say a minute ago was going to gush forth and prove once more that gender is thicker than blood. He was going to be the one against two again.

He spoke before she could. "This isn't up for debate. I'm her father, and my decision stands."

Carrie moaned, stomped her foot.

Brenna put her hand on the girl's shoulder. "Oh, we know that, right, Carrie? Mike is your dad. He's only looking out for your safety."

Carrie gawked at her as if she'd just broken a female bond in effect since the Middle Ages. "Miss Sullivan!"

Mike echoed her, expressing a different kind of shock. "Miss Sullivan?"

"I was just going to say that I'd reconsidered. I'll go to the game and the *three of us* can sit together. Then if I see any kids from your class sitting near us, I think your dad would let you go join them as long as he can see you." She gave Mike a look that dared him to say no. "How would that be, Mike?"

Carrie scuffed the toe of her sandal in the dirt for a moment and then appeared to conclude that the compromise was better than nothing. "Okay, I'll do that," she said. "What about you, Dad?"

Mike switched his gaze from his scowling daughter to her sweetly smiling teacher. "I guess that would be all right," he said at last. "As long as Miss Sullivan knows the kids you'll be sitting with."

"Oh, boy. Football," Brenna said with feigned chirpiness. "I can give Carrie tickets at school tomorrow, and I'll meet you two somewhere in the middle of the bleachers about ten minutes before the game, okay?"

"Middle of the bleachers?" Mike repeated. "Are you talking fifty-yard-line seats?"

"I'm not even sure what that is," Brenna said. "But my friend's husband is the coach and she's always offering to let me sit with her. She says her seats are in the middle somewhere."

"Then they'll do fine," Mike said.

"See you then." Brenna got in her car, turned around and drove off. And Mike was left wondering if this was going to be the best game he'd ever been to or the worst—fifty-yard-line seats and all.

"I CANNOT BELIEVE I am doing this," Brenna said as she drove onto the grassy field that served as overflow parking on game nights. "And even more alarming, I can't believe I've been *thinking* about doing this most of the day."

She'd fussed over what to wear to this game and finally settled on jeans and a nice blouse. And now she was practically late. Did these games always start on time? she wondered, or was it okay to be fashionably late? Probably not the latter.

She headed toward the glow of flashlights directing her to a parking space at the end of a line of cars. She waved to the high school maintenance man as she followed his beam into a narrow spot. "Thanks, Phil."

He peered into her car. "Is that you, Brenna?"

"'Fraid so."

"I've never seen you at a game before."

"No, you haven't," she said, cutting her engine.

"Should be a barn burner tonight. Both of these teams were nine and one last year."

"Well, goody," she said, getting out of her car. "Nothing I like better than burning barns." Like everyone in town, she remembered that the Mount Union Ravens had enjoyed a winning season last year. But unlike most of her fellow citizens, she hadn't observed one play.

But there was no way she was going to miss this game tonight. In school today, Carrie had questioned her several times about showing up. Diana had been so excited about sharing her prime seats with her best friend that she'd told half the faculty that Brenna was going to attend. Even some of the players, the ones who took her home ec class for what they figured would be an easy passing grade, said they heard she would be in the stands.

Okay, so she would do her duty, this once, and show school spirit and help a lonely kid form a few bonds of friendship. But try as she might to deny her interest in one particular brooding male who was meeting her at this game, his possible eagerness at seeing her again was really occupying her thoughts.

"Do not make the mistake of thinking of Mike Langston as just another guy, Brenna," she warned herself as she went through the stadium gate. "He's not interested in you as anything other than a buffer between him and his daughter...if that."

She was well aware that Mike wasn't the typical sort of man she usually dated. He wasn't out for a good time. He wasn't a good conversationalist or an educated up-and-coming career-oriented type. He wasn't looking for a clever, fun-loving woman to be by his side. And what if his current job was the most he'd ever accomplish?

Could Brenna really care for a man whose goals didn't exactly mesh with hers? She had long ago decided that she wasn't going to backslide into the life she'd worked so hard to escape. "It's just as easy to love a rich man as it is a poor one," her mother told her often enough, always ending her words of wisdom by lamenting that she hadn't followed her own advice.

Her mother's words had been mercenary and self-serving, but they'd also stuck, and Brenna had ventured down the dating road with one principle guiding her steps: marriage was fine, if it happened, but she had to think about her future and the strides she'd made escaping that run-down trailer. She also had to accept that she would probably end up supporting her parents, which could prove difficult on a teacher's salary.

So why was her heart pounding as she approached the middle of the bleachers? And why did it threaten to stop altogether when she looked up and saw Mike Langston looking nothing like a mechanic from Alvin's Garage?

"Miss Sullivan, up here!"

Brenna waved at Carrie and climbed up to the fourth row of seats.

"Hi, Bren," Diana said. "Look who's here? Our favorite mechanic." She slid down and nudged Carrie and Mike to do the same. Brenna sat in the last space beside Diana.

Carrie leaned across her father and Diana and spoke to Brenna. "I see some kids from my home ec class in the next section. Do you think I could go sit with them?"

Brenna stole a close-up glance at Mike and swallowed a sigh. His dark hair, seeming longer now than when she'd first met him, was expertly mussed. The tousled look was perfect for his rugged, slightly bearded face. And the short-sleeved beige knit shirt tucked into a pair of faded black jeans fit his solid chest oh so well. One booted foot tapped against the seat in front of him.

"What do you say, Dad?" Brenna asked. "I can take her over and make sure she settles in."

"Okay, but try to pick a seat where I can see her from here."

"You're not going to stare at me all night are you, Dad?" Carrie asked. "You'll give everybody the creeps."

"I'm here to watch a football game, Carrie. But if my eyes wander over to the next section a few times, just know that you'd better be sitting where Miss Sullivan takes you."

Carrie half stumbled over her dad and Diana in her haste to be away from the adults. "I'll see you at the end of the game," she said. "Mrs. Montgomery invited us to go for pizza after. I'd really like to."

Mike glanced at Diana, who nodded. "I suppose that would be all right," he said.

"Great." Carrie hurried down the steps.

Following her, Brenna looked over her shoulder at Diana and Mike. "Be right back. Don't let them start without me."

She spoke to Mary Sue Mayberry, a student she knew well, and introduced Carrie as a new arrival to Mount Union High School. Mary Sue was friendly and asked Carrie to sit with them. Once Brenna was certain that Carrie was welcome in the group, she returned to her seat, but Diana wasn't there.

"She went down to the fence to wish her husband good luck," Mike said when Brenna stood looking down at the two vacant spaces on the bench.

Sure enough, Diana was giving the coach a thumbs-up sign…before she glanced up, saw Brenna and delivered a coy half grin. Diana had known exactly what she was doing when she left her seat empty.

You couldn't be more obvious if you were dressed as my fairy godmother, twinkling wand and all, Brenna thought.

"Have a seat," Mike said. He stared in the

direction of his daughter. "Who are those kids she's with?"

"Don't worry," Brenna said, still observing the seat beside Mike. "They are all good kids from nice families. Carrie's in good hands."

"Despite my daughter's claims, I don't bite," Mike said as he patted the bleacher seat.

Deciding to act as an adult, Brenna slid in beside him. After all, she and Mike would be seated side by side in the midst of hundreds of screaming fans. Hardly a compromising situation even though she maintained a couple of inches between them.

"So, what do you know about football?" he asked.

"I know it's bad when our guys drop the ball. I know it's good when they run over the goal line."

He smiled. "Yes, that's the point of the whole thing. But there are a number of details involved in making that happen—and in making sure the other guys don't."

"I assume you know all about these details?"

"I have some knowledge on this subject. I'd be happy to fill you in on the basics if you'd like."

He wanted to fill her head with stats and arrows and *X*'s and *O*'s about something she didn't give a hoot about? Not wanting to take away his enthusiasm, she gave him an earnest look and said, "If you think it's something a woman with a total ignorance of sports can understand, sure, give it your best shot."

What was so different about Mike Langston? She almost looked forward to being educated by him, despite the subtle heat that thought brought to her face. Maybe she understood that he was having a hard time, and she simply didn't want to discourage him. Or maybe she liked the sound of his voice, soft and low and with a faint vibration that made her skin tingle. She smiled back at him. "But don't expect me to remember any of it tomorrow."

A little more than two hours later, the Ravens had chalked their opening game into the win column, Brenna knew more about football than she'd ever imagined possible and she was debating whether or not to go to the pizza place with Diana, Mike and Carrie. Usually by this time on a Friday night she'd be well into the Texas two-step at the Riverview Tavern with a banker dressed in a custom Western shirt and three-hundred-dollar cowboy boots. A banker whose persistent calls she hadn't answered during the game.

"Pizza, huh?" she said as they all walked to the parking lot. If she didn't go to the Riverview, she'd at least have to call Alex with an excuse.

"Bobby will meet us there," Diana said.

"You should come, Miss Sullivan," Carrie said. "A lot of your students will be there, too."

Just what I want to hear. Nevertheless, when Brenna reached her car, she promised to meet the others at Vinnie's for pizza and beer. And hopefully no football talk.

THE EVENING HAD turned out pretty well. In fact, Mike hadn't felt this relaxed in months, certainly since he'd been called back from the Middle East. While he'd been overseas, he'd forgotten the enjoyment in witnessing the simple everyday combat of teams on a football field. While explosions had sounded all around him in Afghanistan, he'd forgotten the heart-pumping rhythm of a high school band. When the brilliant trails of rockets lit the night sky in the war zone, he never thought of the sparkle of a majorette's baton twirling in bright stadium lights.

And now, sitting in a cheese-and-garlic-scented room with cheap prints of Italy adorning the walls, he was even more content. His daughter was on one side of him. The pretty home ec teacher was on the other. And in almost three hours Brenna hadn't interfered in his fathering techniques. She hadn't expressed an opinion or subtly criticized. She'd just been a pleasant companion.

He figured it was only a matter of time until she brought up that rather astounding announcement he'd overheard his daughter make the night before. "He doesn't even know me," Carrie had said, and her words had cut deep.

Not that he could argue with her. He didn't know his daughter. When she was young and he'd been home on leave, he'd marveled at her, been amazed by her. He'd tossed her in the air until she squealed. He'd pushed her on a swing until she'd giggled with delight.

Later, when she was older, he'd slipped her a twenty so she could go to the mall. He pretended not to hear the middle school gossip and teen-idol talk among Carrie and her friends. And when he flew back across the ocean to the dangerous job that had filled him with such pride and would someday enable him to go to college, he didn't think about the fact that his daughter was becoming more of a stranger with every mile.

And then, when his wife was taking her final breaths, he'd promised to protect and care for a once-delicate creature who had somehow turned into this opinionated, demanding, vulnerable, lovely young woman. The army had rules. Football teams had plays. But Lori hadn't given him even a hint about how to take over her job.

"Hey, there he is, the man of the hour!"

Brought back to the present with the jubilant shout of one of the restaurant patrons, Mike looked at a familiar man coming through the door. Bobby Montgomery, Diana's husband.

With humility that seemed as natural as his easy stride, Bobby nodded to folks he knew and came to the table, where he leaned over and kissed his wife. She took her purse from the seat she'd been saving beside her, and he sat. He immediately teased Brenna about being at the game and asked her what she thought about that gutsy fourth-down call he'd made in the third quarter.

Brenna stared at him as if he was speaking a foreign language. "Look, Bobby, I'm going to join the crowd and say congratulations on the game. If you expect any more in the way of sports banter, you're going to have to be satisfied with what you hear from my coach." She indicated Mike with a nod.

She leaned back so the two men could see each other. "I don't think you guys have met. Bobby Montgomery, Mike Langston."

They shook hands. "I've seen you around," Bobby said. "Heard you're a top-notch mechanic."

"I had top-notch government training," Mike said.

Bobby pulled out his chair. "Welcome to Mount Union."

"Mike was at the game," Brenna pointed out. "He probably remembers the fourth-down call."

"Oh, yeah," Mike said. "You must have a lot of confidence in your second-string quarterback to let him throw that pass on fourth and three."

"I do. The guy has worked hard and he's

showing real promise." Bobby ordered a beer and leaned forward, elbows on the table. "So, you like football, Mike?"

"Played it all through school," Mike said. "Defensive back, mostly."

Carrie looked up at him with something almost like admiration in her eyes. "Weren't you given a special award?" she said. "All-state or something like that?"

Shocked that she'd remember that detail of his life, he shrugged. "It was a long time ago, Carrie."

"All-state, huh?" Bobby said. "And you played a tough position. What did you think of tonight's game?"

What he really thought about the defense wasn't anything the coach would want to hear, so Mike simply took a swallow of beer and said, "You got a win, Coach. That's what counts."

Obviously Bobby was no slouch at picking up on innuendo. He gave Mike a thoughtful stare before saying, "Oh, no. You're not going to get away with that vague statement. You can tell me the truth. This was just our first game, and I'm always looking for ways to improve."

Mike rubbed his hand over his mouth. He'd be better off to keep his opinions to himself, but then, he'd never been one to do that. "Your offense was pretty stellar, Coach," he said. "But the defense…well, it's my area, and I saw some minor things. A couple of your linemen were off-balance in the three-point stance. On more than one occasion, their timing was sloppy."

"Hold it," Bobby said, and Mike figured he'd just made an enemy of the man the town obviously revered.

"Look, I'm sorry. I shouldn't have said anything…" Mike paused when Bobby got up from his chair, walked to the end of the table and sat next to him.

"You'd have better luck delivering a solid punch if we both got up and went outside," Mike said.

"I don't want to hit you," Bobby said. "I just might want to hire you."

Mike hid his shock behind a false chuckle.

"Tell me what else you noticed," Bobby said. "Fact is, I know the defense was off, but I couldn't put my finger on what was wrong. I'm more of an offense guy, but I think you picked up on the problem."

Mike grinned. If he couldn't be close to a battlefield discussing strategy, this was the next best thing. He barely heard Diana when she leaned close to Brenna and whispered something that ended with, "We've just lost our men for the rest of the night."

"You may have lost yours," Brenna said, "but I'm pretty sure Mike is his own man."

"Not so fast, gentlemen," Diana said. "Bobby, if you get Mike to help with the team, he should give equal time to Brenna to help her get the Cultural Arts Center up and running. She needs him just as much as you do."

Brenna swallowed a gasp before it slipped out. "Oh, I don't think…"

"Mike would be perfect for that project," Diana said. "He's obviously got skills. I'll bet he knows one end of a screwdriver from the other."

Mike looked at his daughter. "Didn't you tell me something about the center the other day, Carrie?"

"Yeah, Miss Sullivan mentioned it to me. It's supposed to be good for the teens in this town."

"What do you need?" Mike asked, glanc-

ing first at Diana and then Brenna. He hoped
he wouldn't regret the question.

"Tell him, Bren," Diana urged, and then
didn't give Brenna time to answer. "Just re-
pairing, light remodeling, building shelves
and such."

"I guess I could devote a few hours," Mike
said, wondering how in the span of a few
minutes, he'd been coerced into having an
active role in this community.

"Great!" Diana said. "Won't Mike be a big
help, Bren?"

Brenna's smile looked forced. "Sure.

Brenna dropped her forehead to her hands,
and Mike thought she might have groaned.
Well, okay. He'd show up a couple of nights
to help her. If she didn't want him there, he'd
quit coming. No problem.

CHAPTER SIX

"WHAT IS IT with men?" Diana said. "They've just spent the past three hours focused on football. You'd think that would be enough. But no, they're back on the same topic."

Brenna couldn't let her friend get away with her attempt to play innocent. "Never mind that," she said. "I can't believe what you just did."

"What did I do?"

"That subtle-as-a-tornado ploy you just used to trap Mike." She used her best imitation of Diana's voice. "'Help Brenna with the center. You know one end of a screwdriver from the other.'"

"I have no idea what you're talking about." Diana smiled. "You do need help with the center, don't you?"

Brenna huffed. "You know I do, but I can recruit my own volunteers. Besides, Mike has enough going on in his life."

"Then he could have said no," Diana pointed out. "And I resent your use of the word *trap*. When a man runs right into the net, like Mike just did, he wants to be trapped."

He did agree rather quickly, Brenna thought, not that Diana was excused for her behavior. "You could have asked me if I minded if he worked at the center." She frowned. "The last I heard, I was still in charge of this project."

"Of course you are," Diana said. "But we're friends. I can't imagine you'd resent me helping you find qualified workers."

"If that's really what you were doing."

"Naturally that's what I was doing. After all, you gave up your normal Friday night activities to go to a football game because his daughter asked you to. It's only fair that Mike do you a favor."

"I'm not sure I can work with him," Brenna said. "Remember how he reacted to my little battery mishap."

"Sure I remember. He charged the battery for what seemed to me a fair price, and you drove off happy."

"I wasn't happy," Brenna said. "He made me feel like an idiot for leaving my lights on."

Diana gave her a look that said *Duh*.

"Okay, it was idiotic, but the guy definitely has attitude."

"And so do you," Diana said. "So quit worrying. I got him in the net. Now you train him."

Brenna glanced at the two men who were huddled together, drawing plays on napkins and talking strategy. "We might as well not even be here," Brenna muttered to her friend. At least the two jocks hadn't heard a word she and Diana had uttered.

Diana nodded toward the door to the pizza shop. "Don't look now, Bren, but here comes a bunch more just like them."

Six boys and a couple of girls came into the restaurant, and the quiet ambiance exploded with testosterone in the throes of celebration. Diana's son, Charlie, led the group to a large booth in the corner.

"I imagine Charlie is feeling pretty good about the win tonight," Brenna said.

Motherly pride showed in Diana's eyes as she watched the group find seats around the big table. "I'm sure he is. All those kids seem pretty happy."

Before sitting, Charlie broke away from the

crowd and came over to their table. "Hey, Mom, what did you think of the game?"

"I thought you all did a great job," she said. "Congratulations."

"Thanks." Charlie looked at Mike and waited for his dad to introduce them. "How do you do, sir?"

"Fine. Good job tonight," Mike said.

"You were at the game?"

"Sure was. Enjoyed myself."

Charlie nodded and turned his attention to Carrie. A grin of recognition spread across his face. "I know you," he said. "I've seen you in the cafeteria."

Carrie's face lit. "Yeah. We have the same lunchtime." She put her hand out. "I'm Carrie."

"I thought that was your name. I had to ask about a half-dozen kids before I found someone who knew it."

Carrie positively beamed.

"I'm Charlie. You're new here, aren't you?"

"My first year."

"Oh. Cool. How do you like Mount Union High?"

Brenna was prepared for one of Carrie's typical negative comments, but the girl only kept the smile in place and said, "It's great. I'd like to meet more kids my age, though," she said.

Brenna gave her a cool-move-kid look on the sly, and Carrie smiled.

"Well, yeah, you need to do that." Charlie paused, looked over at his crowd. "Why don't you come sit with us? You won't be the only girl. I'll introduce you to some of the guys on the team, and more kids will be showing up in a few minutes."

"I'd like that," Carrie said, turning to her father. "Dad, I'm going…"

Mike stared at Charlie before concentrating on his daughter. "We've just ordered our pizza," he said. "You don't want to leave before it arrives."

"She can eat with us, Mr. Langston," Charlie said.

"Yeah, Dad. I can eat with them."

Brenna gave him a pointed look, urging him to give in. "Yeah, *Dad*. Pizza's pizza, isn't it?"

He scowled. "Okay, go ahead, but just for a while. We're not going to stay too late."

She bounded up from her chair. "Thanks, Dad."

Brenna lightly touched his arm. "Good decision, Mike."

He turned his beer in his hands. "What choice did I have? You women were ganging up on me again." He managed a smile. "But I can keep an eye on her from here."

"Be sure and stare at her a lot," Brenna said. "It'll make her feel loved."

Mike pretended he didn't hear the jab.

Mostly empty glasses and only a few crusts of pizza remained on the trays at the adults' table when the order at the corner booth arrived—three large pizzas to feed the group that had grown to twelve.

Bobby leaned back in his chair and rubbed his eyes. "I'm beat. What do you say, Di, finish your beer and let's go home?"

"Sounds good." She looked at Brenna. "You leaving soon?"

"I'll go when you guys do. Mike?"

"The kids just got their food," he said. "I'll have to wait around until Carrie's done, I guess."

"What the heck, I'll keep you company," Brenna said. She caught Diana's smile before refocusing on Mike. "I suppose we can talk about the Cultural Arts Center, now that you're going to be involved."

"Sure. You can tell me all about it."

Bobby called for the check just as Carrie left her booth and came over. "We're not leaving, are we, Dad? We just got our order."

"No. I'll wait till you're done."

Charlie walked over and stood behind Carrie. "You can go if you want, Mr. Langston. I'll bring Carrie home. We live out the same way."

Heavy creases appeared in Mike's brow. He released a long breath and said, "That's okay. I'll wait."

Carrie leaned down and spoke in her father's ear. "Dad, that is so lame! Go home!"

He narrowed his eyes at her. "Are you kidding? I'm waiting."

Bobby folded his arms on the table and said, "I'm sure it will be okay, Mike. Charlie just got his license, but he's a careful driver, and the car is safe."

"You heard him, Dad," Carrie said. "Charlie is a good driver."

"I'm sure he is," Mike said, "but I'm saying no. You go on back and eat your pizza before it gets cold, but when you're done you're riding home with me."

Carrie crossed her arms over her chest and spoke through gritted teeth. "Dad, I'll be fifteen in another two weeks. I'm old enough to ride with boys. And I'm old enough to make my own decisions."

Mike's face flushed. Brenna could see the effort it was taking for him to remain in control. He pursed his lips before answering. His voice was level and deceptively calm. "Carrie, I've told you the way it's going to be. Now go on back and eat your pizza. It's almost eleven o'clock."

"That's not late! Jeez, Dad!"

Carrie walked around to Brenna. "Miss Sullivan, can you talk some sense into him?"

Brenna put her hands up in a gesture of self-defense. She thought Mike was being overly cautious and intractable, but what could she do?

Carrie stood her ground, and then glanced back once at Charlie before giving Brenna her most pitiable look. "Please, Miss Sullivan, talk to him. I'm having such a good time."

Brenna sighed, asking herself why she was getting involved—again! "Mike, if it makes any difference, I've known Charlie for four years. He's a great kid." She regarded Diana and Bobby. "And now you know his parents." She smiled and nudged his arm, trying to keep the situation light. "It's just a ride home. Maybe you should…"

She never finished her sentence. Mike grabbed her wrist and practically lifted her from her chair. "Carrie, go back and eat your pizza. Brenna, would you come outside with me, please?"

He'd asked a question, but Brenna knew it was a demand. Still in Mike's grip, she took a couple of steps toward the door. She heard Diana say, "Bren, you want me to go with you?"

She shrugged off Diana's concern. "It's fine. We'll be back in a minute."

And then, with Mike's hand firmly against her back, she preceded him out the door and around the restaurant to the alley where deliveries were made.

"I HOPE YOU'RE HAPPY," she said when they were in the shadows of the alley.

Mike pointed to his face. "Does this look like the face of a happy man?"

She squinted in the darkness, cocked her head left and right as she made an exaggerated effort to study him. "For you? Maybe."

"I'm not in the mood for jokes," he said.

"That wasn't a joke."

This woman was determined to drive him crazy while she undermined every one of his attempts to be a careful, protective father. Just when he was beginning to think he might be able to trust her, work with her on the arts center project, just when she'd done a fairly decent job of smoothing things out between him and Carrie at the cabin, she had to butt in where she didn't belong once more. How could any sane person think a responsible father was going to allow his daughter to ride home with someone who was practically a stranger?

He forced himself to take a deep breath. Maybe stranger was a bit of an exaggeration, but Brenna had to know she was pushing his buttons.

"What did you think you were doing in there just now?" he asked.

"Helping to improve your relationship with your daughter."

"That's not your job."

She smirked at him. "I wouldn't even consider it my job if you were doing yours."

The blatant criticism was too much. When he couldn't think of a comeback, he said, "This is so not your business, lady!"

A snort burst from her mouth or her nose, or somewhere, and Mike knew he'd gone too far. But so had she.

"Lady?" Coming from her lips, the word sounded like the worst sort of insult. "Did you just call me *lady?* The calendar says we're in the twenty-first century, Mike."

He scratched the back of his neck. He wasn't a chauvinist. Never had been. "Sorry. That was uncalled for, but you get my motor racing, and not in a good way."

"That's your problem. Believe me, Mike, racing your motor in any way hasn't been my intention."

He decided to use logic, the one tactic that had always worked for him during his years in the army. Until Carrie. Until Brenna. "I don't know you all that well, Brenna, but I'm assuming you don't have any children."

"Of my own? No."

"Then of the two of us, I'm the only one who does. I'm thinking that makes me a bit more qualified than you to make parenting decisions."

"One would think so," she said. "But in your case…" She shrugged off the rest of her answer, effectively forcing him to conclude her thought. "And besides, I interact with about a hundred and ten teenagers every day. Doesn't that qualify me to have an opinion?"

"Not about the way I raise my daughter."

She didn't respond for a long time, and Mike became conscious of several physical effects of her silent treatment. The nape of his neck itched under his collar. He heard his heartbeat in his ears.

And while he found standing still increasingly uncomfortable, Brenna just continued to stare at him with an intense sort of scrutiny he figured was designed to make him squirm. Starting at his head, she worked her way down his body and back up. Analyzing, drawing conclusions, arming herself for a verbal attack, he supposed.

Unfortunately, her investigative stare only made him more aware of her eyes, as green and dark as a moonlit meadow, and her mouth, as she ran her tongue over her bottom lip in concentration. And suddenly he didn't mind being the object of her inspection. In fact, he was enjoying the way her gaze raked his body. He blinked, shook his head. Again, she was making him crazy.

"What are you doing?" he said before he made a fool of himself for giving in to impulses he hadn't exercised in way too long. "Why are you staring at me like that?"

"I'm letting you have your way."

He forced a chuckle. "Yeah, right."

"No, really. You're right. Carrie is your daughter, so I'll just say what you want to hear from now on."

"Which is what?"

"You're doing a great job with her, Pops."

The sting of her sarcasm almost felt like a slap in his face.

And she didn't let up. "She's one happy kid, isn't she? Keep up the good work. You certainly don't need my advice."

She stepped away from the wall where they'd been talking. "With that I'll say good night."

He grabbed her arm. "Oh, no. You're not leaving now."

She looked down at where his grip locked onto her upper arm. "Pardon me?"

"Why the one-eighty, Brenna? I can recognize sarcasm, but besides that, you sound serious, like you've really changed your tune."

"Oh, I have," she said. "You can make Carrie into Mount Union's first bubble girl if you want. I'm through. I've told you that Charlie's a good kid. You should be thankful she met someone who has good parents and good values. Carrie couldn't be safer with anyone else in town."

"I'm not questioning the kid's integrity."

"Then you're just questioning Carrie's?"

"No. She's a girl, that's all. It's different."

"Oh, come on, Mike. You don't believe that. Trust is trust."

He smirked. "Yeah, and pizza is pizza. I guess that's the way you look at life. Black is black and white is white."

She pried his fingers from her arm. "I didn't ask for this. This whole involved-teacher thing isn't me. I don't like football. I don't spy on students. If your daughter hadn't come looking for me a week ago, I probably never would have seen a student outside of the classroom."

"So you've just become a busybody with my kid?"

"Guess so. Nuts, isn't it?"

She locked those enormous green eyes on him again, and he felt weak inside. Mike Langston, elite army ranger, a man who'd been prepared for nearly every dangerous situation the army could conceive of, was fighting to gain mastery over trembling knees and a racing heart. The army had never prepared him for this kind of adrenaline rush.

"And you know something else?" she said, her eyes seeming to light up the alley with her anger, her indignation. Mike rubbed his finger around his collar. Even at night the Georgia breezes were hot.

He tried to speak, but his mouth opened and closed like some mindless guppy's.

"I definitely don't put up with Neanderthal fathers." She started to walk away from him. "Good night, Mike. I'll see myself out of the alley. And don't worry. You're officially relieved from any responsibility at the Cultural Arts Center. I can find someone else who knows what a screwdriver is for."

She was everything in a woman that he didn't like. Opinionated, bossy, outspoken, interfering. Yet he was suddenly overcome with panic. He didn't want her to go. Not like this. He said the word before he gave himself time to think. "Wait!"

She turned, stared.

"Don't leave. I'm…"

"You're what?"

He swallowed. "Sorry?"

"Is that a question?"

"No. I am. I'm sorry." And he was. Only he wasn't exactly sure what he was sorry about. Certainly not for protecting his daughter. He'd promised Lori. Certainly not for expressing his opinion. In the army, his opinion had been respected, sought after. So what was he sorry about?

Her face softened right before his eyes. And he thought he'd never seen such a beautiful transformation. His heart still raced and his mind still struggled to understand what was happening to him.

She walked back. "Look, Mike, you're a good man. I know that. You're swimming upstream against the current of waters you've never tested before."

She placed her palm on his arm, where the skin was exposed under his short sleeve. He thought his heart would leap from his chest.

"Something has made you not trust yourself," she said. "I don't know what, and—you'll like this—it truly is none of my business. But you're about the most uptight guy I've ever met. You're wound up. You've got to cut loose a little."

He took in a deep breath, felt his chest expand with the breeze from the creek that flowed just south of the alley. "Yeah, okay, I'll do that. No problem."

She gave him a sympathetic smile as if she knew it was indeed a huge problem. "I've got a suggestion."

"Oh. What?"

She placed both hands on his face. He gulped air, let his eyes close for just an instant so he could feel the exquisite softness of her palms. And then her lips were on his. Urgent, moist, just the right pressure for coaxing an uptight man to cut loose. It wasn't a long kiss. If it had been, he'd have died of suffocation because his ability to breathe had stopped. And the kiss wasn't invasive. But it was spectacular just the same because it had been so long since anyone had really kissed him. And because it came from her.

She stepped back, dropped her hands.

"Nice," she said. "You're a good kisser, Mike."

He didn't really believe her. He wasn't the one who'd done the kissing just now. Maybe he used to be a decent kisser, but he hadn't practiced in a year and a half. Except for the gentle press of his lips when he kissed his wife as she lay dying... *No, don't revisit that day.*

He wanted another chance. He started to reach for her when a voice invaded their privacy.

"Mike, you out here?" It was Bobby.

"Brenna? Everything okay?" Diana followed.

"We've got company," he said.

"We've got friends," she said. "It's nice to have them."

She walked ahead of him out of the alley. "We're fine. Just having a little discussion."

Diana stared at her. A subtle smile curved her lips. "I can see that."

Mike, thankful his brain was in gear again, pulled his wallet from his back pocket. "I've got to settle up the check." He handed Bobby a few bills. "Will that cover my share?"

"Oh, me, too," Brenna said, reaching into her pocket. "What do I owe?"

Mike waved his hand. "I've got this."

"Okay. I owe you."

No. No, you don't.

"Come by the field house on Monday, Mike," Bobby said. "We start practice around three o'clock. Can you adjust your work hours at the garage to sit in a couple of days, see how we do things?"

"Alvin is a Ravens supporter," Mike said. "I don't think he'll mind if I leave the shop early." He rubbed his fingers over his lips. "Oh, another thing. I guess it's okay if Carrie rides home with your son…as long as there are no stops between here and there."

Bobby smiled. "Up to you, Mike."

"I want her home by twelve, though," Mike said. "I can count on Charlie to be on time, right?"

"If he isn't, he'll answer to me."

"Fair enough."

"All's well that ends well," Brenna said. "See you all later."

She went to her car, and Mike headed back to the restaurant to tell Carrie his decision. He stopped at the door and watched until Brenna's car had sped down the road before he let out the breath he'd been holding.

CHAPTER SEVEN

ALL THE WAY home Brenna was smiling. She'd really knocked Mike Langston for a loop with that kiss. His complete jaw-dropping surprise had been evident in the tensing of every muscle in his body. And speaking of muscles—whatever the army did to train their soldiers, it worked.

She'd kissed him for the shock value, to get him to relax, make him see that life was short and everyone ought to include some spontaneous fun, whether you're thirty-something or almost fifteen. But the strangest thing was that she was a little astonished herself. Sparring with Mike had some built-in rewards. She'd told him he was a good kisser, and now, thinking back, she realized she'd been too conservative with her praise. He was a *darned* good kisser.

Imagine what that moment would have been like if *he'd* initiated the kiss. That thought kept Brenna's smile in place as she got out of her car and walked to her front door. Brenna had kissed a number of guys, some so-so, some quite skilled. Mike Langston was unlike any of the others. For the first time she wished she had a dog or a cat or even a hamster—some living, breathing being she could talk to about how she'd left Mike speechless. And about how she was having trouble moving beyond that memorable kiss. She liked the guy. He wasn't her type, of course. Too regimented, too narrowminded, definitely too old-fashioned. Or was it too principled? Principles weren't bad, but he definitely went overboard adhering to his.

Mostly she and Mike had different sets of values. Not that Brenna's were better or more worthy than his, but she'd lived this long with her belief system and wasn't about to give up her goals of security and independence. Still, Mike was a challenge, and she enjoyed trying to figure him out—for now.

In lieu of a pet, Brenna spoke to a photo on her dresser as she shed her jeans and blouse and reached for her chenille robe. "Sandy," she said to the smiling face of the ten-year-old girl standing next to her in the picture. "I have a hunch that Mike and I are going to butt heads about a lot of things. But I also have a very good feeling that he and I are going to kiss again."

Brenna and Sandy Richards had been best friends in elementary school. Sandy was the only one Brenna confided her deepest, darkest secrets to. Sandy knew about Brenna's mother's despair, her father's lack of ambition, all the hand-me-down clothes Brenna had altered to fit and detailed with inexpensive trims. Sandy had been there when Brenna taught herself to sew so she could make new clothes of her own.

The two women still talked and emailed, and Brenna visited her when she was back in that trailer for the day or two at a time she visited her parents. She didn't need Sandy for moral support so much now, but tonight, when she had something to talk about, it was nice to know Sandy was there in spirit.

"The man is frustrating, certainly not a candidate for the long term," she said to the photo, "but I can't remember when I've had so much fun." She knotted the tie on the old robe and padded barefoot down the hall to the living room. She planned to watch a little late-night TV before going to bed. Her mind was too occupied with Mike to turn itself off just now.

Before she picked up the remote on the coffee table, she saw headlights reflected in her front windowpane. A vehicle slowed to a crawl and stopped. Curious, she went to the window. Her street was normally quiet, everyone tucked in bed by eleven. Peering through a slit in the blinds, she saw a pickup truck. A blue one.

Her heartbeat accelerated. "My gosh, what's he doing here?" Her first thought was that Mike hadn't allowed Carrie to go home with Charlie after all, and he'd brought his daughter here so Brenna could act as referee again. But she dismissed that idea right away. Mike knew how she felt about Carrie riding with Charlie. Surely he wouldn't come to her to smooth over an argument with his daughter.

The truck door opened, illuminating the dome light. Mike was the only passenger. Brenna raked a few tangles from her hair with her fingers. No time for other primping. He was already walking onto her porch. She frowned down at the soft but decidedly unsexy bathrobe that had seen her through many Georgia nights and assorted crises. Oh well, Langston might as well see the down-home side of Brenna Sullivan. That was what he got for showing up unannounced.

She paused, took a couple of deep breaths after he knocked and opened the door. "Well, howdy," she said.

He appeared awkward, insecure, and for some reason Brenna found that endearing. He quickly took in her appearance from head to painted toes and said, "You're ready for bed."

"Yes. And?"

"Well, I have a few minutes."

"Until what? You run the risk of being late for the curfew you gave Carrie? Wouldn't want to do that." She looked at the clock over her fireplace. "You have forty-five minutes, to be exact." Propping her arm on the side of her door, she smiled. "So, how do you want to spend them?"

She waited. He didn't speak, but his eyes were alert, his expression anxious. Something was definitely bothering him. "Are you waiting for me to suggest how we could fill those forty-five minutes, Mike?" she finally said. "I have a few board games inside."

"I thought we could talk."

"Okay." She opened the door wider. "Come on in."

"No. I mean, no, thanks. Maybe we can talk out here."

"On the porch?"

"Yeah. It's nice and cool." He shifted his weight from one booted foot to the other. "Unless you were planning to go to bed now."

Any number of comments came to her mind, but Mike obviously wasn't prompting her for the usual flirtatious remarks. She settled for, "Not on the porch, I'm not."

She pointed to the swing hanging from her ceiling. "Sit. I think I can scrounge up some lemonades."

When she came back out with two glasses, Mike was perched stiffly on the swing, his feet planted solidly on the floor, his hands dangling between his knees. His gaze focused out over her shrubs before she cleared her throat and handed him a glass.

She sat next to him, leaving plenty of space between them. "So, what do you want to talk about?"

He took a sip of the lemonade and said, "How old do you think I am?"

This was a detail she usually guesstimated right away when she met a new guy, but she hadn't considered Mike's age. He had a teen daughter so he was definitely old enough to vote. She thought a moment. "Thinking back to when we were in the pizza shop, I'd say about sixty."

He narrowed his eyes in confused concentration before a corner of his mouth lifted in what passed for a grin. "Funny. I don't suppose you're ever going to run out of jabs at my parenting skills, are you?"

"I got a million of 'em."

"Okay, now seriously. How old am I?"

She made a show of studying him. He was an interesting-looking man. There was nothing soft about him. His dark hair, though mussed and longer than he might have liked it as a soldier, was coarse and thick. His jaw was squared, his eyes intense. Every line had been earned from experience. Even the slight stubble of beard that had grown since his last shave was rough-looking. She fisted her hand to resist touching it with the tip of a finger.

"That's enough time, Brenna," he said. "You don't need to count every gray hair."

"All right. I'm guessing thirty-five, thirty-six."

"People always guess my age as more than what it is. But you're close. I'm thirty-three."

"We're only three years apart," she said.

"Wow, you're thirty-six? That's surprising."

Her mouth opened in shock. "Younger, Mike. Younger!" When she realized he was grinning with triumph, she added, "Okay, you get a point for that one."

"I got a million of 'em."

This was cute Mike. Brenna could learn to like him. "Don't gloat," she said. "Now, why is it so important that I know your age?"

"Well, you can count backward, right? I'm thirty-three. My daughter is going to be fifteen in a couple of weeks."

"You're a young dad."

"Young, yes. It's possible I'm also insensitive and clueless, too—all those things Carrie has been pointing out to you." He clenched his hands between his knees. "But there is one thing I know plenty about."

"What's that?"

"I know what a kid's mind is on when he gets a girl alone in his car. I know because I've been there. I was seventeen when Carrie's mother and I… Well, we made a mistake."

"I should point out that times have changed. Abstinence is practiced by lots of teens today. And not all boys are alike. For instance, you didn't have Bobby and Diana as parents."

He conceded her point with a nod. "No, I didn't. My parents weren't bad people. They just sort of left me on my own."

"You hadn't heard of protection back then?"

"Of course. But I wasn't so experienced at the time. I sort of forgot."

Brenna figured she could be called insensitive herself if she said what she really thought. Too bad Mike hadn't had a teacher like her to explain all the hazards of dating and marrying too young. She'd already volunteered to teach a family-life course at the Cultural Arts Center. The school board had cut the budget for the publicly supported semester-long class two years ago. Kids needed to have certain facts before they started dating, and they should know that a baby is a twenty-four-hour responsibility. Unfortunately, many teens didn't have someone to go to for honest dialogue on these important topics.

"Thanks for not commenting on how stupid I was," he said.

"You weren't stupid. You simply didn't have someone you could trust to talk with you about these matters. I plan to drill the message of protection into my family-class students when the center is open."

He seemed surprised. "I assumed the Cultural Arts Center was just for music and theater and things like that."

"It is, but in a larger sense, it's for any class that has been cut due to budget restraints. And the word *cultural* covers a large realm of topics." She paused as an idea suddenly occurred to her. "For instance, you could even teach a class for girls on simple auto repairs."

He shook his head.

"What? You don't think our fragile Southern belles should learn how to change a tire?"

"I know better than to admit that to you."

"Everyone should know what to watch for when they're driving an automobile—how to know when your oil is low, when the engine needs water… I don't know, lots of potential problems."

"You've got a point," he said. "I guess I could give it a try."

She wanted to get back to the subject that most interested her—Mike's past—so she redirected her next question. "So you and your girlfriend found yourself in an age-old pickle?"

"That's right. I keep thinking of that movie title *It Happened One Night*."

"And Carrie is what happened?"

He nodded. "I never regretted having Carrie, though I had to put some plans on hold while I tried to earn a decent living for my family. And I cared for Lori—that's my wife's name—I really did. We'd been going together for a while, but that night in my car was the first time…"

"I get the picture. All it takes is one time."

He looked down at his shoes. "Yeah. Lori and I planned on having another kid one day, when I got out of the army. We finally saw the wisdom in having a plan."

Brenna rested her elbow on the back of the swing and gave him a serious look. "Carrie may not have been planned, but she has turned out pretty great, Mike."

"I know. I love her. I really do." He raised his face and met Brenna's gaze. "I haven't been there for her as much as I should have been, but Lori was a good mom. Those two got along like they were best friends. Don't get me wrong. Lori had to discipline her, but she had a way of doing it that was gentle, caring. That was the kind of woman she was."

"She sounds like a wonderful person. I'm sorry for your loss."

He rubbed his thumb and forefinger over his eyes. "Thanks."

She sensed there was more to the story but didn't force him to tell it. Whatever he hadn't said was probably intensely personal and, she was certain, painful.

After a few minutes he said, "I tried to make a go of being a husband and father. I enrolled in college but only lasted a couple of semesters. Working at night and going to school in the day—I couldn't cut it. I never was a particularly good student."

"So you joined the army?"

"The reserves at first so I could be close to my family. But I wasn't making enough money so I went full-time. The army paid me extra to go overseas. From that point on, I made enough to support Carrie and Lori."

Knowing that must have been a tough decision for a young dad, Brenna said, "What were you hoping to study at college?"

He chuckled in a self-deprecating way. "You probably won't believe this since my specialty in the army was mechanics, and that's what I'm doing now. But I had it in mind to become a teacher, a history teacher. You wouldn't guess it to look at me, I suppose, but I read a lot. I'm fascinated by why things happened, how history repeats itself no matter how much we think we've learned. It's all cyclical, you know."

"Enthusiasm and passion for your subject matter is the most important quality of an effective teacher." Brenna twisted her body on the swing to look more clearly into Mike's eyes. "Why don't you go to college now? You can start with a few classes a couple of nights a week."

He gave her an incredulous stare. "You're kidding, right? Now I've got Carrie to look after full-time?"

"She's old enough to stay home without you for a few hours. Or you could drop her off at my place when you go to school." *Yikes, did I just say that?* "We have great universities nearby in Augusta and Athens."

He shook his head. "An education is not really in my budget right now."

"Get a government loan. Use the military benefits that must be owed you."

"I don't know. I'd feel pretty stupid walking around campus with a bunch of freshmen. Besides, I don't know if I could succeed. I haven't studied in a long time."

"You just told me you read a lot. What do you think studying is? It's reading, listening and doing." She smiled. "I know you are good at reading and doing. The listening might take some practice...."

He laughed. "I'd better quit coming up with excuses. You seem to have an answer for all of them."

She placed her hand over his knee and then pulled it back. Perhaps he would resent the familiarity. Or misinterpret it. But for this one moment she felt she was making a connection with Mike.

"Look, the army worked well for you for a long time, enabled you to take care of your family. But you're not likely to go back now, so why not think of your future and what you really want to do? This point of your life could present a really worthwhile opportunity."

"I thought I wanted to come here," he said. "Start over in a safe, comfortable space where Carrie and I could get to know each other." He rubbed his nape. "But you can see that isn't working out too well. All Carrie talks about is going back to California, how much better California is than Georgia. Carrie is my responsibility now. She's my future. I have to consider her needs."

"Of course you do," Brenna said. "But you're new at this fathering business, and you're likely to make some mistakes. Despite all that, Carrie loves you. I can see that even if you don't."

"Then why do I feel like everything I do is a failure?"

"You'll get the hang of it. Don't put so much pressure on yourself to have all the answers now."

He leaned back in the swing, resting his head on the back and looking up at the ceiling. "That's just it. I didn't have time to ask Lori all the questions. By the time I got to her, she wasn't strong enough to fill me in on all the details of our little girl's life." He blinked rapidly. "Little girl? Ha. That's the way I remember her. And when Lori said I should protect her, keep her from harm, that's all I could think about, and all I think about now. Keeping a promise by protecting our little girl."

"That's instinctive, Mike," Brenna said. "Dads want to protect their daughters. But Carrie isn't so little and she needs more from you than just protection."

He sat up straight again and looked at her. "Maybe you can help."

Brenna almost laughed. "You want my help? There's a one-eighty if I ever heard one. Remember, I don't have kids of my own."

He had the decency to look guilty. "I'm sorry I said that. You don't have to have kids to be good with them."

She felt the need to correct him. "I'm good with them as a *teacher,* that's pretty much it."

"That's not true. You can help her with the things I can't, you know. Girl stuff."

"Girl stuff?"

"Shopping, clothes, that kind of thing."

She couldn't help noticing he hadn't mentioned boys. For a girl Carrie's age, the topic of boys was definitely girl stuff.

He looked around Brenna's porch, pointing at various objects—hanging flower arrangements, the wreath on the door, the colorful metal umbrella stand. "You have all these… things. I'm thinking it would be okay if you took Carrie shopping sometime. Her birthday's coming up soon, and I don't have any idea what to get her."

Oh, no. She wasn't falling into that trap. "Or maybe you could take her shopping. It's another opportunity for you, Mike, to get to know her."

He shook his head. "If I'm in a woman's store more than two minutes, I get the shakes. The walls start closing in."

"That's ridiculous."

"It's true. The one time I took Carrie to a decorating store to buy things to fix up her room, she started fingering everything, smelling every candle, plumping every pillow. I was ready to jump out of my skin."

"You poor baby. Did she buy anything?"

"No. She said I made her nervous. The whole trip was a disaster. That's why I thought you—"

"I'm not your answer, Mike." Just thinking of such a personal commitment to Carrie made Brenna cringe. Should she tell Mike about her past so he would understand her reluctance? Sure, maybe offering friendship to this one child would turn out okay, but it could lead to another child, another year… and another, until who knew… Marcus all over again.

"Mike, you should understand something about me," she said.

"What?"

"I made a vow a long time ago that I wouldn't get involved in my students' lives on a personal level. I've already broken that rule numerous times where Carrie is concerned."

"I don't understand," he said. "Why wouldn't you want to get involved? Kids are your business, aren't they?"

"Teaching them is my business. Being their buddy isn't." He still looked confused by her attitude so she added just enough to make him consider her position. "Look, a few years ago, I got mixed up with a middle school boy who had some problems. I tried to help him out, and I only made things worse. Much worse."

"How could you make things worse?"

"Believe me, I did." *And the kid ended up*

*in the hospital and I've never forgiven myself
for the way I handled the situation.*

"I'm just talking about a trip to the store. I
figured you two would enjoy it."

"It's not that I wouldn't enjoy it. It's that I
don't want to develop that level of intimacy
with someone else's daughter. If you need a
counselor for Carrie…"

His lips thinned. "Don't go there, Brenna.
In California, that's all I ever heard. Counselor, therapist. Carrie didn't want to go, and
I don't want to force her. She's okay. Or she
will be."

"Fine. I think she'll be okay, too."

"Brenna, I'm just looking for a favor from
you."

"I think you're looking for a way out of a
situation that makes you uncomfortable."

"Okay, that, too. But it would mean a lot to
me. You'd be a great role model for Carrie.
She already likes you."

"I like her, too…."

He sensed her weakening and pushed
harder. "Then say you'll at least think about
it. It's not like you have to go tomorrow or
anything. Her birthday's two weeks off. You
set the date."

He waited, his expression hopeful. Could she do this again? Should she? The circumstances were obviously different now. Carrie wasn't suffering anything similar to what Marcus had.

"Well, will you think about it?"

"Okay, I'll think about it, but no promises. There's a bed and bath shop in Augusta."

"That'd be great, Brenna."

"I only said I'd think about it."

"I know." Despite his apparent appreciation, his eyes narrowed.

"What's the problem now?"

"I was just wondering. I'm not a rich man. You've seen the cabin. It's pretty basic, nothing fancy. What do you suppose a room makeover for a teenager will cost? Would a hundred bucks do it?"

Brenna had spent more than that on her down comforter. Maybe this was her way out of this dilemma. But she heard herself say, "Yeah, I think we can manage to make a few changes on a hundred dollars."

He set his nearly untouched lemonade on the floor but didn't stand.

"Is there anything else, Mike?" Brenna

asked. "Your reason for stopping by was to ask me to go shopping with Carrie?"

"Not entirely."

"So there's something else?"

He half grinned. "I owe you, that's all."

"You owe me? I haven't agreed to do anything yet. I've only given you some advice, and that's free."

He leaned closer to her on the swing. "No, not for the advice. I'm still not sure I'm even going to take any of it."

She smiled. "Figures. Then what do you owe me for?"

"Back in the alley, you gave me something, and I've been thinking about returning the favor."

She clutched the lapels of her robe. "You were furious at me in the alley."

"I know, but then you gave me that kiss."

"I was trying to make a point."

"I didn't know what to make of that kiss, Brenna. I'm not really looking for a relationship."

For a moment she could only stare back at him. Then she said, "Mike, it was a kiss, not a marriage proposal."

"Well, sure, I understand, but I know you

don't go around kissing guys all the time, and…"

"Actually, you don't know that," she said. "Kissing you didn't mean I was ready to attach you to a ball and chain. I didn't mean to terrify you."

"It wasn't terrifying."

She sighed. She had no idea where he was going with this conversation. "Gee, that's good to hear."

"I said I owed you, remember?"

She nodded.

He wrapped both hands around her upper arms and held her tight. "I figure I should give back what you gave me."

She started to speak, but her words were muffled by the press of his lips. Soft yet hungry. And extremely satisfying.

He pulled back. "There, we're even."

She let out the breath she'd been holding. "And now I'm a little terrified."

He smiled. "I've got to go. There's a curfew…"

"Right."

He stood and walked briskly to his truck. Brenna remained on her porch swing, her hands clutching her robe, her face warming to the roots of her hair. Here she was, in the baggy old robe she'd had for years, her hair bushy in humidity-frizzed waves, and she'd never felt more beautiful in her life. Or more confused. But at least she now knew what a kiss initiated by Mike Langston felt like.

CHAPTER EIGHT

"WHAT? YOU KISSED HIM?"

Brenna put a finger to her lips. It was Saturday morning. She and Diana were at the crowded Mount Union Diner having coffee. "Lower your voice," she said. "Do you want the whole town to hear you?"

Diana complied and spoke in a loud whisper. "I just knew something had been going on in that alley. Bobby thought so, too."

"It shouldn't have happened," Brenna said. "But you know how I am—spontaneous and not always on my best behavior. Mike had been yelling at me—again!"

"And of course you weren't yelling back."

"Well… Anyway, I just wanted to loosen him up, make him see that life doesn't have to be so serious all the time. A kiss seemed like the best way to do that."

Diana grinned. "I see. And did he find your tactic the least bit amusing?"

"I'm not sure. With Mike, how can you tell? But after he allowed his daughter to ride home with Charlie, he stopped by my house."

Diana allowed the waitress to refill her cup before focusing on Brenna again. "Now this is getting really interesting. Did you talk about what happened in the alley?"

"No." That was sort of a lie, but Brenna didn't want to admit that Mike returned the kiss or that she liked it. "He was all serious again, talking about his problems with Carrie, asking me to take her shopping. He only stayed a few minutes."

"He's really got it for you, Bren."

"Don't be ridiculous. The only thing he's got for me is contempt and enough of a begrudging admiration that he can ask a favor of me. He's smart enough to know that he's got some weaknesses in the dad department."

Diana shook her head in deep concentration. "You're wrong. If a guy like Mike—the strong, silent type—makes it a point to come over to your house at eleven at night, that's not contempt."

"He's just desperate for someone to help him with Carrie—so desperate he would come to me." The waitress put their check on the table. Brenna knew they should free up the space so another group could sit, but she hadn't yet made her point. "This situation is becoming too involved for me, Diana. I can't forget that I'm not the mothering type...."

"So you've said, but maybe you are the girlfriend type."

"No. I won't let a relationship with Mike develop. I can't. There's no future in it for either of us. You know I'm dating Alex. And now, thanks to you, Mike will be working at the center. And Bobby's roped him into helping the football team. I'll see him nearly every day, which will only make things more uncomfortable."

Diana tapped her wristwatch. "And why exactly are you telling me this when you know I have to meet Bobby at the bank in ten minutes? What can I do about it?"

Brenna did have a suggestion she'd thought about much of the previous night. "I'd like you to convince Mike not to work at the center, tell him you made a mistake and that I have enough volunteers. I can't work with him, Diana. We don't get along." *And I'm afraid I could really like him and I don't want to.*

"Sounds like you were getting along just fine Friday night."

Brenna couldn't argue that point. People who don't get along generally don't end the night with a dynamite kiss. She tried a different approach. "We're so different," she said. "I can't imagine him taking directions from me."

"Didn't you just remind me last night that you're in charge of this project?"

"Yes. So?"

Diana fished in her purse for her wallet and placed some bills over the check. Then she smiled and said, "Then act like the woman in charge, Bren, and handle your own personnel problems." She walked to the door, but stopped and said, "Don't forget the barbecue tomorrow. You were at the game, which makes you part of the celebration. So try to celebrate, okay?"

MIKE COULDN'T REMEMBER when he'd had a worse weekend, at least since coming home from Afghanistan to say goodbye to his wife. The downward slide had begun Friday night when he'd made a darn fool of himself in front of Brenna Sullivan. He'd ended up looking like a middle school kid who didn't know the first thing about women when he'd used that line about returning the kiss.

And that word she'd used. *Terrified.* He hadn't been able to put it out of his mind. It wasn't a word that any well-trained army ranger liked to hear in any situation, especially one involving something as simple as a kiss.

Granted, Mike did have a few shortcomings when it came to women, but he wasn't a complete dunce. He'd married young, but in high school he'd enjoyed modest popularity. In the army, women recruits came on to him occasionally, but he'd told them he was married—seriously married—and the advances stopped. Ultimately, Mike hadn't been with any woman other than his wife in fifteen years, so for him, that kiss from Brenna had not been simple.

After a nearly sleepless night, he'd been called into work on Saturday. And when he'd come home in the afternoon, Carrie had fluctuated between euphoria about "meeting a boy" and despair that she was stuck in "this awful cabin another Saturday night."

Though dog-tired, he'd suggested going to

Augusta to a movie. She'd turned down his offer, saying he'd never agree to see a flick she would pick. Even when he said he would, she declined, went in her bedroom and spent the night on the computer. He heard her giggle a few times so he assumed she'd found someone to chat with who was far more interesting than her father. Possibly Charlie Montgomery.

Now it was Sunday morning, 9:00 a.m. and his fantasy of sleeping late had been destroyed by the rockin' sound of Justin or Robin or some other teen heartthrob playing full volume through the four small rooms of the cabin. Mike stumbled into the kitchen to find Carrie flipping pancakes in one of his grandmother's old cast-iron skillets.

"Hi, Dad. Sleep well? I made breakfast. I thought maybe I could get a dog. Would that be okay?"

His brain buzzed with the effort of trying to block out drums and guitars so he could keep up with her disjointed chatter. He plopped down in a chair and said, "Not especially. I can see that. We'll talk about it… after coffee."

She set a mug on the counter in front of

the steaming coffeepot. "I made that, too, but I've never made coffee before so it might not be any good."

He dropped two loaded teaspoons of sugar in the nearly black liquid she set before him and took a sip. Way too strong. He'd have to put coffee on the shopping list. But the caffeine jolt opened his eyes. "It's fine. Can you turn down the music a little?"

"Oh, sure." She scurried into the living room and cut the volume on her iPod. A smile settled on Mike's face. He actually heard a bird chirp in his backyard.

She came back to the kitchen and resumed flipping pancakes. He noticed she was wearing an outfit she must have brought from California. A too-short skirt with glittery stuff on the back pockets and a tank top with a big cloth flower of some kind over her right… He averted his gaze after deciding he wouldn't allow her to wear that getup to school.

She put a plate of pancakes in front of him. Normally Mike couldn't even think of food until he'd been awake an hour. He usually fired up with coffee at home and ordered a biscuit or a doughnut from the guy who stopped at the garage every morning in a mobile truck café. But his daughter was in a good mood, and he wasn't about to spoil it, so he poured on the syrup and dug in.

Carrie fixed a plate for herself and sat opposite him at the table. "It's a nice day, isn't it?" she said.

He glanced out the window. "Yeah, it's nice."

"Good day to go outside and do something."

This was getting weird. Did she want to go somewhere outside with him? Dare he hope? "I suppose."

She drummed her fingers on the tabletop. "I hope something comes up," she said. "I finished all my homework last night."

He swallowed and gave her his full attention. "Are you waiting for me to suggest something?"

"Oh, no. You rest today, Dad. You had to work yesterday. You need a day off."

"Well, if I'm going to be resting, what's going to come up?"

She showed him a brilliant smile. "Who knows? I just believe in possibilities. You can never tell, right?"

Oh, he could tell. He could tell he was being set up.

A half hour later the pancakes were gone and the kitchen was clean. Carrie sat on the front porch rocking idly in one of his grandmother's old wood slat chairs. The raucous sounds of an electric guitar alerted Mike that her custom ringtone had kicked in on her cell phone. She answered on the first chords. Mike went to the front door and listened.

"Oh, hi." Her voice positively floated. "Yes, I think it's going to be okay."

A pause. Then, "No, I haven't asked him yet, but hold on. I will now."

Mike hurried away from the door and picked up a magazine.

Carrie came in the house, the phone clutched in her hand. "Dad, this is Charlie Montgomery."

He nodded.

"He…ah, asked me to go somewhere with his family today."

"Where?"

"To this place just outside of town called the Riverview Tavern."

Mike shook his head. He'd heard of it from the guys at the garage. "It's a bar."

"It's a restaurant."

"It's mostly a bar, and it's probably a good seven, eight miles from here."

She frowned. "So what? I said we were going with his family. You know them."

Aware that the phone connection to Charlie was probably still live, Mike kept his cool. "Tell Charlie you'll call him back. We'll discuss this."

"Why can't you tell me now? Why do you have to make everything such a big production?"

"Carrie…"

She put the phone up to her ear. "I guess I have to call you back." She waited. "What? Oh, okay."

Holding the phone toward Mike, she said, "It's for you."

Ambush phase. Mike wasn't about to be caught unprepared. "I don't need to talk to Charlie. Tell him you'll call…"

"It's his dad on the line."

"Oh." Mike took the phone. "Bobby?"

"Hey, Mike. I was going to call you this morning. Looks like the kids beat me to it."

Didn't Bobby Montgomery know that dads should stick together? Next to soldiers, cops and firefighters standing by one another, it ought to be the most important male bond. "What about?"

"I should have mentioned this Friday night when we were all together. A friend of my family's, a native of Mount Union, opened a restaurant called the Riverview."

"I've never been there," Mike said.

"It's a nice place," Bobby continued. "Anyway, this guy is having a barbecue today for all the players and their friends and family. Quite a crowd. This party has sort of become a tradition after the first game of the season. Since you might be a Raven come Monday, I wanted to invite you and Carrie, of course. Be a good opportunity for you to meet a lot of people."

And a perfect opportunity for Carrie, as well. She could mingle to her heart's content while he maintained a close watch. "I appreciate that," he said. "Carrie and I will be glad to come. What time?"

"The official start is one o'clock, but here's the thing, Mike. Charlie, Diana and I are going early to help get things ready. Charlie was kind of hoping that Carrie could ride along with us." He paused. When Mike didn't say anything he added, "I'll be doing the driving and Diana and I will watch out for the kids. You don't have to worry."

Mike supposed he was right. And he couldn't come up with a logical excuse to deny his daughter a ride to the party. "Okay, then," he told Bobby. "You want me to drop Carrie off at your place?" In the background Carrie squealed with triumph.

"We'll pick her up. About a half hour from now if that's okay."

"That's fine. I'll see you all there later."

He disconnected Carrie's phone and handed it to her. "Keep this with you at all times."

"I will." She grinned at him. "And, Dad, thanks. You don't have to hurry now, see? You can take your time, even go back to bed awhile if you want."

"I'm fully rested." He gave her another once-over. "Are you wearing that outfit?" When he saw the pout start to form, he quickly amended, "Never mind. Go on and do whatever you have to do to get ready. They'll be here soon."

"Thanks, Dad." She waited a few seconds before closing the gap between them and giving him a quick hug. The only other time he remembered Carrie hugging him was after the funeral. This was definitely better.

Mike fiddled around for a couple of hours trimming some bushes, reading, cleaning up. Then he went to take a shower, wondering just who would be at this shindig today.

At one-thirty, he pulled into the parking lot at the Riverview. The building looked much like he'd thought it would—lots of neon signs, though not lit in the daytime, a tin roof and weathered wood siding. A porch extended across the front and around the side. The lot was full of pickups, SUVs and small, older cars probably belonging to teens.

He found a spot near the back of the parking lot, where the restaurant bordered the river. When he got out of his truck, he was assailed by the scent of rich, sweet and tangy barbecue sauce. A huge iron smoker near the building's back deck hissed steam from under the cover and through slits on top. Mike's mouth watered. Nothing beat authentic barbecue.

To the beat of fiddle and guitar strings of a live country band, he entered the restaurant. He didn't figure he'd know anyone other than his daughter and the Montgomerys, but that was okay. He was here for one reason—to keep his eye on Carrie. He spotted her right away in the main dining area. She was standing near the platform where the band played. Charlie was next to her, his hands in his pockets. Other than the occasional smile she gave him, he wouldn't have assumed they'd come together and would probably leave the same way.

Satisfied that his daughter was okay for now, Mike escaped the noise and headed into the bar, where he could adapt to the environment with a beer in his hand. And then he saw Brenna.

Surprised, he stopped, stared at her and reminded himself that she didn't even like football. But of course she'd be here anyway. He figured she liked parties. She looked much more appropriate to the atmosphere than he did in his beige cargo shorts, gray-and-blue U.S. Army T-shirt and sandals. Brenna had on a denim skirt that flared just above her knees, tan cowboy boots with fancy blue stitching and a scoop-neck short-sleeved white blouse that looked as though it came from the vineyards of Tuscany—not that he'd ever been there.

Her curly red hair was secured in a high ponytail with a blue ribbon. She could have been fresh off a bluebonnet Texas meadow. And just as inviting to a man who hadn't seen a meadow in a long time.

He stood out of sight and wondered what he should do. Retrace his steps and escape to his truck for a couple of hours? Or put the awkwardness of Friday night behind them and go up and talk to her? Of course he should. He'd gone on numerous night raids in the Middle East. Mortar shells had whizzed by his head. Bombs had exploded on dusty roads ahead of his vehicle. He was a ranger, one of the army's elite. So he straightened his spine and walked up to her. She was alone, leaning on the bar and speaking to the middle-aged bartender.

She seemed to sense his approach and turned around just as he reached the bar. He allowed himself to believe that her expression showed pleasure. "Well, look who's here," she said. "I've heard your name a lot today."

"Really? What'd I do now?"

She smiled. "The town is all abuzz about a former all-state defensive something-or-other helping Bobby with the team."

"That word's out already?"

"It's a small town, remember?"

"That's fine, I guess, but I'm not here so much for football as I am…" He let his sentence trail off, knowing she would finish it.

She glanced into the main dining room. "For guard duty?"

He shrugged.

"You want a beer?" She looked back at the bartender. "This is Lou Sanderson. He owns this place."

Mike shook his hand and placed his order.

"I hear you're going to be helping Bobby out with the defense," Lou said as he set down a frothy cold bottle.

"I'll be on the field for practice tomorrow. We'll see how it goes." He started to take his wallet from his back pocket.

"No tab today," Lou said. "On the house along with all the ribs, wings and beans you can eat."

"I appreciate that." Mike took a pull on the bottle and spoke to Brenna. "I'm glad you're here."

"Really?"

"Yeah. I was wondering if we could go find a table somewhere and have a talk about…"

He never finished. A tall man came out of the hallway to the restrooms and strode over to them. He immediately looped one arm around Brenna's shoulders, pushed a perfectly cowboy-curled banded straw hat back from his forehead and said, "All taken care of, missy. I'm ready for a return to the dance floor."

Mike disliked the guy instantly, although it wasn't his general nature to form such quick opinions. But this urban cowboy was too much in his designer Western shirt with the shiny buttons and embroidered cacti. If his jeans had been any tighter, he'd have had to lie down to breathe. And his boots. Snake-skin with a point sharp enough to kill an ant in the corner.

Brenna patted the hand that dangled next to her throat as if the guy were a child and said, "Mike, this is Alex Cameron. Alex, Mike Langston."

"Howdy," Alex said in a refined voice that was much more Southern drawl than Texas twang. His grin, however, was Texas-sized and about as phony as the rest of him. "You know my little cactus flower, Brenna?"

"I do," Mike said. "We're…ah, acquaintances."

Right. She was an acquaintance he just happened to enjoy kissing.

"You never know what to expect when Bren's around," Alex said. His words were slurred.

Mike suffered through a brief replay of Friday night's kisses and couldn't argue.

Brenna scooted out of Alex's hold, turned him around and nudged him toward the dining room. "Okay, Tex, let's swing to a couple of songs, and then maybe you and I should get some food."

Alex held his hand out to the bar. "One more, Lou, if you don't mind."

Brenna shook her head at Lou before concentrating on Alex again. "It's only two o'clock, Alex. You'll never make it to the buffet table at this rate."

"Aw, honey…"

Mike headed toward the exit as Brenna and Alex went into the dining room and the dance floor. Taking a seat outside and nursing his beer, he couldn't help wondering what Brenna saw in that jerk.

THE TEXAS TWO-STEP was suddenly the Texas barely-managed-one-step. Tired of leading, Brenna grabbed hold of Alex's arm and tried to get him to a table where they could sit down.

"Hey, the song's not over," he said, trying to keep time with the music. "And anyway, I'll bet Lou's got my beer ready."

She leaned against him to help him stand without swaying. "Alex, don't you think you ought to give it a rest?"

"Hey, I had a big breakfast. All those eggs and sausages are soaking up my brews."

"Yeah, right. Still, let's avoid the bar for a while."

He gave her a sorrowful look and drawled, "You're a bossy gal for sure. But I want to finish this song."

"All right, although this is the last one. We need to eat."

Fortunately Brenna wasn't able to complete the dance. Her cell phone vibrated in her pocket. She pulled it out and recognized her mother's number. "I've got to get this," she said to Alex. "Go sit down and wait for me."

"Don't go, Bren," he said. "Dance to the end."

"I can't." She looked around the room, spotted one of the single moms who had a son on the football team and waved her over. "Hey, Elaine, can you finish this one out with Alex?"

The woman was only too happy to oblige. After all, Brenna was partnering her with a coveted date—Alex Cameron, rising young Augusta financier, who was incredibly good-looking and had inherited money to spend.

Relieved to be free of her burden, Brenna watched them twirl and stumble across the dance floor as she headed toward the back door of the restaurant and the quiet of the creek-front deck.

She connected right away. "Hi, Mom."

"Ohh…Brenna baby…"

Her mother's voice hitched, and Brenna prepared herself for bad news. "What's wrong, Ma?"

"It's Carl."

"Daddy? What's happened to Daddy?"

"We're at Mercy Hospital."

Brenna pressed her hand over her heart. "What? Why?"

"He got a temp job cleaning out the gut-ters at the office of the trailer park. He was so happy to get it, as you can imagine." Alma paused and took an audible long breath. "He'd just gone over there about an hour before…"

Brenna's patience began to fray. "Mom, just tell me what happened!"

"It's a two-story building, and your dad was up on the ladder. Part of the gutter gave way, and the ladder slipped."

"Oh, no. Mom, is he okay?"

"When he fell, Brenna, he twisted his leg pretty bad. I called an ambulance. I had the good sense to tell the paramedics to take him to County, but they didn't. They took him to Mercy because it's closer."

"That's normal, Mom. It's what they're supposed to do."

"They say Carl's leg is broken. It's what they call a compound fracture."

Knowing the diagnosis was serious, Brenna tried to keep her voice steady. "I understand. What are they going to do?"

"They have to operate, Brenna. Put in pins. But they won't do it here at Mercy because we don't have insurance." Alma started to cry.

Brenna closed her eyes, leaned against the railing on the deck and drew in a deep breath.

"They can't just refuse to treat him, Mom. They have to do something."

"Oh, they did," Alma said. "They put this partial cast on him and told me to take him to County for the surgery. They'll do it for free over there."

Brenna recalled the conversation she'd had with her mother a few months ago. Alma told her they'd stopped paying their health insurance because her dad was approaching the age of sixty-five, and he would soon be covered by Medicare. Soon but not yet. Brenna had argued with her, but Alma had been adamant that the minimal risk was worth saving the money.

Getting angry wouldn't help anything now, so Brenna said, "Okay. Are you able to get him over to County?"

"No. They said he'd have to be transported in a private ambulance. I called a company and they are sending one over to take him. But the thing is…"

Brenna knew where this was going. The thing is, the Sullivans didn't have the money to pay for the transport.

"They won't take him unless I pay. It's two hundred and twenty-five dollars, Brenna. I have to pay them up front. And Mercy asked me what I could pay here for what they did."

"What did you tell them?" Brenna held her breath.

"They asked if I could pay at least 10 percent. I said I could. I thought it would be okay. We have a little in our checking account."

"How much, Mom?"

"I owe two thousand here, honey. I told them I'd pay 10 percent of it. They'll bill me the rest."

"Do you have that much, plus the money for the transport?"

Her mother's sobs tore at Brenna's heart. "I only have fifty dollars. Carl's Social Security check comes in a few days…"

"It's all right, Mom. Don't cry. I can help out. I need to transfer some money from my savings account to your checking account. It will take an hour or so. This is Sunday…"

"Oh, Brenna, I'm so sorry. I just didn't know what to do. I guess I could have driven your father to County myself, but the doctors…"

"No, Mom. You did the right thing." Brenna knew her mother was too stressed out to transport her injured husband across the county. "For now, Mom, just tell them at Mercy and the ambulance company that the money is coming. You can go ahead and write them both a check."

Alma sniffed loudly. "Brenna, you are such a good girl. The Lord blessed us when He gave you to Carl and me."

As usual, her mother's obsequious gratitude only made matters worse. At the heart of it was Brenna's belief that her obligations to her parents would never be over. She sighed. "Mom, I've got to go and get this straightened out. It'll be okay."

She disconnected and allowed herself a few seconds to calm down before going back inside. She realized her hands were shaking. Staring over the water, she drew in several gulps of air. She had to get to her computer at home, where she'd stored her bank account numbers. She'd left her car at Alex's cabin this morning, and he was certainly in no shape to drive her to get it. And anyway, Alex's cabin was at least a thirty-minute drive away. Brenna didn't have that much time.

She could ask Diana to drive her home. She knew at least a dozen other people who would agree to help, as well. She entered the restaurant again, walked through the public rooms to the door leading to the front porch, where she'd watched one of her friends go a few minutes earlier.

It seemed as if her footsteps guided her, not her conscious thought, because when she stepped out onto the porch, she saw the steadiest, most dependable person she knew in Mount Union. Again without thinking, she walked up to Mike Langston.

CHAPTER NINE

MIKE NURSED HIS beer alongside two other Mount Union citizens who appeared to belong to this party about as much as he did. After watching Brenna waltz off with her date, he'd been relieved to join the pair of anti-cowboys at an outside picnic table. The three were involved in a lively conversation about motors and horsepower, and Mike had found his comfort zone.

One of the men stared across the deck and lifted his bottle in a greeting. "Look who it is—my favorite teacher. Howdy, Brenna. You are lookin' fine today, girl."

Mike twisted around to see Brenna urgently clipping across the wooden floor in her fancy boots.

She stopped at Mike's shoulder. "Hi, Duane, Stuart. Do you guys mind if I borrow your buddy here?"

Both men gave Mike a suggestive grin.

"Just bring him back the way you found him, Bren," Duane said. "We were just getting to know this guy."

"I promise." She looked down at Mike. "I need a favor."

He stood. "Okay. What do you want me to do?" Secretly he was kind of hoping she wanted him to deck the boyfriend.

"Can you run me back to Mount Union? I don't have my car, and I need to get to my house right away."

"What about Roy Rogers? Can't he take you?" Mike regretted the flippant question the moment he asked it. Truthfully, he wouldn't want Brenna riding anywhere with the blurry-eyed Alex.

As if reading his mind she said, "You saw him. I don't want to get in a car with Alex."

Mike enjoyed playing hero, and he got an extra kick out of one-upping Alex. "I'll take you," he said. "Just let me tell Carrie."

"You're a lifesaver." She took his hand and led him to the dance floor. "You find Carrie, and I'll tell Alex I'll be back in a while."

Alex, struggling to keep time to a slow country song, was snake-wrapped around a tall, lanky blonde. Brenna frowned. "On second thought, just tell Carrie. We'll be back before Alex even knows I'm gone."

Mike explained the situation to his daughter, who reacted about as he'd expected. "Sure, Dad, see you later." She didn't even look at him. Mike pointed a warning finger at Charlie, who had his arm around Carrie's waist. Brenna tugged him toward the door.

They got in Mike's truck, and he backed out of the parking lot. Brenna sat straight, her eyes on the road. She chewed on a fingernail.

"Want the air-conditioning on, or the windows down?" Mike asked.

"Let's have some fresh air. I think I need it for what I have to do."

Mike couldn't remember being with Brenna when she wasn't confident, bossy and totally together—until now. He draped one arm over the steering wheel and stole a glance at her. "What's going on, Brenna?"

Her eyes narrowed. "It's nothing. A personal problem. Wouldn't interest you."

"You'd be surprised what interests me," he said. "I'm normally a good listener, though you might get a different opinion from my daughter."

He waited, but she didn't provide any information.

He cleared his throat. "So, why are we rushing to your house in the middle of a party? Seems rather strange behavior considering your love of football."

She gave him something like a genuine smile. "I need to arrange a money transfer, that's all," she said. "I promised to send someone a loan."

"I see. Someone in town?"

"No."

Though it was probably a dumb idea, Mike decided to probe deeper. "And this person has nowhere else he can get the money? No other source but you?"

"That's about the size of it."

Another silence during which Mike focused on the road. "Do you want to hear some music?"

"Not really. After the band at the Riverview just now, I think I'm tired of foot-stomping decibels."

"Okay." He drove into town and was relieved when they passed a location that would introduce a neutral topic, maybe get Brenna to open up and at least acknowledge his existence. Mike nodded out his window at a venerable brick building. "Isn't that where the Cultural Arts Center is going to be?"

She leaned across the gap between the seats and looked. "Yeah, that building was the town's original library, built in 1912."

"Looks to be in reasonable condition. Hard to destroy a brick structure."

"I suppose. It definitely has good bones."

"Or a good spine, in this case," Mike said, trying to lighten the mood. When Brenna gave him a confused look he added, "Books used to be there, right? Spine. Get it?"

"Oh. Clever." She said the words but without conviction.

"So when do we get inside to start working?"

"In a week or so." It was a vague answer, another indicator that she wasn't into talking right now. "Turn here," she said. "This is my street."

As if he didn't know that. He slowed and pulled in front of her house. "You want me to go in with you? I promise to mind my own business."

"Sure. You may as well cool off in my air-

conditioning. I think there's a beer in the refrigerator."

"No, thanks. What about some lemonade?
Any left over from Friday night?" Just mentioning Friday night, those kisses, made him
realize that he needed to cool off.

"I think so."

She unlocked the front door and preceded
him inside. She immediately went toward a
hallway, explaining that her computer was in
her office. "Make yourself at home," she said
as she left him in the living room.

Her instructions were easy to follow. He
looked around at the furnishings that defined
Brenna and decided that almost anyone would
feel at home in and be impressed with the immaculate, comfortable space. The room was
small and minimally decorated with quality
pieces. A plush beige sofa with accent pillows took up one wall. Two chairs flanked an
old stone fireplace. Tasteful artwork, low-lit
lamps and a pair of expertly crafted built-in
cupboards completed the welcoming atmosphere. After getting the lemonade, Mike sat
on the sofa and put his feet on a soft leather
ottoman. He did indeed feel at home. A sig-

nificant step for a man who hadn't felt at home anywhere in years.

After a few minutes he wandered to the fireplace to get a better look at a pair of pastoral watercolors on each side of the mantel. He wondered where Brenna bought them. A local artist perhaps. They seemed to capture the green hills of the Georgia countryside.

Brenna's voice carried down the hallway. Despite knowing he was eavesdropping, Mike edged closer. Her words conveyed frustration and more. Worry. A hint of desperation.

"I did this as fast as I could," she said. "It's Sunday. The banks aren't open, and I had to arrange an electronic transfer."

There was a pause before she added, "The funds should be there now. Tell the hospital to check your account balance."

Mike heard a soft but rhythmic tapping as if Brenna were drumming her fingernails on her desk. "Yes, I know it was hard for you to ask for the money." She sighed. "I know you'll pay me back. Just do what you need to for now." Her normally steady voice vibrated with obvious concern. "This is all I have. I'm tapped out. You just have to make this work."

There was another pause during which

Brenna sniffled. Mike walked closer to the door to her office and peered in. He knew he was violating her privacy, but he wanted to be there if she needed support. She murmured a quick, "Tell him I love him, and I love you, too," and disconnected. Mike heard the familiar chimes of a computer shutting down.

She sat in her office chair for nearly a full minute, just staring at the black monitor. Finally Mike coughed into his hand. She turned suddenly. "What are you doing there? Did you listen to my conversation?"

"I didn't intend to, but I heard you from the living room. It sounded like you were upset, and so I came into the hallway…"

She swiped at her eyes with an index finger that she dried on her skirt. "This was private," she said. "You had no right."

He leaned on the door frame. "Okay." He used the perfect comeback for her accusation. "But sometimes, and I think you'll agree, we do things whether we have a right to or not. Sometimes we just sense a need and step in."

Her eyes widened with recognition and maybe a grudging admiration. "Point taken." She stood. Despite the cowgirl boots with two-inch heels, she seemed small and vulnerable. "So what all did you hear?"

"Pretty much all of it. You mentioned a hospital. Is someone ill?"

She closed her eyes for a moment and took a deep breath. "My father. He suffered a compound fracture of the leg today. That was my mom I was talking to. She's trying to get a hospital to operate…" Her voice broke and she inhaled to steady herself. "I mean, she found a hospital but it's across the county and…"

Mike was aware that some hospitals gave emergency treatment and dismissed indigent patients to other facilities. "Your parents are asking you for money? Don't they have insurance?"

"No. My mother let it lapse, obviously not a good decision. This isn't the first time I've had to cover their expenses, but this is the worst." She looked back at her computer, as if staring at it would change the bottom line she'd just seen on the monitor—her bank balance. "I…I only have forty-eight dollars in my savings account now. Forty-eight dollars. I can't remember my balance ever being so low."

She squeezed her eyes shut. Two tears spilled over her bottom lashes. "This is ridiculous. I don't tell guys my bank balance. It's not like you can help by lending me a bunch of money."

"Yeah, forty-eight dollars seems like a lot to me."

"I'm a private person. And I don't cry... well, hardly ever." She sniffed again. "Don't you have a handkerchief or something?"

He patted his pockets though he knew he didn't even own a handkerchief. To compensate, he handed her the tail of his T-shirt. "Will this do?"

Surprisingly, she took the hem and dragged it under her eyes, leaving a trail of mascara like storm clouds on the blue fabric. "I can get that stain off," she whimpered. "I'm a home ec teacher, remember?."

He chuckled and suddenly she was pressed up against him with her head nestled where his shoulder met his neck. She emitted a tiny sob, sighed and finally said, "I'm glad you're here."

For a moment he forgot to breathe. He rubbed her back, awkwardly at first since he hadn't held a woman in a long time. He'd forgotten how soft and fragile-feeling female bones were. He wanted her to feel protected. He was an army-trained protector after all, and he hoped he was good at it. "It's going to be okay," he said. He smiled, though she couldn't see it. "Think of all the things a really good home ec teacher can do with forty bucks. Probably put together a whole Thanksgiving dinner with change left over."

She laughed softly into his T-shirt. "Actually, I'm rather proficient at turkey roasting. This holiday maybe I'll fix one for you. You've earned it today."

He turned her in his arms and led her to the sofa. She sat and he settled in next to her. "I think maybe you should talk about this," he said. "Talking helps, or so I've heard." An odd observation from a guy who'd refused to even talk to his army chaplain when his wife died. "Is your father going to be all right? Are you upset because you're worried about him?"

She clasped her hands in her lap and stared at them. "I am, but I know he'll be fine. He'll get good care once the county hospital has the money worked out. And I'm not upset about lending money, not really. I've sent them money before, a few hundred here and there."

He was baffled. "Then what, Brenna? You're obviously strung out about something."

"You wouldn't understand."

"I might."

"No chance. You're happy living in that cabin with all the things your grandmother left in it."

"Yes, I'm okay with it, but what does that have to do with anything?"

"You'll think I'm a terrible person."

That was the last statement he expected to come from her mouth. Confident, knowledge-able, opinionated Brenna Sullivan, a terrible person? Even if by some ridiculous stretch of the imagination he did think that, he couldn't believe that she'd think it of herself.

He stared at her profile. She still concen-trated on her hands. "First of all, do I seem like the kind of father who would ask a ter-rible person to take his daughter shopping? Second, as troublesome as Carrie can be, she is a good judge of character. I don't think she would have become attached to you so quickly if you were a terrible person. And third, you're just not a terrible person. Nosy maybe, but not terrible."

She rubbed a finger under her nose and

took in a deep breath. She was regaining control, and he was almost sorry. Holding her had been unexpectedly nice.

"I'm so ashamed," she said after a moment. "I don't even know why I'm telling you this, but we're so opposite. And I've gone this far. You've seen me at my worst now."

"I thought I'd seen you at your worst when you were swatting mosquitoes in my driveway."

She didn't smile, and he considered cutting the one-liners. Whatever was bothering her was serious. He placed his hand over hers. "Why are you ashamed, Brenna?"

"Look around this place," she said.

Okay. He could do that even if the request didn't make much sense. "It's nice. You've done a great job decorating and fixing it up…." At least he supposed she had. He hadn't had much experience in decorating anything but an eight-by-eight tent, and that didn't require much skill.

"I have, haven't I?" Her voice was flat, hollow. "You're sitting on a fifteen-hundred-dollar sofa. Those chairs over there by the fireplace cost, well, you don't want to know. Everything in here I either bought new or picked up at antiques shops." She raised her face and seemed to be examining her belongings for the first time. "I guess it's obvious that I don't mind spending money on myself."

"There's no harm in that," he said.

"That's what I thought, so I spent and spent. Like this house. I didn't need a three-bedroom single-family home. I could have managed in a one-bedroom apartment when I moved to Mount Union. But no...Brenna Sullivan has to have more than she needs, more than she can reasonably afford."

Since he'd never had excess money, Mike had a hard time relating. But he tried. "Hey, this house was probably a good investment."

"Great. I think most people are like you, Mike," she said. "They prioritize so they can acquire the things they need and they sacrifice the things they can do without."

He wasn't sure he liked being lumped in with the people who made do, even though it was true, especially because Brenna wasn't in this group.

He shook his head. "I don't see where this is going, Brenna. You're single, you make a decent living, why shouldn't you have nice things?" He gently squeezed her hands and gave her one more chance to appreciate his humor. "Unless you really stole all this stuff."

"No. It's all bought and paid for or on a payment plan. Lately I've been able to manipulate my credit cards so I can get most everything I want."

"Okay. But I still don't see why you're ashamed."

"I'm ashamed because, deep down, I don't think I can survive without all this stuff. I need these things to validate who I am, to make all my sacrifices seem worthwhile."

"How long have you felt this way?" he asked.

"Since you… Well, maybe today has been a harsh eye-opener for me." She stared into his eyes, and he couldn't deny the cold reality in hers. "You can call me shallow, Mike. I won't blame you if you do. But I need these things to make me feel good about myself."

"You're really confusing me, Brenna. I don't see how a teacher can be called shallow. You give so much of your time and energy to kids…"

"But I don't. Not anymore. At least until Carrie. I don't understand why I've become so involved with her. I'm basically selfish."

He let go of her hands and half turned on the sofa, putting distance between them. "Are you deliberately trying to paint an unpleasant picture of yourself? Because if you keep it up, it just might work."

"I'm telling you what I'm really like whether you want to believe it or not. I'm a good teacher. I am, but that's because I love my job. I like the salary, the benefits, the vacation time, the crafting and creating I do in the classroom with my students. There is nothing I would rather do every day other than go to Mount Union High School and be with those kids."

"Only the first three of those reasons are selfish," he said. "The last one at least makes me believe you have what it takes to be a good teacher."

"I told you that passion for a subject is the most important requirement for being a successful teacher. I have that."

"A little knowledge about kids and a certain amount of empathy helps, too, I would imagine."

She shook her head. "I can't afford to be empathetic or sympathetic. Years ago I learned a very hard and painful lesson about interfering in a student's life."

He'd known for a while that she'd had a heart-wrenching story to tell. "Do you want to tell me about that?"

"I don't like to talk about it. Just know that my interference only made life much worse for that kid. Much worse. So I simply don't allow myself to care too much anymore. That's why I took this job in Mount Union. It's a middle-class community with strong family values, a good school system and excellent parental support. The kids aren't needy, at least not like Marcus…" Her voice trailed off.

"So Mount Union is ideal if you want to maintain your isolation?"

She shrugged. "And it pays well."

"And allows you to buy all this stuff and give a chunk of your salary to your parents?"

"That's what has been happening."

He rubbed his forehead. "Why exactly do you give money to your parents? They can't support themselves?"

"Not well enough. It's a long story."

He waited while she breathed deeply.

"I grew up in a single-wide trailer. Not one

of those fancy ones. A run-down, beat-up hunk of metal in an overgrown park that my parents still live in today. I lived there while I went to high school and college and saved money. And I haven't slept there one night since the day I graduated."

"If you believe that makes me think any less of you, you're wrong. If anything, I admire your determination to get out of that situation."

She smiled. "Thanks. And I knew you would believe that. But here's the thing. I've come to admire you, too. You're in a situation that isn't easy, like I was. You're practically a new dad. You lost your wife, moved, and you're trying to make the best of it."

"Are you saying we're alike?"

"Oh, we're not alike. Not at all."

He wasn't sure he wanted to hear that.

"You've recognized a greater purpose in your life—your daughter. And because of her, you've given up your dreams of college, your career in the military…"

"You make me sound pathetic."

"Just the opposite. You're living simply, honestly and honorably."

"And you're not?"

"Not like you." She stood and spread her arms to encompass the room. "I'm certainly not wealthy, but I amass things anyway. I live above my means and certainly above my needs."

"But you're supporting your parents."

"I'm helping out when I need to. And here's the really horrible part. I resent every dime I give them, and then I feel guilty for days because I resent it. My parents are stuck. They can't get a break, whether it's their fault or not. And I've escaped that life. I live better than they've ever dreamed. I could help them out of that trailer park, but I don't want to. I don't want to give up a darn thing I've got."

He didn't want to believe her brutal honesty. Deep down, he was convinced she was selling herself short. "You obviously care deeply about your parents."

"Sure. I love them, I guess, but I'm not willing to compromise my life in any significant way to help them have a better one."

"But according to you, that's exactly what you've been doing."

She sat down next to him again. "Only when their situation is dire," she said. "Here's one for you. I've been in this house for four years, and they've never seen it. And that's because I'm afraid that they'll ask to stay. I couldn't let that happen. I don't want them here. Right or wrong, I don't want them to be my greater purpose."

"Brenna, being responsible for a dependent child is a lot different than being responsible for one's parents. You can't compare the two."

"Yes, I know that. But I could be responsible for them. I have the space. I could do much more than I do."

She took his hand this time. "You've become a friend to me, Mike, whether you intended that or not. Granted ours isn't a friendship that just coasts along. It has needed work and will continue to need it if it will grow. We both know we are about as different as any two people can be."

He wasn't sure he knew that. "Okay."

"Why do you think I date Alex? Other than the fact that he's semi-gorgeous, a trait that may have eluded you since you're a guy."

"You tell me."

"I like him. We have fun. We go to good restaurants, the theater, things like that. And he's successful."

Mike frowned. "Somehow you've made that last quality stand out more than the others."

"I'm sorry, but his success is part of what attracted me to him. I found it easy to like someone with his qualities." She paused before adding, "I told you I'm shallow. I guess that proves it."

"Yes, you did." *But I wasn't convinced—didn't want to be.*

"I don't know if Alex will ask me to marry him. I think he's leading up to it. If he does ask, I'd be foolish not to consider his proposal. We could build on what we have."

She hadn't mentioned love or any reason that should lead to marriage in Mike's view. He spoke without emotion, just stating the facts as he understood them. "And Alex could alleviate some of the guilt you have about your parents by bankrolling them." *Something I could never do.*

"Well…he could."

"And someday you could have a bigger house and more pretty things."

"I suppose."

He'd heard enough, and he tried to ignore the almost physical stab of disappointment by looking at his watch. "We'd better get back to the tavern. I don't want to leave Carrie too long. And you'd be smart not to leave Alex on his own, either."

A wisecrack remark, he knew. But after the conversation they'd had, he wasn't much concerned with pleasing Brenna Sullivan. Not that he ever could. He knew that now.

Neither spoke as Mike passed the old library building and headed out of town. When they were almost at the Riverview, Brenna finally cleared her throat and said, "You haven't had much to say, Mike."

He kept his eyes on the road. "Don't know what *to* say."

"Obviously you're upset about what I told you, and now I'm worried that my honesty will affect our friendship."

He didn't answer.

"It's not a crime to want to protect what you have," she said in a small voice.

"I guess that depends on your definition of *protect*." He should have let the subject drop right there, but he didn't. "It's not a crime to marry someone for money, either, but it sure does go against all the laws of nature as I see them."

He pulled into the Riverview lot and

jammed his gearshift into Park. "You'd better hightail it inside, Brenna, before your cash cowboy finds another filly."

She stepped out of the truck and glared back at him. "Now you're just being ridiculous. And narrow-minded."

Mike stayed in the pickup, watching her walk toward the restaurant and thinking about what she'd said. He *had* been ridiculous and petty. Like a child who had his favorite toy suddenly snatched away from him. He shook his head. "Problem is, Mike," he muttered, "you never had a chance with this toy in the first place."

He waited until Brenna had gone inside and then he got out of his truck. The last thing he wanted to see was her with Alex, so he'd check quickly on his daughter and leave. He hoped Carrie would agree to go with him. Maybe she would have had enough of barbecue and beans herself.

No such luck. Mike walked into the main dining room and saw Carrie linked up with other teens, the same ones from the pizza shop. They were involved in some kind of dance where they all seemed to know the same steps. Mike stood off to the side and just watched. He was learning that fitting in was tough when you didn't know which foot to put forward first.

CHAPTER TEN

BRENNA WAS STEAMING. She didn't want to see Mike. She didn't want to see Alex. She couldn't even ask the friendly bartender for a beer because she knew she'd be the one driving when she took Alex home and picked up her car. Thank goodness there were iced colas in a cooler at the end of the bar. Brenna picked one up, wiped the ice crystals off and took a long swallow.

She tapped her boot on the rough wood floor. *It's going to take more than a soda to cool me off right now.*

She supposed she could find Alex and convince him to leave, but to do that, she'd have to put up with his slurred speech and unfocused eyes. And that was after she'd peeled his latest dance partner from his arms.

She inched along the wall separating the bar from the dancers until she could peek around the partition without being seen.

There he was, arm draped around Loretta Stone, lips moving awkwardly in time to the words of a country song. She didn't worry that Alex was after anything more than a dance with Loretta. He was loyal to one woman alone, and thankfully he didn't over-indulge with booze often.

She'd just started into the room to retrieve her date when she realized she'd have to pass Mike to get to Alex. Bumping into Mike again while tempers were still hot was not something she wanted to face. She retreated behind the wall once more and waited to see what Mike would do. He approached Carrie on the dance floor and started talking to her.

"No, Dad. I'm not going. That's not fair!"

Brenna didn't realize she had a talent for lip-reading. Or maybe Carrie was just being superexpressive about not wanting to leave.

Brenna hid herself more securely behind the wall. She couldn't let Carrie realize she was near or the girl might enlist her help in persuading her father to let her stay. Mike didn't need another reason to be angry with her. Poor guy. Brenna almost felt sorry for him. He wouldn't win this argument with Carrie without invoking a parental edict, something that would embarrass his daughter and only widen the gap between them. Mike wouldn't do that, so he would probably just have to leave on his own, and let Carrie ride home with the Montgomerys.

The women in Mike's life were not making his life any easier. One had outright defied him. The other had undeniably disappointed him.

Thankfully Alex spotted Brenna after a few more moments. He stumbled over to her.

"Hey, babe, where you been? In the ladies' room?"

Unbelievable. "Yeah, that's right, Alex. I've been in the bathroom for two hours."

He grinned. "You must have eaten some powerful beans."

She looped her arm with his to keep him upright. "Okay, we'll go with that. It's time to leave, Roy Rogers." She smiled, thinking of Mike's reference earlier. "Wave goodbye to all those brokenhearted women you're leaving behind."

The grin stayed in place as if his lips were glued. "I don't care about their hearts, Bren. You're the only lady that matters to me."

"I know, Alex." She led him to the exit. "Just don't step on my feet, all right?"

Thirty minutes later she drove Alex's car up a narrow, landscaped pathway that ended at the log cabin where he spent many of his weekends. His parents had built the place a few years before to give the busy, career-oriented family a place to unwind. Alex had definitely fulfilled his parents' dream of unwinding. He was asleep in the passenger seat, snoring loudly.

She jostled his shoulder. "Wake up, Alex. I can't carry you inside."

He opened the passenger door and stepped out. "You're coming in, aren't you?" His voice was sleep-filled and groggy.

"To watch you sleep it off? I don't think so." She got him in the door and watched while he flopped onto the sofa. "I'll phone you later," she called from the porch.

"'Kay." He was asleep before she'd locked him safely in the cabin and walked to her car.

Brenna was halfway home when her phone rang. Diana's face smiled up at her from the screen. Brenna activated her speaker. "Hi. What's up?"

"Where are you?" Diana asked. "I've looked everywhere for you."

"You're still at the Riverview?" When Diana said that she was, Brenna explained her quick trip home, minus the details about her argument with Mike. "When I got back to the tavern, I clearly saw I would have to drive Alex home."

"Wise decision," Diana said.

"Why were you looking for me?" Brenna asked.

"I've got good news. Stan Peterson, that new Mount Union commissioner, stopped by the barbecue and told me the council had voted to turn the library building over to your committee. They need to run some standard inspections before you go in—electric, plumbing, stuff like that—but he said you could start working in there on Wednesday."

In three days? Brenna had told Mike it would be at least a week or more. She was hoping their disagreement would have faded into insignificance by then and maybe they could still work on the project together with no hard feelings.

"Aren't you going to say anything?" Diana prompted. "It's great news, right?"

"Of course."

"You'll tell Mike? I know Bobby will see him tomorrow at practice, but if you see him first…"

Easier said than done, Brenna thought. Mike was probably still chewing on the bitter realization that his new lady friend was a shallow, greedy hypocrite.

Brenna disconnected and set her mind to bridging the gap that now existed between her and Mike. Maybe, if she was successful, this sudden, miserable, empty sensation in her stomach would go away. She didn't like thinking she'd offended her new friend. But had she really?

She shouldn't regret telling him the truth. If he was putting her on some sort of unrealistic pedestal, he should know she didn't belong there. Maybe Mike would never understand Brenna's motives for the decisions she made, but surely they could still work together. She had to try.

She thought of the kisses they'd shared on Friday night. She'd kissed him first, but she'd left the alley confused and uncertain herself. And the impulsive kiss he gave her on the porch later—she'd enjoyed that kiss, too.

She couldn't think about those possibilities now. Mike wasn't her type. She definitely wasn't his. It was not that they were prime examples of the "Haves" and "Have nots." But they were definitely card-carrying members of the "Wants" and Want nots." Still, she could save their fragile bond. She could have a relationship with him and his daughter. For the sake of the Cultural Arts Center, if nothing else.

So a plan formed in her mind. When Brenna reached town, she passed her street and kept going for three more miles. She pulled onto Mike's overgrown road and headed for the cabin, confident she could establish trust between them. She would reveal the details of one of the most disturbing incidents of her life—the one she never talked about. She would tell him about Marcus, make him understand.

When she got out of her car, Brenna immediately noticed the eerie calm, almost as if no one lived here. Even the woodsy sounds of insects and small animals seemed muted, allowing just the beat of her heart to accompany her faltering steps to the old porch.

She knew Mike was home. She'd parked

next to his truck. Maybe he was napping. She considered leaving, coming back later, but no, she wanted to do this before Carrie arrived home with the Montgomerys. Brenna raised her fist, opened the screen door and tapped lightly.

The door opened at once. Mike, barefoot and dressed in army-issue shorts and a Fort Pendleton T-shirt, stared through the screen. His shoulders, usually so military-squared, slumped slightly.

"What a surprise," he said, crossing his arms over his chest.

"May I come in?" Four little words, yet they'd been so hard to say.

He paused, staring at her, and then finally held the screen for her. She walked inside. The room was just as it had been before. The old but comfortable plaid couch was covered with newspaper. An iced tea and a computer were on the coffee table. The monitor showed a pet-rescue site.

"Shopping?" Brenna said, nodding toward the computer.

"Carrie mentioned wanting a dog. I'm just seeing what's out there."

"A dog would be nice. You certainly have room for him to run."

"Yep."

Neither spoke for a few moments until Mike stacked the newspapers and asked if she wanted to sit. She did and he took the chair next to the fireplace.

"This will be a cozy room in the winter," Brenna said.

"Suppose so." He frowned. "Though it might be a bit simple for some people's tastes."

Don't take the bait, Brenna.

"So…" He settled one leg over the opposite knee. "I assume there's a reason for this visit."

No niceties. Brenna's mouth went dry, and she desperately wanted a sip of that iced tea. She refrained from lifting his glass. Sharing wouldn't have bothered her, but Mike was obviously still holding on to his anger.

"I didn't like the way we left things earlier," she said.

"I thought our points of view were pretty clear."

"I know. But…" Her voice crackled with hoarseness. "Can I have a sip of your tea?"

He nodded and she picked up the glass. The sip turned into a gulp.

Her confidence, bolstered by a couple of beers earlier in the day and the refreshing coolness of the tea, returned. And with it, a spark of anger. She reminded herself that she hadn't done anything wrong. She'd been honest with Mike, and now she was being made to suffer for it as if she'd wounded him irreparably.

"Look," she began, "you can make this difficult for me, or you can make it easy. Either way, we are committed to working on the center together, so we have to make peace."

She tried to read his stoic face for a sign that she was getting through to him. Nothing.

"Unless you want to back out of the project."

"I don't want to back out. I've got nothing against the arts center, or that century-old building that's being repurposed for a new use." He swept his arm around his living room, encompassing the primitive old furniture that now held Carrie's backpack and Mike's lunch box. "As you can see, I'm quite fond of finding new uses for old things."

That shouldn't have sounded like a dig, but oddly it did. Just because she liked fine antiques and pretty new things...

"I hope you're not waiting for me to apologize for something," she said.

"What should you apologize for? Telling the truth about yourself?"

Her thoughts exactly. "Good, we agree on that, then. I am sorry if I altered an opinion you had mistakenly formed of me. If we're going to be working together, I don't feel there should be any illusions—"

"Oh, you took care of that. No illusions. And, like you said, we're just friends anyway, working buddies."

He stood. "That's it, then?"

Was he suggesting that she leave? "No! I haven't even gotten to the reason that brought me all the way out here."

Again he crossed his arms, his remarkably fabulous, masculine arms. "Okay."

She took another sip of his tea. "As long as we're being honest, I thought it was important for you to understand how I feel about my teaching position."

"I think I do. Good salary, vacations…"

"I knew you thought that."

"Only because it's exactly what you told me."

She couldn't argue. She did say that, but

he deliberately left out the part about how she loved her work in the classroom. "Those things make me sound shallow, and it's not the whole picture."

He didn't sit again, just stood there, legs spread, eyes narrowed, almost combative. "If it will make you feel better to fill in some blanks, Brenna, go ahead."

When she'd decided to come to the cabin, she'd intended to tell him the truth about her past teaching experience. Now she wasn't sure. But she was here, and the tension between them was still crackling. She cleared her throat. "Remember I told you there was an incident from my past when I was at another school?"

"Yes. I believe you let slip the name Marcus."

The man remembered everything! "I was teaching seventh grade then, a difficult age, both for kids and teachers."

"I'll take your word for that."

"Anyway, I was employed in a poor district, low budget, lacking equipment and mostly disinterested parents who dropped their children off as if it were free day care."

"I get the picture."

"Marcus was in my class. He was a sweet boy, a trait that stood out because so many of the boys were tough guys practicing for the adulthood they would soon grow into. Marcus was sometimes bullied because of his size. He was small, thin. His clothes were often torn. His mother had run off, and so he had no one to mend them. I kept an eye on him when I could in case he needed someone to come to his defense."

Mike nodded. His eyes suddenly reflected a serious interest.

"And sometimes I noticed he had bruises on his arms."

"From the other kids?" Mike asked.

"No. From his father, as it turned out."

"That stinks."

"Yes, it does. When I asked him about the bruises, he denied any abuse at home, but I knew it happened. The days he had the marks, he had trouble concentrating. His schoolwork suffered. The situation couldn't be ignored."

"It shouldn't have been," Mike said.

"I took the advice of a superior and called the DCF, that stands for Department of Children and Fam…"

"I know what DCF stands for, Brenna."

"Okay. A representative from DCF visited the home. She didn't discover solid evidence, but she was disturbed enough to call and tell me she was putting a weekly check on the address. Marcus and his brother would be watched carefully."

"What happened then?"

"Marcus wasn't in school the next day. I was concerned, scared for him, really. But it wasn't until the end of the day, when I was home watching the news, that I saw the story."

Tension lines popped in Mike's temple. "What did you hear?"

"Marcus had been hospitalized for severe injuries. Neighbors had heard his screams and called the police. The father was arrested, the brother taken into DCF custody and Marcus... Well, an ambulance was called." Her voice hitched. "He almost didn't make it."

Mike's fists clenched several times.

"I went to the hospital to visit him, just one time. I couldn't believe what I saw. His little jaw was wired shut. If he knew I was even there, he didn't show it. He wouldn't, or couldn't, speak to me. His arm and one leg were in casts. There were bruises..." She stopped, looked at Mike. "Could I have my own tea, please?"

He hurried into the kitchen to get her a glass.

She drank and continued, "He stayed in the hospital a long time, more than two weeks. When he left, his father was in jail and his brother was in foster care. Marcus had weeks of rehab before he was sent to foster care, also. I heard he didn't live too far from Darius, that's his brother, but after that, I don't know what happened."

Her throat was parched, her eyes burning, but she was almost done.

"I never saw him again. I quit at the end of the school year and began filling out applications for another position. I couldn't stay there, not after what I'd done."

Mike sat next to her on the couch. "What *you'd* done? Brenna, what are you talking about?"

"For months, for years, I couldn't get the image of that child out of my mind. He had suffered so. If only I hadn't made that call…"

Suddenly Mike's arm was around her, and he was patting her shoulder. "You can't believe that. Not making the call would have meant you were ignoring the problem."

"But I felt every bit as guilty as Marcus's father was. I didn't strike that poor little boy, but I started the whole thing. With good intentions, yes, but you know what they say about the path to hell being paved with good intentions. That applies to me."

"What was the alternative, Brenna?" Mike asked, his arm strong and sturdy, supporting her. "You couldn't have gone on pretending everything was okay with that kid."

"But if I had, at least Marcus wouldn't have suffered such horrible injuries."

"Or he would have suffered them anyway, at another time, for another reason. You ultimately got him out of that situation."

"I don't even know what happened to him," she said, her voice choking. "I've always been too afraid to find out. What if he never got well? Maybe he turned to crime or drugs. I don't know." She grabbed for her purse, but it wasn't within reach. "Do you have a handkerchief?" she said.

He stretched the hem of his T-shirt. She took it, smiled at his blurry face and dabbed her eyes. "This is getting to be a habit."

"No problem. We have a dependable ringer washer out back," he said.

"You don't!"

"No. We're not that backwoods." He handed her the tea glass, and she took a swallow.

When she was relatively assured she was in control again, she said, "I wanted you to know this, Mike. Maybe it explains some things to you."

"I'm glad you told me. This goes a long way toward explaining your reaction to seeing Carrie at your house that first night. I'm sorry this happened to you, Brenna."

"I won't ever go back, not to that sad, underfunded school district, not to that single-wide trailer where I grew up. I'm not good with sadness. And I'm really not good at living with my questionable decisions." She laughed softly. "I know it sounds awful, especially to a guy like you, a man who has fought for his country and lived in unbelievably remote and deprived conditions, but I need my life to be easy."

He removed his hand from her shoulder and threaded his fingers on his lap. "Okay, Brenna. I get it. There's nothing wrong with easy."

"So we can still be friends, like we were just getting to be?" *But without the kissing.* "I want to go back to the way things were, maybe build on our friendship."

"Sure, pal. We're friends." He chuckled. "Can't say how we'll be as working partners, though. Who will be boss?"

She smiled. "Me."

"Figures."

"Good. Because we can get in the building on Wednesday."

"Really? I'll be there as soon as I get out of football practice." He grinned at her. "You people are turning my life upside down. You know that, don't you?"

"You mean us Mount Union people?"

"Exactly. You've got me jumping through hoops I didn't even know existed."

"That's okay. I'm thinking your life needed a little handstand."

He opened his mouth, but never uttered a sound because the front door swung open. Carrie stood on the porch and hollered, "Thanks. That was so much fun." Then she bounded inside.

"Dad! Who's car..."

She stopped, stared at Brenna. "Miss Sullivan. What are you doing here?"

Thankful Carrie hadn't walked in when she was drying her eyes on her dad's T-shirt or when Mike had his arm around her, Brenna rose from the sofa and straightened her skirt. "I… We were talking about the Cultural Arts Center," she said. "Your dad is going to help me with that project."

Carrie dropped into a chair. "I heard about that." She frowned at her dad. "Is there anything going on in this town that you're *not* involved in? First football and now this center thing. I won't be able to go anywhere without running into you."

"Not true, Carrie," he said. "You can avoid Alvin's Garage, where I still have to make a living," he said.

"Don't worry. I won't go there."

"Did you have fun at the barbecue?" he asked.

"Well, yeah, except for that completely embarrassing thing you did."

Mike flashed Brenna a here-it-comes look.

Carrie leaned forward in the chair to capture Brenna's attention. "He actually came up to me while I was line dancing with a bunch of kids. Said I had to leave, we were going home."

Brenna smiled. "Oh, how awful."

"Yes, I know! It was so humiliating, and he acted like he even enjoyed it."

"I think that's my cue to leave," Brenna said. "Mike, thanks so much for listening to me today. And for your input." And then to clear up any misconception Carrie might draw, she added, "The center is going to be a great place for enrichment classes and activities for teens."

"You're welcome," Mike said. "Anytime."

She reached the door, but turned around before leaving. "Just one thing, Carrie."

"What?"

"I've known lots of teenagers, and I can't think of one who hasn't complained of being humiliated by their parents. On the other hand, I can't think of one parent who has ever told me they enjoyed it." She smiled at Carrie while pointing to Mike. "You might want to give Dad a break once in a while. Just sayin'. He's a pretty good guy."

CHAPTER ELEVEN

At 3:15 p.m. on Monday, almost an hour after students had been dismissed, Brenna was still in her classroom. She'd already graded papers and was now restocking baking supplies in the kitchen cubicles. This was a task she usually assigned to students, but she wasn't in a hurry to leave. Not today.

Diana walked by her open door, did a double take and entered the room. "What are you still doing here?"

"Just finishing up some detail work. I'm leaving soon."

"Need help?"

"No, I can manage."

Diana walked over to the windows of Brenna's second-floor classroom. "I'll just close your blinds then and…"

"No!"

Diana gave her a shocked look. "We always close the blinds before we leave for the day."

"I know, but I'll do it."

Setting her tote on the floor, Diana gazed out the window, taking in the view of the field house and football stadium. Brenna pretended not to notice.

"Oh, I get it," Diana said.

Brenna wiped down a perfectly clean counter. "What exactly do you think you get?"

"You have a great view of football practice from these windows. The guys ought to be done with their meeting and will come out to the field soon."

"Oh, right," Brenna said, not surprised by her friend's logical conclusion but determined to make light of it. "You know how I love football."

"I know how you *used* to feel about football. Something tells me your attitude is changing fast."

"Don't be silly." Brenna hurried to her desk and took her purse from the drawer. "Come on, let's go. I'm ready."

Diana parked her hip on the corner of the desk. "Not so fast. I've been waiting for the chance to ask you about your car being at Mike Langston's yesterday. Now seems like the perfect opportunity. It's just the two of us.

Nothing to interrupt our conversation except for a few dozen panting, grunting males about to charge outside—" she pointed out the window "—right over there."

Brenna frowned. "You saw my car, did you?"

"We did drop Carrie off at home, Bren. Couldn't very well miss the silver bullet with its dented bumper." She grinned. "What's going on? You'd better tell me before I jump to all the conclusions I want to be true."

"Nothing's going on," Brenna said, surprised by the defensively high pitch of her voice. "I went over to tell Mike about the Cultural Arts Center being available to us on Wednesday." For added effect, she said, "You told me to tell him, remember?"

"Yeah, I remember. So the visit had nothing to do with Alex being a pie-eyed dolt and Mike being a truly decent, dependable potential boyfriend?"

"You say that like you've known Mike your whole life."

"I guess. But some people you can just tell are good folks. Like you. I've known you for four years, and you've only disappointed me once."

"Don't start on Alex again," Brenna warned. "I'm well aware of your opinion of him. And anyway, we haven't taken anything like a permanent step forward in our relationship."

Diana shrugged. "Did you talk to Mike about anything other than the center?"

Brenna felt a flush creep into her cheeks. Mike had been consoling and gentle and understanding. She blinked. "Well, sure. We talked about his daughter. And I suggested some courses he could take at the Georgia State branch...." She hadn't done that yet, but she intended to—practically the same thing.

"What? Hold on. Mike's going to college?"

"He wants to be a teacher."

Diana's grin turned coy. "Isn't that an interesting bit of news?"

"Fascinating," Brenna said. "He'll only be one of about three and a half million teachers in this country."

"And it takes him right out of that dating pool at Alvin's Garage."

Brenna started to defend the crack she'd made the day she and Diana met Mike, but Diana didn't let her. "I'll leave you alone to close your own blinds," she said. "And to enjoy whatever views this fine Georgia afternoon presents to you." She slung her bag, stuffed with papers, over her shoulder and went to the door. "See you tomorrow, Bren."

Her footsteps had no sooner faded in the hallway when Brenna heard the shouts and pounding footsteps of Ravens testosterone. The boys were on the field. And so were their coaches. Bobby, with a clipboard in his hand, and Mike Langston, seen for the first time in his coaching gear, tight-fitting navy blue shorts, a gray collared shirt and a matching ball cap.

Brenna sat at a student desk and leaned her elbows on the windowsill. "Carrie might not want to see her dad at school," she said softly, "but I don't mind it a bit."

She could allow herself a few guilty pleasures, couldn't she? Mike wasn't her ideal man, but the guy was very admirably muscled. Even a woman with set goals, such as herself, could appreciate that. And he was turning out to be a *very* good friend.

FRIDAY NIGHT, BRENNA smoothed back a curly lock of hair that had come loose from her bandanna and fallen on her forehead. She checked her watch. Almost 8:00 p.m. She still had an hour to clean up before Alex would arrive at her house to take her for a late dinner in Libertyville. She had time for just a few more swipes of the chosen soft beige with the paint roller.

She and Mike and a few other volunteers had been at work in the Cultural Arts Center all three nights since being allowed in on Wednesday. Today, the other helpers had abandoned them over an hour ago, saying something about dinners and movies, shopping and family time. Carrie was with the Montgomerys again, at the pizza place, where Bobby was unwinding before the Saturday night game.

Brenna finished the wall and passed by Mike on her way to the janitor's closet, where she could put the roller in a bucket of water to soak. He looked down at her from near the top of the nine-foot ladder, where he had climbed to install energy-efficient bulbs in the many overhead light sockets.

An almost audible sigh escaped her lips. When Mike found the right woman, she would be one lucky gal. Loyalty, honesty and sincere caring were qualities any woman would appreciate. "I'm done for today," she said.

"Okay. I'll probably stick around for another hour or so. Carrie has a ten o'clock curfew so I've got some time."

As she headed to the closet, she swallowed a gulp of remorse at having to leave him here alone.

"What's going on in here?"

Boone's official baritone filled the building entrance. Brenna held up the roller so it wouldn't drip on the old wood floor. "Hi, Boone. We're just working on the center."

Mike came down from the ladder. The two men greeted each other with a fist bump before settling on a traditional handshake. Obviously any hard feelings between the two men the night Carrie had gone missing had long faded. Good. They were about the same age and had many of the same interests. Brenna had heard that Boone never missed a Ravens game unless he was on patrol. He'd been the Ravens tight end—whatever that was—when he went to Mount Union High School and he liked to fish and talk carburetors and stuff. Brenna always hoped he'd find the right woman, who would be good to him and let him lavish her with adoration. Unfortunately, Brenna wasn't that woman.

Realizing her thoughts had turned romantic, Brenna continued into the closet and set the paint roller in a bucket. When she joined the men, she joked, "Did you think the old library had turned into a crime scene, Boone?"

"Not exactly. I know about the center for the kids, but when I saw a light on in here, I figured I'd check." He grinned. "Just doing my job, ma'am. You two are working late."

"I'm about to quit," Brenna said. "But you can keep Mike company."

"Wish I could," Boone said. "But there's a whole town out there that needs my attention." He smiled that country-boy grin that let many speeders think he could be charmed into ignoring citations. They were soon set straight.

"Don't forget to lock up," he said and left the way he'd come in.

"He's such a good guy," Brenna said. "I wish he could find a nice, sweet girl and settle down with a kid or two."

Mike chuckled. "Then don't let him talk to me. When he hears my tales of fatherhood, he'll run off screaming into the woods."

She play-punched his shoulder, grateful

that the past few nights had only strengthened their friendship.

She could have left right then, but she lin-
gered. A few more minutes couldn't hurt.
Alex could wait while she showered.

"The walls look good, Sullivan," Mike
said.

"And your bulbs are bright, Langston."

"Hey, wait till you see this." Like a kid
with a new toy, he walked to the nearest wall,
turned a knob, and the room grew pleasantly
dark. "Dimmers in case we need to project
something on a screen." He walked back toward her. "Nice, huh?"

She gave him a subtle grin. "Mike, have
you ever been in a darkened room with a
bunch of teenagers? Recipe for disaster, my
friend...."

"Whoa, hadn't thought about that."

The light in his eyes dimmed, too, as if he
were thinking about the ramifications now.
Or something else having nothing to do with
teenagers. He reached up where her mind-of-
its-own curl had come loose again and tried
to push it under the edge of the bandanna.

"Forget it," she said. "A losing battle."

"I can get a pair of scissors and eliminate the problem."

"Don't you dare!" She grabbed his hand next to her face and swallowed hard. His gaze settled on her eyes and soon slid to her lips. She felt him inching closer and dropped her hand. "Mike…"

He reached behind her and tugged on the bandanna. It fluttered to the ground. Next he took hold of the old tie in her hair and pulled it loose. Her hair fell around her shoulders just before his hands fisted the unruly strands.

His lips were on hers before she had a chance to back away. Or maybe it was before she tried to. Either way, he was kissing her long and hard and wonderfully. She sighed into his mouth. "What are we doing?" she murmured.

"I don't know, but I keep wanting to do it."

The huge, round schoolhouse clock, which had been in the library for decades, ticked loudly, insinuating its presence into the haze of sweetness that had overtaken her. The time. Her date. She took a step back. "We shouldn't."

"Why not?"

"The timing just isn't right. You've been widowed less than a year."

"I don't care," he said. "I need this…"

His words sobered her. "I know you do. I understand, but I can't be the one to meet your needs, Mike. Unless you need me to be your friend. I can do that. I can be there for you. I would do anything for you. I trust you more than anyone I've ever known."

He drew in a ragged breath before averting his gaze. He seemed to be staring at the old clock when he said, "Lori didn't…"

There was so much anguish in those two words. Brenna put her hand on his shoulder. "She didn't what, Mike? What are you trying to say?"

His hand clenched. "Never mind."

"Oh, no. You're not getting away with a never mind. Not after I blubbered my guts out to you, not once, but twice in the past week."

She took his arm and led him to a bench near the old Dewey decimal card drawers. The bench looked about as comfortable as a pew in a pilgrim's church, but it was the only option. "Sit," she said.

He did.

"What did you mean when you said 'Lori didn't'?"

"It doesn't matter now."

"Of course it matters. It matters to me." She waited for him to say something, and when he didn't, she prompted, "I think you meant that Lori didn't trust you. Is that right?"

He turned his face to stare into her eyes again. "Weren't you leaving?"

She glanced at her watch. Alex would be at her house in twenty minutes. "I have time," she said. "I'll leave when you do. You must be starved. The apples I brought have long since worn off." She smiled at him. "You're not getting away without talking to me. So tell me, why do you think Lori didn't trust you?"

A long breath escaped his lips. His shoulders slumped. "She did trust me. At least I thought she did. For the first years of our marriage she trusted me enough to consult with me on every decision."

"Even when you were overseas?"

"Especially then. And especially after Carrie was born. We emailed several times a day when I wasn't in a combat zone. We Skyped. We spoke on the phone at least three times a week. She knew I was staying with the army for as long as I needed to in order to make a nice living for her and Carrie. And so I could finish up a little ahead and maybe start those college classes."

Brenna was beginning to see where this discussion was headed. She was starting to think of Lori Langston as a caring and kind woman, a woman who didn't mind giving up her own goals when her husband was such a good man. "Did she talk to you about any problems she might have been having?"

"That's the strange part," he said. "I didn't think she had many. I think now that she didn't want to worry me with home-front problems. Maybe knowing I couldn't do much about any situation, she didn't dwell on anything bad. She said Carrie was a good baby and a bright, healthy child. She included me on the milestones of our daughter's development. And when I came home, I'd catch up on what I'd missed."

He sighed. "We were a happy family, at least as happy as any family could be under the circumstances of our quick marriage and my enlistment. When she…" He paused, swallowed. "At the end, I only had thirteen months to go on my last reenlistment. I would have been stateside even sooner."

Brenna shifted, put her elbow on the back of the bench. "I can undersand why she didn't want to bother you with her problems. She didn't want to distract you. That must have been hard on her, but it certainly doesn't mean she didn't trust you."

"But when it really mattered, she didn't. For five months she knew about that tumor in her brain. She knew it was bad, but maybe she had kept hoping that the doctors could fix it. I don't know. We went on communicating by email and sent pictures back and forth like we always had. The pictures of Carrie showed a smiling, typical teen. The pictures of Lori ended up being just head shots taken from a distance so I wouldn't notice the weight loss. You'd think I would have caught on. But I didn't. She was my wife. I would have thought she was pretty if she'd had a paper bag over her head."

"Why do you think she didn't tell you about her illness?" Brenna asked.

"At this point, I can only guess. She knew I'd come home. And I would have. Maybe on days when she didn't feel so weak, she actually thought she'd get better or at least hang on until my time was up. Maybe the illness progressed faster than she'd thought it would. Or, like you said, maybe she didn't want to distract me while I was in a combat zone. Bottom line is, she didn't say a word until the end, and she didn't let Carrie tell me, either."

"Who did eventually tell you?"

He explained about the base chaplain pulling him from mess hall one morning and informing him that he had been granted immediate leave to go home. He shook his head with a bitterness that brought an ache to Brenna's heart. "A handful of people stateside knew," he said. "Until the military chaplain, no one said a word to me. It was as if Lori convinced everyone that my goals and safety were more important than her life— or that she believed *I* thought they were. She let herself grow worse every day, alone, so I would keep my mind on staying safe and not give up any of my stupid benefits."

His indrawn breath was shaky. He looked at the ceiling. "To this day, I still can't figure out what kind of man she thought I was. Did she think I wouldn't be able to handle it, that I'd fall apart? Did she secretly not want me there with her? Did she believe I didn't have the right to know?" He scrubbed his hand down his face. "Or did she believe I was so selfish that I wouldn't want her suffering to interfere with my plans?"

"No, Mike," Brenna said. "Anyone who's met you knows that you are an unselfish person."

"Yeah, well ask my daughter what she thinks of that opinion."

"She'll come around. Carrie knows that you've sacrificed so much to bring her here, where she's not bombarded with bad memories every day. She knows you're helping with the football team, the Cultural Arts Center." Brenna placed her hand on Mike's knee. "You're a giving man, Mike. Carrie will appreciate that someday, even if she doesn't fully now."

A smile trembled on his lips. "If I live that long. Anyway, Lori left me out of the most important aspect of her life, of *our* lives. She didn't trust me with the truth, for whatever reasons she had for doing that. I asked her when I finally did come home, but she was so weak by then…" He clenched his hands between his knees. "I live with that every day.

With the realization that she didn't want me to know."

Brenna gave his knee a gentle squeeze. "I'm so sorry, Mike."

"I'm a big boy," he said. "I'm coping with this a little better every day. Someday maybe I'll even be able to forgive her and myself, for not seeing the signs, for not knowing."

"That's the first step."

"At the end, at her bedside, she just gave me daddy lessons, made me promise to protect our daughter."

That explained a lot. "And you're fulfilling your duties as a dad. Protecting Carrie as your wife asked you to. You can't keep blaming yourself because you didn't know your daughter as well as you could have," Brenna said. "You're a good dad. Carrie wouldn't be coping half as well as she is if it weren't for you."

"That's up for debate."

"Not at all. Look at the strides she's made in a few short months. She's reached out to me, made friends, might be on a pathway to calling Charlie her boyfriend. She's a normal fifteen-year-old girl, Mike, complete with mood swings and obstinacy and the typical view that her parent is clueless."

"Yeah, she's all that."

Brenna rubbed her palm along Mike's bare arm. "What can I do to help?"

He turned on the bench and looked into her eyes. With his free hand, he cupped her cheek. "You already have, Brenna. You've listened, and you've said some things that will stick with me." He smiled at her. "Too bad you have this goal to avoid involvement in people's lives. Contrary to what I thought at first, you're pretty good at interfering."

She smirked. "Only where you're concerned." She leaned into his hand. "For you, my friend, I would gladly be Miss Buttinski whenever you need me to be."

His eyes reflected an inner anguish. "As long as certain lines between us are drawn, you mean?"

Suddenly the lines he was talking about seemed insignificant. He was hurting, and she desperately wanted to help. But that wasn't all. His hand on her face felt so good, so natural. It would be so easy to close the few inches between them and kiss him. It was what he wanted. It was what she could give him. What could one more kiss matter? She leaned toward him…

"There you are!"

Mike dropped his hand as if it had caught fire. Brenna jerked away from him, spun around. "Alex! How long have you been there?"

"Just walked in the door. I went to your house and it was closed up tight."

Mike clasped his hands and released a long, trembling breath. Brenna checked her watch. Yikes. "We were working," she said. "I lost track of time."

"Luckily I remembered you said you'd be here," Alex said, approaching the bench. "So I came to drag you out before we both starve to death."

He stuck his hand out toward Mike. "You were at the Riverview, weren't you? Mike, is it?"

"That's right."

Alex grinned. "Looks like Bren has met her match in the volunteer workaholic department." He reached down, took her elbow. She rose and stared down at Mike.

"I'll see you soon," she said. "Carrie and I are going shopping tomorrow, so you might want to polish up your credit card. She's talking about making this a birthday to remember."

"I think letting her buy what she wants is the safest way to please her."

The reversion to the safe topic of Carrie had seemed awkward, and Brenna's efforts to make her goodbye seem lighthearted fell far short of her goal. She resented the slight tug Alex administered to her arm. Yet an unbidden relief flooded her. She'd almost given way to temptation, abandoning her goals. Her life was well thought out. Certain things mattered to her. And she'd do well to remember that honorable, steady Mike Langston couldn't ensure that she'd never go back to that trailer.

CHAPTER TWELVE

THE NEXT MORNING at ten o'clock, Brenna pulled in front of Mike's house. After feigning a headache the night before and sending Alex home early, she felt rested and ready to traipse through the shopping mall with Carrie. And ready to see if Mike was okay this morning.

She shut down her engine, checked her hair in the rearview mirror and started to get out of the car. If Mike invited her inside for a cup of coffee, she'd take him up on it. Alex had walked into the center at an inconvenient time, and Brenna wanted to at least make sure the lines of communication between her and Mike were open. But he didn't come outside to greet her.

Wearing a short denim skirt and blouse, Carrie came out the door, her shoulder bag thumping against her hips. Her hair was in a ponytail that hung just over her bare shoulder. "Bye, Dad!" she called as she came down the porch steps.

Brenna, fighting off stubborn disappointment, sank back into the driver's seat. No coffee. No Mike. Okay.

Carrie got in the car, and Brenna put the gearshift into Reverse. No point hanging around. Maybe after she dropped Carrie off...

As she drove away from the cabin, she saw Mike in her side mirror. He stood on the porch dressed in jeans and a short-sleeved T-shirt. He had a coffee mug in his hand. He'd obviously seen her looking in the mirror. He raised his hand for a slight wave. She honked her horn.

"So, you ready to shop till we drop today?" she asked Carrie.

"Yeah, I even got the credit card. Dad said I could spend a hundred on stuff for my room and a hundred on clothes." She smiled. "I haven't even had to remind him too many times about my birthday. I think he remembered."

"Sounds like he's being very generous," Brenna agreed.

"I figure we should go to a really cheap

decorating place so I can fix up my room and still have most of the money left for clothes."

Remembering what she'd told Mike yesterday, Brenna smiled back at her. Carrie really was a normal teenage girl. Mike didn't need to worry all the time. "You're the boss today, Carrie," she said.

"Are we going to the mall in Libertyville?" Carrie asked.

"I thought we would. It's closer than Athens or Augusta, so we'll have more time to scope out the stores."

The girl settled back in her seat and gazed out the window. "Good. They have really excellent clothing and decorating places there." After a moment she said, "Can I turn on some music?"

"Sure." Brenna hit the four-lane road to the bigger town and drummed her fingers on the steering wheel in time to a young singer with a sweet voice. "What's your dad doing today?" she asked when the song ended.

"Oh! I forgot to tell you!" Carrie's eyes were bright with excitement. "Dad said maybe we can get a dog. He's measuring the backyard for a fence, and he might go to the home improvement store to get posts and stuff."

Good for you, Dad. "I think that's great," Brenna said. "Have you started looking?"

"We'll go to the shelter tomorrow. Dad said I have to limit the dog to under thirty pounds."

"That still gives you lots of options."

"Why don't you go with us? That would be so cool. If you and I both agree on the same dog, even if he's bigger, Dad will have to agree to take him."

Brenna felt a surge of temptation. She'd never had a dog as a kid so hadn't really thought about having one. But it would be fun to be in on the experience. Common sense soon won out over her inclination to say yes, however. *No, Brenna. You're not part of this family.*

"I don't think so, Carrie." She laughed. "You're not talking me into being a coconspirator in this deal. You and your dad are on your own."

They talked about school and activities and cafeteria food as the miles ticked away. Brenna carefully broached the subject of Charlie with an innocent question about how their friendship was progressing.

Carrie answered with a sigh and silence

before finally admitting that she really liked Charlie. "He's as cool as any of the guys in California," she said. "And he's so cute."

"I guess I have to agree with that," Brenna said. She'd always had a special fondness for Diana's son. He was a good kid, exactly what she'd told Mike that night in the pizza shop. "Your father doesn't mind you hanging out with Charlie?" she asked.

"My dad minds everything," Carrie said. "But he has loosened up on the Charlie thing a little. And the dog thing. He may actually become human if he keeps this up." She twisted her purse strap in her hand. "And I'm trying, too," she said. "Just like you told me the other night. Dad's not so bad, really."

"No, he's not, and I'm sure he appreciates your efforts."

When Brenna asked about the girls she'd introduced Carrie to at the football game, Carrie was still enthusiastic. "They are all so much fun," she said. "They go places and do the coolest things. And they have parties and hang out all the time." She frowned. "I'm not allowed to do all the stuff they do," she said. "But when I'm with them, it's such a blast. They know how to have a good time without parents constantly looking over their shoulders."

"I'm sure their parents keep a close watch on what they do," Brenna said. At least she hoped that was true. Anyway, how much trouble could a few teenagers get into in quiet little Mount Union, Georgia?

FIVE HOURS LATER, her feet aching from walking the length of the mall at least three times, Brenna pulled up to the cabin. She figured Mike would be anxiously standing at the door keeping vigil, but he was nowhere to be seen. Carrie thanked Brenna for taking her, jumped out of the car and grabbed sacks from the backseat. She ran onto the porch.

"Dad! Don't come in my room!" she hollered in the front door. "I want to put everything out on my bed, then you can see."

Well, good, the shopping expedition had been a success.

Brenna got out of the car and waited, her keys in her hand. Maybe Mike would come out. She hoped so.

She heard water running from the side of the cabin and gingerly stepped over the gravel pathway to see what was causing the noise.

Mike was definitely home. He stood near the side of the house, one hand flat against the log wall for support. His other hand held a garden hose over his head. Water sluiced over him, soaking his bare chest and the waistband of his jeans.

She cupped her hands around her mouth, and when sufficient air had filled her deprived lungs, she shouted, "Hey!"

He looked up, dropped the hose and twisted the faucet handle. "I didn't hear you drive up," he said.

"Oh. Ah…" *Words, Brenna. You know what they are. Combinations of letters formed together to make sense.* "We just got here," she said.

He reached for his T-shirt hanging over the back of an old lawn chair.

"How'd everything go?" he asked, slipping the shirt over his head. "I hope Carrie didn't wear blisters on your feet."

"Not at all, and I think the shopping went really well. We tortured your credit card."

He smiled. "I thought you would." He walked closer to her. "So I can put a check mark in the success column for the fifteenth birthday?"

"You can."

"Pardon my appearance. It's hot today."

Indeed it is. "No sweat. What have you been doing?"

"Got a few fence posts in. Looks like we might be getting a dog tomorrow."

Exhibiting her ignorance, she said, "Why the fence? Can't you just let him run? As Carrie points out, this is the boonies."

"Really shouldn't. There are panthers and other critters out here. Besides, I want Carrie to help me put in a garden, and I need to keep the deer out." He looked over Brenna's shoulder. "Where is she, anyway?"

"In the house. She's putting everything on her bed so you can see what you bought."

He laughed. "Swell. I take it I'm supposed to think everything is way cool."

She smiled. "If you know what's good for you."

He continued to the front of the house, and Brenna fell into step beside him. Even after his dowsing, she could feel the heat radiating off his bare arms. Or maybe off her arms. Either way...

"Thanks for doing this," he said. "And

by that I mean thanks for getting me out of doing it."

"No problem. I usually don't have to be persuaded to go shopping."

"Well, I'm sure you did a better job of advising her than I would have."

He climbed the steps to the porch but didn't invite her to follow him in. "We've got a game tonight. You're coming, aren't you?"

"Wouldn't miss it," she said. "You know how I love football." She smiled at the familiar sarcasm, only now the sentiment didn't seem all that sarcastic.

"You can come in if you want. I've got to grab a quick shower and get dressed in my official gear, but it won't bother me if you're here."

Why did his sudden disinterest get under her skin? Isn't this exactly the kind of relationship she wanted with Mike? Casual, friendly. Hang out or don't.

"No, I'll get going," she said. She wanted to tell him that she'd passed on an invitation from Alex to see a small theater production in Athens tonight so she could attend the game. She'd had to promise that she'd go with him to a wine tasting and jazz concert on Sunday, though. But right now Mike didn't seem as if he'd appreciate her sacrifice.

He waved from the front door and went inside. Brenna got in her car and backed away from the cabin. The rest of her weekend was looking bleak. She'd never really liked jazz.

CHAPTER THIRTEEN

DURING THE NEXT two weeks, Mike decided that no one seemed happy, least of all him. The Ravens football team had lost their most recent game, and Bobby Montgomery was taking the heat from the townspeople. Even Charlie, the star running back, was moody, and his reticence caused Carrie to worry that her first love was going to dump her.

"What does *dumping* even mean?" Mike asked Brenna one night at the center. This particular night, he was even more down than usual because Brenna looked exceptionally cute in shorts and a tank top and with her hair up in a funny twisty thing with cherries printed on it. They'd been working for days to get the old building ready for the teens to enjoy it, and now that they were in the home-stretch, he was sorry the project was nearing completion.

"Come on, Mike," she said. "You know

what *dump* means in dating terms, don't you? Or have you never been dumped, and it's not part of your vocabulary?"

"Oh, I've been dumped," he said. "Plenty of times. But you have to be going steady for that to happen. Do you think Carrie considers that she's been *going* with Charlie?"

Brenna tried to wiggle the soundproof partition she'd been bolting to a wall of the library. Apparently deciding it was secure, she turned her attention to Mike. "Open your eyes, Dad. Everyone knows Carrie and Charlie have been going together."

He carried a stack of chairs into the classroom space blocked off by Brenna's partition and began putting them in rows. "So they've been kissing and stuff like that?" A stupid question, but he'd been doing his best to avoid thinking about any physical part of Carrie's relationship with Charlie.

"Considering I saw him kiss her in front of her locker the other day, I'd say that's a safe bet."

"And he gave her a necklace with her birthstone in it for her birthday," Mike said. "Seemed a little too personal to me."

Brenna didn't comment.

Mike made a growling sound deep in his throat. "What am I supposed to do now that you've given me this information?"

"Have you talked to her about dating, health concerns, preventing unplanned pregnancy, things like…"

"Whoa! Hold on. No, of course not. I figure her mother covered all those topics."

"Maybe she did, but I'd suggest you grow a backbone and at least ask Carrie some questions."

He set down the last chair. "Can't you…"

"Talk to her for you? No, I can't," she stated emphatically. "You're the parent, and this discussion definitely comes under parent-child guidelines."

"But you're my *friend,* aren't you?" He hated the sound of that dreaded word spoken as if he was some obstinate kid. He'd thrown it out there as if it were a rock he'd tried to hit her with.

"Don't start," she said. "As your *friend,* I would do most anything for you. But talking to your daughter about sex isn't on the list."

"What if she came to you and asked questions?"

Brenna sighed. "I suppose then I would talk to her, but only if I had your permission."

"You have it. I'll tell her that you want to talk to her about girl stuff."

Brenna moved one chair about two inches. She was becoming a perfectionist about every detail in the center. "You're hopeless," she said to him.

"And there's another thing."

"What?"

"Those girls Carrie has been hanging around with. I'm not so sure they're not manipulating her."

Brenna shook her head as if she couldn't believe what he'd said. "In what way?"

"She follows everything they do. What they wear, where they go, everything."

"Mike, that's what kids do. They're basically pack animals."

"Maybe, but I don't like the little tricks she's using to get me to agree to let her do things. That's not like Carrie."

That wasn't exactly true. Mike remembered the pancake breakfast Carrie had made for him when she'd wanted him to let her go to the Riverview with the Montgomerys. Carrie wasn't beyond a few manipulations of her own, but lately she'd been pushing boundaries more than ever.

"I introduced her to those girls," Brenna said. "I know each of them. Allison is a cheerleader. Mary Sue is president of the Circle Service Club. They're also normal teenagers, and like most kids, they test their limits. It's part of growing up."

"I don't know..."

"How are Carrie's grades?" Brenna asked, an obvious attempt to get Mike to relax his attitude.

"Okay, I guess. How is she doing in your class?"

"Fine, a solid B." She sat in one of the chairs and rubbed her shoulder. "Quit worrying, Mike. You're making more of this situation than you should. You ought to be glad that Carrie has made friends.... For heaven's sake, she even goes to football games!"

He supposed she was right. Brenna knew about his promise to Lori. Maybe Brenna didn't understand the full impact of his pledge to his dying wife, but she understood the responsibility he felt for his daughter's upbringing and care. Lori hadn't trusted him with her end-of-life decisions, but if she was looking down on them, she'd know she could trust him to protect their daughter. Even so, he had lightened up on Carrie. Most times, maybe once or twice a week, he even let her ride with Charlie to events.

Mike sat down, leaving one chair between him and Brenna. "Okay. You've made a good point. And I'm doing better."

She smiled. "Fine. Now are we through talking about you because I want to talk about me."

The opening he'd been waiting for. "Okay. How's Alex?"

She smirked at him. "I said *me,* not Alex."

"I thought you two were joined at the hip, or the heart, or something." He was being a jerk, and he knew it. But sometimes it was easier to play the dolt than it was to deal with real emotions, especially the ones he couldn't seem to control where Brenna was concerned. He hadn't kissed her, or gotten close in any way, since that Friday night when Alex had walked in on them. And each day, when they worked together, when they happened to see each other in school, his self-control grew more difficult to manage. He found himself thinking of her with Alex, and he was surprised he hadn't ground his teeth down to the gums. And when he didn't think about that, he thought about what it would be like if she were with him instead, and that was even worse.

He was so occupied with collecting his thoughts he barely heard her response to his comment about Alex.

"Since you asked, we're taking a break," she said.

"What?"

"We're taking a break," she repeated.

"What does that even mean?" he asked. "Did you split up? Are you seeing other people? I don't know what any of this modern-day dating stuff is all about. New terms. New definitions…"

"It means, Mr. Thick Head, that we've agreed not to see each other for a while."

"Since when? How long is a while?"

"Since a couple of days ago. And I don't know."

"Did you dump him?"

She exhaled a long breath. "Is that what you'd like to believe?"

Yes! "Maybe."

"Well, truthfully nobody dumped anyone. It just sort of, I don't know, fizzled."

He tried not to smile. Brenna might feel really lousy about this.

"I guess Alex brought up the separation first," she admitted.

He'd rather the split happened the other way, but at least this was encouraging.

"He said I was acting differently, like I wasn't into the relationship the way I used to be."

"Did you deny it?" He didn't want to ask so many leading questions that she'd quit talking, so he added, "I mean, he's your Mr. Wonderful, right?"

She gave him a freezing stare.

"Sorry, but did you try to convince him that it was all in his imagination?"

"No, not exactly."

He held his breath. Could this mean she was really growing tired of Alex? Or could it mean she was becoming interested in someone else—someone less perfect, with less money, education and success? He needed more information. "So was it his imagination, or did you really want to break up with him?"

She huffed with obvious impatience. "What do you think, Mike?"

"I don't know! One minute he's your Mr. Everything. The next you don't even seem all that upset after breaking it off with him. What's going on? Why…"

"You can be so dense!" She turned a full ninety degrees on the chair so she could look directly into his eyes. "We've been working here side by side every night for two weeks. Even when I rubbed my shoulder a minute ago, practically begging for you to massage it, you kept your distance."

"That was a sign? Rubbing your shoulder was supposed to tell me something?"

She just stared at him.

"How was I supposed to know you wanted me to massage your shoulder? You asked me to back off, and I have! It's not what I wanted."

"I certainly wouldn't have known that by how you've acted. Suddenly it's like I have this horrible disease or something."

He chuckled and her face grew scarlet.

"What's so funny?"

"This whole thing. I can't figure you out. You told me you just wanted to be my friend.

Now you're saying you're disappointed because I haven't been coming on to you. I'm more than a little confused here, Brenna."

"It's more than just the shoulder rubbing. There have been other signs," she said as if it made all the sense in the world.

"Oh yeah? Mind telling me what they were so I won't blow it with another woman down the road?"

She stared down at the chair separating them. "This is all my fault. I should have been more obvious." She looked up at him again. Her eyes glistened with an emotion he'd never seen before, but he sensed he was the center of it, and that was a good place to be. She inched closer to him. "If this chair weren't here…"

He knocked the chair over.

And suddenly her hands were wrapped around his nape, she'd yanked him none too gently across the open space and her lips were on his. Her head moved, slowly, temptingly, and all the emotions he'd kept stored up for weeks found an outlet. He hardly recognized the growl that came from his throat as he deepened the kiss.

Too soon for him she pulled back. A long,

sweet breath came from the lips he'd just kissed.

"So what does this mean exactly?" he said, his voice raspy. "Are we dating now?"

This time she chuckled. "Dating, Langston? Is that the best you can come up with to describe what's going on?"

"I guess we've never really had a date," he said.

She spread the fingers of one hand and began listing. "Let's see. We've had arguments, deep discussions, pizza and a few kisses. But a date? No, never."

His grin originated from deep inside. "Will you go out with me tonight? Right now." He glanced at his watch. "It's Friday night, still early. We can go to dinner or something…"

"What's your curfew tonight, Mike?"

"Doesn't matter. I'm taking you home with me."

The light in her eyes dimmed and his heart sank. He was rushing things. That wasn't good for either Brenna or him. But the kiss had been so encouraging.

She pulled away from him. "Mike, I don't think so. You have a daughter, remember?"

Time to backpedal his way out of this. "I

wasn't suggesting anything inappropriate, Miss Schoolteacher."

"No?"

"No. I just thought you'd like to meet my dog."

"Uh-huh."

"Carrie won't have a problem with you meeting Buster. She's been hoping you'd drop by. Besides, she's not due home until eleven, and lately that means eleven-fifteen."

He stood and grabbed her hands. She rose and he took the opportunity to kiss her again. "And between now and whenever we hear Charlie Montgomery's car in the drive, I can get in a few more of these."

"Okay. Sounds like a plan, then." She grinned up at him. "I can't wait to…meet your dog."

THE NEXT WEEK flew by for Mike. He didn't argue with Carrie. The Ravens won their weekend game. The Cultural Arts Center would be ready for the big reveal on Sunday. And he'd been with Brenna every evening. They had the date thing down, though their dates mostly consisted of grabbing dinner after working on the center or cooking something up at the cabin so Mike could be home with his daughter. Brenna understood and supported his need to be around when Carrie was home. With the one exception of not having enough alone time with Brenna, Mike was content.

There hadn't been any point in hiding the relationship from Carrie. She was too bright not to catch on, and Mike was too happy to pretend. So they settled into a comfortable foursome. Mike, Brenna, Carrie and Buster, the fifty-pound Labrador mix who'd managed to claim every chair in the house as his own.

Mike and Brenna didn't talk about the future, which was okay because the present was working out just fine. They both had agreed to take things slowly and see how this new and exciting phase of their "friendship" progressed. Each time Mike kissed her, whenever he held her hand, whenever he laughed at something she said, he felt a little of the old, bitter Mike dissolve, leaving the beginnings of an optimistic believer in its place.

Unfortunately, one aspect of Mike's life still troubled him. His relationship with Carrie had improved, but he certainly didn't think his parenting skills were the reason.

Brenna continually told him that everything with Carrie was fine. She was popular. Her grades were good. Charlie was a great boy. And the girls she hung out with were from good families.

So why did Mike feel as if he was losing control over his daughter? He rarely refused Carrie anything these days. When she wanted to go out, he let her, though he still insisted on maintaining a curfew. When she asked to ride in cars with other kids, he usually asked a bunch of questions and then gave in. When he asked her where she'd been and what she'd done and she answered, "Here and there" and "Not much," he let it go.

As long as she returned to the cabin relatively close to when he expected her, he tried to tell himself everything was fine. He didn't need to keep such tight reins on his daughter. Brenna was right. She was a normal kid, doing ordinary things with other normal kids.

Still, the promise he made Lori kept coming back to haunt him. He'd pledged to protect their daughter and he'd gone from smothering her to being "the greatest dad ever." Mike didn't know much about being a father, but even he knew a title like that often meant that dear old dad, despite scoring points with his offspring, wasn't doing such a good job.

"I can't believe the change in you," Brenna said one night as they were doing dishes. "You've really loosened up and you've made friends. People know you and like you."

"Wasn't I likable before?" he asked her.

"Not as much," she said. "I mean I liked you, sort of, but now you just fit in everywhere, with the adults, the kids, the other teachers." She playfully slapped him with the damp dish towel. "You're a really great guy, Mike. You've come so far from that quiet, withdrawn, overprotective man you were when we first met."

It was not that he wasn't happy that Brenna liked him this way. There wasn't much he wouldn't do to please her. She had been a kind of savior to him, bringing him back from the darkest time of his life. And that was all good.

But in the back of his mind, he couldn't erase the thought that he was failing somehow. Throughout his life he'd never relied on other people's opinions and advice, and now he seemed to be taking Brenna's word as easily as if she'd given it to him with a cherry on top. Brenna couldn't be wrong about Carrie, could she? She was a teacher after all. She knew kids.

So he tried to relax, take each day as it came and strove to be happy. He had a bit of extra money now, thanks to a small stipend Bobby had arranged for him to receive from the school board. He decided he liked Charlie well enough. He accepted that Carrie was old enough to go out with friends and make many of her own decisions. But this was an awful lot of accepting for a guy like Mike.

SATURDAY NIGHT, THE day before the Cultural Arts Center was to be opened to the public, Mike and Brenna were at the cabin celebrating an afternoon game victory. They'd picked up a pizza and a six-pack of beer and intended to discuss the event the town council had planned to showcase the center. Carrie was out with Charlie and a few other kids.

Mike popped the tops on a couple of beers, handed one to Brenna and took a long swallow from the other. He lifted the lid on the pizza box and the spicy aroma filled the small room.

"We did it, Brenna," he said, tapping his

beer can against hers. "We turned that old building into something important and lasting. You were right to commission the library for the new purpose."

She smiled. "I couldn't have done it without you and the other volunteers. We all should be very proud. I can't wait until tomorrow when the whole community will see what we've done in a few short weeks."

He passed his hand down the loose waves that fell to her shoulders and held a strand up to the light.

"What are you doing?"

"Just trying to decide," he said. "I can't tell whether I like your hair this shade of red or with streaks of Hot Summer Beige running through it."

She laughed. "Many nights I didn't think I'd ever get the paint out."

He leaned in for a quick kiss. "I'm not the only one who's changed, you know."

"Are you talking about me? I haven't changed."

He leaned back and studied her resolute features. "Are you saying that after all this work you haven't relaxed your own attitudes about teaching and becoming involved?"

She bit the pointed end off a piece of pizza. "Sorry, but no. Working on this building is far different from working on problems in a student's life. I still feel as I always have. I will continue to do my job, teach to the best of my ability and let the professionals handle the emotional turmoil." She frowned. "And before you say it, yes, I realize I've violated that principle many times with regard to Carrie."

He wondered if he didn't know her better than she knew herself. He understood her reasons for feeling how she did. What happened to her with the young boy who'd been abused by his father during her previous job was heartbreaking. But he'd hoped she'd come to see that she had a lot to give her students. She could be a friend, an advisor and a role model.

Apparently reading his thoughts, she said, "I've done it again, haven't I?"

"Done what?"

"Ruined some sort of ideal you had of me. Sorry, Mike, but I'm still the same person I was when you met me. Just because I've taken Carrie under my wing doesn't mean I'm ready to be a confidante and confessor to every student who comes along. Remember, I learned this lesson the hard way."

He didn't want to accept her desire to remain aloof. Carrie idolized her. And he... well, he was falling too hard and too fast. If he hit bottom and found himself alone, he didn't know if he'd recover. Daring to ask the question that bothered him the most, he said, "Does this mean you're the same person in all respects or just the same teacher?"

He held his breath. Were money and possessions still priorities? She'd broken off with Alex, the man who could have given her everything, but had she sacrificed the principles she'd always believed in? Or was she just biding her time until another Alex came along?

She smiled and patted the cushion next to her on the sofa. "No. I've changed in small ways. For instance, I'm beginning to like this cabin."

Not all that he'd wanted to hear, but it was something. And he'd hold on to that for now.

"How's the pizza?" he asked when he sensed they should pursue another topic.

"It's great. Why haven't you had a piece?"

"I like cold pizza. You acquire a taste for

it in the army when you're at the end of the line in mess."

She smiled. "I'm so excited about the unveiling of the center tomorrow, aren't you?"

"Sure."

"I want to be there early so we can attend to any last-minute…"

She halted when his phone rang. He connected to the unfamiliar number. "Hello."

"Mike, this is Boone."

"Oh, hey. What's up?"

"I have some news for you. I don't have all the details. In fact, I hardly have any details, but I thought you'd want to know."

Mike's blood chilled. He looked at his watch. Only five after eleven. Carrie wasn't too late yet. "What is it?"

"A car went off White Deer Trail a few minutes ago and into the river."

He didn't recognize the croak that came from his throat. "Whose car?"

"A witness got a description and the first three numbers of the license plate. Based on that, we think it was Charlie Montgomery's car."

The thudding of his heart practically toppled him. "Who was in it?"

"Don't know yet. I just got the call. I'm on my way out to the scene now."

"Where?" The one word seemed to tear the lining of his throat.

"About halfway between town and your place. A patrol car should have arrived. You'll see the flashing lights if you want to come out…"

Mike disconnected, shoved his cell phone into his shirt pocket and grabbed his keys off the coffee table.

"What is it?" Brenna asked. "What's happened?"

"Accident. Charlie's car…" He ran out the door, only vaguely aware that she was right behind him. She'd barely closed the passenger door to his truck before he was barreling down the dirt path.

CHAPTER FOURTEEN

BRENNA CLENCHED HER hands and prayed, though she didn't do it often enough to feel as if she deserved God's attention. But maybe someone up there would listen tonight, and she didn't know what else to do. "Please let there be a mistake," she said softly. "Don't let this be Charlie's car…"

Mike kept mumbling, "Lori, I'm sorry." Their truck swerved on the narrow road despite the force with which his hands clenched the steering wheel. Brenna didn't know if he was even aware he was driving. He certainly didn't seem to notice her presence in the truck.

After what felt like an eternity, flashing lights appeared ahead of them. Mike didn't slow down until he was practically on top of the two police cars at the edge of the road. Brenna lurched in her seat when he applied the brakes, grateful she'd put on her seat belt.

At least four police officers were present. Boone stood on the riverbank looking down at the tail end of a car, its red lights blinking eerily in the darkness. The other cops were tending to people on the ground.

"Thank goodness," Brenna said, stumbling out of the truck and running after Mike. "Whoever was inside has been pulled out."

Five kids sat on the grassy bank with blankets wrapped around their shoulders. Brenna recognized each of them: boys from the football team, girls she'd introduced to Carrie. But Carrie wasn't among them.

Mike grabbed Boone's arm. "Is it Charlie's car?" he demanded.

Boone nodded. "Yeah. Went off the road about—"

Mike spun away from him, glanced quickly at the five teens and plunged into the water. He shouted Carrie's name and half walked, half swam to the submerged car door.

"Mike, no!"

Brenna barely heard Boone's call. Her mind couldn't process anything other than the horrible possibilities. Carrie was still in the car. So was Charlie, her best friend's son. This couldn't be happening.

Brenna felt frozen, unable to go forward, almost unable to breathe. Every second counted. Maybe there was a pocket of air... Almost as great as her fear was the paralyzing thought that Mike would think this was all her fault. She'd introduced Carrie to this group of kids, all fine kids from good homes, kids who were just normal teens who didn't get into trouble.

Why did she do it? Why did she get involved? She knew better and now another tragedy, another unbearable loss. Her heart was breaking for Mike. How would he live through this? How could anyone reach him now? And how would she cope with such horrible guilt one more time?

Mike reached the car door and appeared to struggle with the handle. He banged on the window. Black water swirled around him. His cries carried up to shore. "Help! I need some help here!"

From somewhere deep inside her brain Brenna thought she heard Boone yell, "Carrie's not in there!" Boone called again, "That door's jammed! Come out." But Mike only doubled his efforts as if he could break the barrier of steel and glass. Boone pointed to another officer. "He's out of his head. We've got to go in and get him."

The two cops followed Mike's path into the river and soon had Mike by his arms and were tugging him to shore. "Listen to me, Mike," Boone said. "She's not in the car!"

Mike's anguished cries stopped along with his frantic struggle against the two men restraining him. "What? What did you say?"

The two officers dragged Mike onto the riverbank. With his forearm holding Mike upright, Boone leaned him against a tree. "Listen to me," Boone said. "Carrie's not here. All these kids got out before we even got here, and your daughter wasn't riding with them."

Even in the darkness, Brenna saw the whites of Mike's eyes as he frantically searched the area, finally settling on the five teens. "But it's Charlie's car."

"Yes, it is. But one of the other boys had the keys."

Mike pushed a huge gulp of air from his lungs. "You're sure?"

"Yes, all five kids are accounted for. Trust me, Mike. There's nobody in that car."

Brenna flattened her hand over her heart,

which had started to beat again. Grateful tears streamed down her cheeks.

Mike's hand fisted over Boone's wet shirt. "Then where's my daughter?"

Boone shook his head. "I don't know, buddy. But she's not in that river, and that's what you need to concentrate on now."

Mike's body relaxed. His hand fell limp to his side just seconds before his body seemed to lose all muscle tone, and he slipped down the tree trunk to the ground. "She's not in the river..." His voice sounded hollow, as if the realization were only now settling in.

Brenna's cell phone rang. She checked the caller ID and didn't recognize the number. "Hello?" Her voice was trembling.

"Miss Sullivan?"

Brenna sobbed, gripped the phone more tightly. "Carrie?"

"I'm sorry to call so late. I tried to reach my dad, but his cell went right to voice mail. Is everything okay?"

Mike's cell phone. He'd put it in his shirt pocket. It must be waterlogged now. "Yes, he's fine. Where are you?" She got Mike's attention, pointed to her phone and nodded. He got to his feet.

"I'm with Charlie in town. We need Dad to pick us up. There's kind of a problem."

"Your dad's right here," Brenna said. "Hold on." She passed the phone to Mike. "She wants you to come get her."

While Mike talked to his daughter, Brenna walked over to Boone, who was drying off with a blanket. "Need any help?" she asked. "I know all these kids."

"They're okay, and unless you have a dry uniform, I'm the same. I feel bad for Mike. He's even more soaked than I am. I tried to keep him from going in the river."

"I know, but he was frantic."

"Sure. I get that."

Boone tossed the blanket into the trunk of his cruiser. "I guess his daughter's fine. That's her on the phone, isn't it?"

"Yeah. She's okay, but what about the rest of them?" Brenna glanced at the five kids huddled under blankets a few yards away. "How did this happen? Why was someone else driving Charlie's car?"

Boone ran his fingers through his sandy-colored hair. "If you get close enough to those kids to smell the air around them, I think you'd begin to have your questions answered."

"They were drinking?"

"No doubt about it, Bren. Not one of them could walk a straight line right now. I'm just glad they had the sense to open the windows as they went over the riverbank. They all crawled out with barely a scratch."

"I noticed an ambulance leaving when we pulled up. No one needed transport to the hospital?"

"No, but they all need a ride home. I'm getting ready to call their parents to come get them."

"Those are going to be some very angry parents," Brenna said. "As well as relieved."

Boone nodded. "But each of them will have to come down to the station tomorrow. We don't take underage drinking lightly around here." He stared for a moment at the sunken car. "And that's the reason why."

"Do you know why Charlie wasn't with them?"

"Yeah, the older kid, Justin, said they wanted to leave the place they'd been hanging out, and Charlie didn't want to drive."

"Smart kid to know his limitations."

"I guess. So Justin took the keys from him and drove off, leaving Charlie and Mike's kid behind."

"Charlie didn't try to stop him?" Brenna asked. She knew how Charlie felt about that car.

"Couldn't say," Boone answered. "But Justin outweighs him by about thirty pounds, so maybe Charlie just let him have his way."

Brenna looked at Mike, who was still talking on her phone. "I wonder if Charlie and Carrie had been drinking, too."

"Wouldn't be surprised," Boone said. "Peer pressure and all that." He paused to glance at Mike. "And he doesn't look too happy."

It was true. Mike looked miserable and grateful at the same time. He disconnected and walked over to where Brenna and Boone stood. "Here's your phone," he said to Brenna.

She stuffed it in her pocket. "How's Carrie?"

"How do you think? In trouble and about to get in even more." He turned and began walking toward his truck. "I'm going to get her now."

Brenna stared at his back. Had he forgotten that she'd ridden out here with him? "I guess that's my cue," she said to Boone. "We're leaving."

"I can give you a lift," he said.

"Thanks, but I'd like to be with Mike. It's been a tough night." For all of them. Brenna hurried to catch up with him. In the back of her mind the fear that he would blame her for what happened took root again. And maybe she was responsible. She had introduced Carrie to these kids, and she had convinced Mike that Carrie was in good company. Bottom line, she'd interfered time and again, just as she knew she shouldn't have.

He'd already started the engine when she got in the passenger seat. He didn't speak or even look at her, just backed up, pulled around a police cruiser and sped toward town.

"Where is she?" Brenna asked after a moment.

"In front of the library."

"The old library? She's at the Cultural Arts Center?"

He nodded once and didn't add any details.

"What were they doing there?" she asked.

"Don't know."

"Were they inside? The doors are always locked."

He speared her with an angry look. "Brenna, I don't know, okay? But something happened and it's not good. This whole night is a nightmare."

"We'll sort it out," she said. "The important thing is…"

His voice was flat and cold when he interrupted her. "The important thing is that I'm through taking advice from anyone. I'm going to trust my own judgment from now on. Carrie is my daughter and nobody is going to tell me how to raise her." He paused, blinked hard and added, "This has been a real wake-up call."

Brenna felt his angry words in the pit of her stomach. She had no doubt that he was referring to her. They drove the rest of the way in silence.

They pulled into the center's parking lot just ahead of Diana and Bobby Montgomery. Carrie and Charlie stood up from a brick wall lined with shrubs when they saw the cars. Bobby parked alongside Mike's truck. Brenna walked around the passenger side and spoke to Diana. "Do you know what happened?"

"I know some of it. Boone called. I can't believe these kids have been so foolish." She watched her husband walk toward Mike. "Bobby is furious."

"At least Charlie didn't get behind the wheel. Justin Hower was driving."

"But Charlie gave him his keys. We've told him never to do that."

Brenna recalled Boone's theory that alcohol and a belligerent Justin might have contributed to Charlie's decision, but she decided Diana would find out this information on her own soon enough. Brenna was staying out of the entire unfortunate incident.

"He also knows to call us whenever drinking's involved," Diana said. "We're not naive that it doesn't happen, but we don't allow it under any circumstance."

"Mike is angry, too," Brenna said. "Maybe we'd better go over there in case things get out of hand."

So far the fathers didn't seem to have said much. Both men were huffing and staring and probably grinding their teeth. Brenna thought if she'd been one of their kids, she would be more terrified than if they'd been yelling.

"Get in the truck," Mike finally said to Carrie.

"Not yet, Dad. There's something you don't know."

He crossed his arms over his chest. His hands were fisted. "That you two have been drinking? Mr. Montgomery and I already figured that out."

"Okay, I admit it. But we only had a little."

"A little is too much. You're fifteen years old, Carrie!"

"I know. You don't have to keep reminding me. But, Dad, that's not the worst of it."

Bobby had pulled Charlie away, and he and Diana were having their own conversation with the boy. Charlie gestured with his hands as if he were trying to explain.

"Start talking, Carrie, and you'd better get it all out in the open now. When we get home, I'm doing the talking!"

"All right, but promise me you won't get mad."

Mike's eyes widened. "Carrie, I left *mad* on that road two miles out of town. Now I'm furious."

"But, Daddy…"

Brenna wondered if she regularly called him "Daddy." It didn't matter. Mike wasn't falling for it.

"Talk!"

"I will! But we have to go inside the building," Carrie said.

The Montgomerys joined them. "Charlie wants to show us something in the center," Bobby said. "I suggest we all go in together." He looked at Brenna. "Have you got a key?"

"Sure," she said before asking Carrie, "How did you kids get inside? The doors are always locked."

Carrie hung her head. "There was a window in the back, and, well…"

"We get the picture," Mike said. Brenna unlocked the front door. "Come on. Let's go."

Brenna preceded the rest of them inside to the all-purpose room. She flipped the switch that controlled several of the overhead lights, and just as Mike had planned, the room was brightly illuminated so all four corners could be seen.

Brenna's heart plunged to her stomach.

All their hard work. All the volunteer hours. So many people from the community had worked so hard to make the center a reality. All the sacrifices made in the past few weeks swam before her eyes as she stared at the destruction. The walls that she had lovingly painted a satin-beige were covered in graffiti. The classroom partitions had been spray-painted with *Losers, geek-freaks* and other similarly unflattering terms. Several empty liquor bottles sat on the floor, their partial contents pooling in telltale puddles on the refinished floors. Numerous plastic cups in garish primary colors sat on the chairs and tables.

Brenna was aware of the others behind her taking in the scene just as she was, but she couldn't summon the energy to turn around.

Carrie's soft voice penetrated the heavy stillness of the room. "I didn't do this, Dad. It was the other..."

"No excuses, Carrie. You were here. You're to blame as much as anyone else." His voice had an underlying tremor of rage.

"But, Daddy, you have to believe me." Carrie's voice cracked. "Justin and Brad, they were the worst. They were making fun of everything the center was supposed to be."

Brenna turned then, a slow, torturous twist of her body. "Is this how the kids really feel about the center?" she asked.

"Some, maybe. But not me, and not Charlie. I think the center is a good idea."

Brenna let out a long, tortured sigh. "How about the rest of the high school kids? Tell me the truth. Is this building just a big joke to everyone or only the few who were here destroying property?"

"I don't know," Carrie said. "I haven't met that many kids. But probably not. Don't be upset, Miss Sullivan. I'll bet a lot of teenagers were looking forward to having this place open. Everyone knows there's nothing to do in this town."

Mike's mouth barely moved as he said, "Oh, you found something to do."

Diana and Bobby had cornered Charlie off to the side and had been hammering him with questions. Bobby looked as if he was ready to explode. Diana, the most caring and compassionate teacher at Mount Union High, just seemed sad. Slowly, they broke apart to begin picking up cups and carrying them to a trash can—an insignificant beginning to what would be a major cleanup.

Bobby's voice carried across the room. "You and your buddies are going to repaint this room, you know that, don't you, Charlie? Not one of you will wear a Ravens uniform again if this place isn't spick-and-span by next weekend."

"We'll put it back like it was, Dad."

"And this doesn't even begin to address the damage to your car. It's probably a total loss."

Charlie muttered under his breath—something about aiming to kill his former best friend.

"And the drinking!" Bobby added. "How many times have we talked about underage drinking?"

"The police are involved, Charlie," Diana said. "Your friends could have been seriously hurt, or they could have been killed."

Charlie rubbed a finger under his nose before depositing cups in the trash. "I tried to stop Justin, Mom."

"That's right, he did," Carrie said. "But they were too drunk…" She stopped. "Or something. Justin was acting like a big bully."

Brenna wanted to talk to Carrie, to ask her what she had been thinking, why she had allowed herself to become involved in such a ridiculous act of vandalism. But Brenna, the only adult not a parent here, reminded herself that this was a family matter. She just moved slowly around the room, checking damage.

Mike rubbed the heels of his hands over his eyes. "The fact is, Carrie, you were drinking, too. You and Charlie?"

She nodded. "Not as much but some. Charlie wasn't going to drive."

"Thank God for that," Diana said.

"And I called you, Dad," Carrie said. "A bunch of times, but you didn't answer."

"That's because my phone fell out of my pocket and into four feet of water when I thought you were inside a submerged car!"

"Oh, Daddy…" Carrie's sobs prevented her from speaking for several moments. "That's why you're all wet. You went in after me."

"Yeah, I did."

Finally Brenna couldn't pretend she wasn't even in the room. The center was her project, and she had certain rights. She walked up to Carrie and asked in a calm voice, "Why the center, Carrie? Even if those kids didn't want to use the facility, I'm surprised. I've had most of you in class. I just don't see why."

"I'm so sorry, Miss Sullivan," she said. "At first we were just going to sneak in here with the bottles. Mary Sue called it a pre-grand-opening party. It seemed like a good idea. We couldn't go to anyone's house, not with the bottles. I didn't think anyone would get drunk. I mean, I never drank liquor before, so I didn't know."

"It just got out of hand, Miss Sullivan," Charlie said, looking around at the destruction. "Way out of hand."

Brenna didn't know what else to say. These were good kids. She'd always thought so. She couldn't stop believing it now. "I've got to call Stan Peterson before the town council shows up here in the morning to start setting up," she finally said. "Obviously we won't be having a ceremony. I'll meet you all outside."

Mike gave her a look that could have frozen Mount Union. "Bobby, can you take Brenna home?" he said. "I want to be alone with Carrie."

His voice wasn't exactly threatening, but it was dangerous just the same. Dangerous to her emotions.

"Sure, no prob..." Bobby started to say.

"My car's at your place," Brenna said to Mike. "I have to go back there to get it."

Mike took Carrie's arm and started toward the exit. "Oh, right. In that case, Bobby, can you drop Brenna at my place before you go home?" He cut another cold stare at Brenna. "Where are your keys?"

"In your house. My purse is on the sofa."

"I'll find it and leave it on the hood of your car," he said. And then, without another word, he quickly led his daughter out of the building.

CHAPTER FIFTEEN

MIKE FLEXED HIS fingers on the steering wheel as he drove. *Stay calm,* he told himself. He couldn't release the awful tension building inside him.

After a few agonizing minutes of silence, Carrie asked, "Aren't you going to say anything?"

Oh, yeah, he had a lot to say. He just figured that if he started now, before he'd had time to sort this mess out in his head, he might regret most of what he said. What had happened tonight was too important for him to speak without thinking first. He'd learned a valuable lesson tonight about trusting his instincts. His daughter had disappointed him, big-time. She could have been killed. How much was one man supposed to handle? "In time," he answered curtly.

"I know you're still mad."

"You could say that."

He slowed when they reached the few yards of road where Charlie's car had plunged over the riverbank. The scene was eerily quiet now. All the police cruisers had taken off. Parents had obviously picked up their drenched kids. The car had been towed. "See those tracks?" Mike said, as he pulled alongside the flattened weeds.

"Yeah."

"That's where I thought you were trapped in an automobile under four feet of water."

"I can't believe you jumped in to get me," she said.

He glared at her. "Why is that so hard to believe?"

"Well, I guess because I wasn't in there after all. I would never have gotten in the car with Justin. I'm not stupid. And also because you and I don't always get along."

He stared at her with disbelief. "So you think I wouldn't risk a soaking to save your life? Jeez, Carrie, you really think that?"

She stared out the windshield as he pulled away from the accident scene. "I don't know."

He choked on his next words. "I thought you were in there. I was crazy to get you out."

"Okay, I get it. Thanks."

Thanks? How about thanks for not having a heart attack? Thanks for not screaming at me in front of my boyfriend? Thanks for making parenting seem like the most impossible job in the world!

The cab of the truck fell into silence once more. Mike thought of Lori, his promise to her. At this moment he truly hoped she couldn't see what was going on down here. He hadn't done such a good job keeping his promise lately. His daughter could have been in that car, maybe would have been if it hadn't been for Charlie. Maybe Bobby's son *was* the levelheaded one. Carrie had been following those other girls like a sheep for days. Who was to say she wouldn't have followed them into the river tonight? Maybe she wouldn't have gotten out... Maybe he would have been too late.

He swerved into the driveway to his grandmother's house without even trying to avoid the holes he'd intended to fill. "There are going to be some changes," he said.

She gaped at him. "I knew it! I knew you would blow this out of proportion. Nothing happened, Dad! We're both back here at this stupid cabin just like always."

He braked in front of the house, turned to stare at her, one arm over the steering wheel. "You broke the law, Carrie! You broke several laws. Underage drinking, breaking and entering, willful mischief, vandalism. I don't know what all, but I expect we'll find out."

She looked as if he'd slapped her. "You mean I could be in real trouble? Could I go to jail?"

He could tell she was close to tears. "I doubt you'll go to jail, but you'll probably appear in court before a judge. You might get probation and community service."

"What about the other kids?"

"I think it's pretty safe to say Justin won't be driving for a while. And all you kids will have to clean up the Cultural Arts Center."

Mentioning the center brought Brenna to his mind. He couldn't concentrate on how this had affected her, not when his own emotions were so raw. But she must have been devastated at the damage to her pet project. She'd chaired this endeavor to help the teens of Mount Union, and it had been those teens who'd destroyed it. Some things just made no sense.

With her fingers wrapped around the door

handle, Carrie said, "Then aren't we being punished enough? Why do you have to change anything?"

"Because everything *has* changed already! And I let it happen. I've taken advice from the wrong people. I've trusted you when I shouldn't have. I thought you could handle more independence." He steeled himself to say the words that hurt the most. "Now I know I've been wrong about everything."

She yanked on the door handle. "This is so like you! Jumping to conclusions just to keep me in this…this prison!" She jumped down, slammed the truck door and ran into the house.

Mike remained in the truck, hoping Carrie's temper would cool before he went inside. Hoping his own temper would cool, as well. But he couldn't stay out here forever. Bobby would be along with Brenna very soon and Mike did not want to see her. If she told him again that these were "really good kids" or to "cut Carrie some slack," he didn't know what he'd do.

He layered his hands on top of the steering wheel and rested his forehead on them. "How did this happen, Langston?" he asked himself. "You used to be so sure of yourself. You knew right from wrong. Granted, you never had the smarts a lot of college guys have, but your common sense led you in the right direction most of the time."

He thought back to his army days, really just a year ago, but now seeming part of a distant past. He'd managed to keep himself alive in a war zone. He'd even helped some of his buddies stay alive, and he did it by following his gut. Then Lori got sick and didn't trust him enough to tell him the truth. Maybe she was right all along. Maybe he wasn't a guy to be trusted with matters of family and children and marriage. Maybe war and basic survival were all he was good for.

He might as well give up on that dream of getting a college education. He'd probably fail at higher education, too, especially if going to night classes meant he had to be away from Carrie for long periods. He couldn't leave her on her own now, not after he'd proven what a failure he was as a father.

Brenna had been suggesting courses he could take to get started with his BA in education. She'd urged him to set reasonable goals so he wouldn't get stressed out. She seemed to know what she was talking about, but hadn't she seemed just as confident when she'd advised him about Carrie? It had taken a while, but he'd finally learned to trust Brenna with the most important person in his life.

But he'd listened to her when he should have listened to the voice in his head, the same voice that had promised his wife that he would protect their daughter. Some protector he turned out to be. Carrie could have been killed tonight.

He raised his head in the cab of the truck and looked at his reflection in the rearview mirror. His eyes were blurry, his face dirty. River mud, he supposed, mixed with the streaks of maddening tears when he'd thought the worst had happened. "I wish you were here, Lori. I wish Carrie had a mother and not just a big, dumb soldier who doesn't know anything about raising a kid.

"Never again," he said aloud, feeling a sudden burst of resolve. "Trust yourself and no one else. No one can take care of your own flesh and blood like you can. No one but you can keep that promise."

This decision had a devastating side effect that he couldn't think about tonight. He'd have to let Brenna go. Just when they were getting started, he'd have to end it. That would hurt for a while, just like other sacrifices he'd made in his life, but he'd get over it. When he saw his daughter safely at home each night, he'd realize that no sacrifice was too great. If Lori was looking down on him, she would be proud of him. She would know that he intended to keep his word even at the expense of his own happiness.

But would he get over it? Brenna had made him happy when he'd begun to doubt that he ever would be again. Her gentle chiding, soft touches, tender but needy kisses—they'd transformed him into a man who'd just started to feel comfortable in his own skin again. And now he'd have to go back to being a single dad again. Single. Lonely. Alone.

When headlights veered through the leafy trees in his drive, he bolted out of the truck. He'd made his decision, difficult as it was. Bobby would be in front of the house in less than a minute. Mike had to find Brenna's purse and lay it on the hood of her car. She was a smart lady in many ways. She'd know what it meant. And then he'd have to go in the cabin and try to be the best father he knew how to be.

"THANKS FOR THE LIFT," Brenna said when she got out of Bobby's car.

"No problem. You going to be okay?"

She leaned into the passenger window. "Sure. I'll be fine. Maybe I'll just run inside a minute and make sure everything's all right."

"Thanks for everything, Bren," Diana said. "And I'm so, so sorry about the center. How did Peterson take the news?"

"He wasn't happy. Wanted to call the police, but I said it might be wise to wait until tomorrow. Some of these kids come from influential families. I'm hoping the parents will make their little darlings do the right thing and we can avoid anything too messy like court appearances. It's bad enough the reckless driving will have to be addressed."

Bobby looked over his shoulder at his son. "I know one set of parents who will make sure restitution is made…. Right, Charlie?"

The boy continued staring down at his clasped hands, which he'd been doing during the entire ride to Mike's.

"And he's going to have to get to the center on his two feet or on his bicycle. His mother and I will decide when he can drive again, if ever."

"Tomorrow I'll call your mom with the paint colors you'll need to buy to do the walls," Brenna said to Charlie.

He finally looked up at her. "I'm really sorry, Miss Sullivan. I didn't mean for you to get hurt, or for Carrie to get mixed up in this. It just got out of hand."

"Yeah, it did, but you'll fix it," she said and backed away from the car. She waited until Bobby had turned around and headed back down the drive before walking to her car. She hoped the purse wouldn't be there, that Mike had just said he would leave it there in a moment of misdirected anger. But the large clasp on the purse's leather strap glistened in the moonlight before she actually could make out the shape of her bag. She sighed, tossed the purse in her car and looked at the house.

Lights were still on in the front room, but despite the cool air, the front door was closed as if shuttered for the night. The air conditioner hummed from the side of the cabin. Other than that, all was quiet.

She took a few tentative steps toward the porch. She couldn't leave things like this. Carrie was hurt and confused. Mike was upset and angry. He was definitely angry with her. She recalled all the times he'd asked her not to interfere. All the times she'd told herself the exact same thing. All the times he'd asked her to forget her pledge to herself and help him with his daughter. And so she'd broken her own promise and let these two sad people into her life and her heart. She had to try to reach him tonight before the bitter feelings escalated and there was no going back.

This was a turning point for all of them. She had to help Mike see that this was a chance to understand each other better, to learn from their mistakes, to go forward with a new sense of trust in each other.

She walked onto the porch and raised her hand to knock. Then she stopped, let her hand fall to her side. The lights inside were suddenly extinguished. The house and the porch were cloaked in darkness. She knew without question that Mike was shutting her out just as surely as he'd switched off the lights.

She got in her car and drove home. Maybe

after a night's sleep he'd see this situation more clearly and he'd call her.

He didn't. Sunday seemed to stretch on forever. Brenna left her house in the afternoon to go to the Cultural Arts Center to see if any progress was being made on the cleanup—and maybe to catch a glimpse of Mike. She ran into Diana in the parking lot. Diana told her that various parents had arrived to monitor the kids and make sure the work was being done correctly.

"I think you'll be pleased with the results," Diana said and then punctuated her optimism with a frown. "Well, I guess *pleased* isn't the right word. How can you be pleased when all your hard work has to be redone?"

"I just want to see the facility open and doing some good for the community," Brenna said. "Carrie was right about one thing. There isn't much for teens to do in this town, and with the interesting classes and activities we're going to offer, I hope the center will fill the void. Mostly, I hope we can reach the students—all of them, even the ones who think the center might not be for them."

"Oh, about one of those classes…" Diana's

voice was hesitant, as if she hated to give her friend more bad news.

"What?"

"Mike has canceled his basic automobile care class. He's decided not to teach it."

Brenna tried not to show her disappointment. Mike would have been a great instructor. The girls would have flocked to his class for obvious reasons—a hunky teacher discussing spark plugs was an automatic draw, and the boys would have wanted to be with the girls. "Did he say why?" she asked.

"No, but I only spoke to him for a few minutes. He stopped to drop Carrie off and left right away."

To avoid seeing me, Brenna thought.

"Is Carrie still here?" Brenna asked.

"She is, and she's working hard. She was asking about you. I think she wants to talk."

No way. Brenna figured Mike would ground his daughter until she was twenty-one if he discovered she was commiserating with the evil Miss Sullivan.

"Why don't you come inside?" Diana said.

"Can't. I've got errands to run. But call if you need anything."

Diana gave Brenna a quick hug. "Again,

Bren, I'm really sorry this happened. Everything was going so well."

"Yeah, it seemed like it. But this event has
reinforced one very important principle. Life
is nothing if not uncertain."

Diana nodded with grim understanding.
"Bobby's going to let Charlie play tonight. I
don't know how effective Charlie will be after
working here all day, but he's busting his butt
now so he can suit up." When Brenna didn't
say anything, Diana added, "You're coming
to the game, aren't you?"

And make Mike uncomfortable on the sidelines? Not a chance. "I think I'll pass tonight,"
she said. "You can spread the word that I'll
be doing other things tonight."

Diana squeezed Brenna's arm. "Mike will
get over this. He's too nice a guy to carry a
grudge. He knows you were only trying to
help his daughter."

"Some help I was," Brenna scoffed. "I introduced her to all the right kids, convinced
her dad to lighten up on the reins, told him
she was 'just a typical teenager.'"

"All that's still true," Diana said. "Show me
one teenager who hasn't gotten into trouble,
and I'll start believing in fairy tales."

"Still, I should have stayed out of the child-raising business. Mike was right when he pointed out that I didn't have any firsthand knowledge on the subject."

Diana's sympathetic expression was almost too much to bear. Brenna had to get away. "Well, I'm off. Got lots to do."

Brenna walked to her car after lying to her best friend. She had absolutely nothing to do. All her spare cash had gone to her parents, so shopping wasn't an option. She'd broken up with Alex, and she didn't even have a football game to prepare for. "Good thing you've got Netflix," she grumbled to herself as she got in the car. "Which sad love story will you watch tonight?" She hoped it was a tale of lost love even more desperate than her own. And that by the end of it, she would believe in happy endings again.

CHAPTER SIXTEEN

CARRIE SAT QUIETLY through her entire home ec class on Monday, and Brenna was concerned. Before Saturday night's drama, the girl had been participating in discussions and kidding around with other students. Today she appeared sullen and angry with the world—and with her teacher.

When class ended, Carrie waited until the rest of the students had left, then she came up to Brenna's desk. Brenna steeled herself for what she knew was coming.

"Hi, Carrie," she said. "Can I help you with something?" Her preservation instincts told her to add, "Something to do with school only," but she didn't.

"Aren't you free for the next period?" Carrie asked.

"Yes, it's my free time. But don't you have class?"

"I thought you could write me a pass to

get in late. I really need to talk to you, Miss Sullivan."

This is what Brenna had been dreading. *Remember what you decided,* she reminded herself. No more getting involved. Stay out of this girl's life. "I don't know that talking is such a good idea, Carrie," she said. "Your father…"

"Is acting like a dictator," Carrie finished for her.

"You gave him quite a scare the other night. You weren't there to see him, but I was. He was frantic that something terrible had happened to you."

"Well, it didn't. I wasn't even in that car, yet he won't let me forget it."

"Carrie, I don't think we should be talking about this. What happened is between you and your father."

"But he's unreasonable, Miss Sullivan!" Carrie plopped down in the nearest student chair. "He drives me everywhere I need to go now. He won't let me talk to Charlie. He says from now on he has to meet and approve of all my friends." Her brown eyes, so like her father's, glistened with tears. "You have to talk to him! He's ruining my life."

Teen drama aside, Brenna could understand Carrie's complaints. But she wasn't surprised by Mike's tightening of the rules. Still, she couldn't interfere, not now and never again. "I can't help you," she said. "But I can at least give you a little advice. Try to be patient. The incident just happened three days ago. Your father is still reeling from the fear of losing you...."

"Which he didn't!"

"I know, but until he found out you weren't in that car, the fear was very real. Give him some time. I'm sure once you convince him that nothing like this will ever happen again, he'll loosen up, give you more freedom."

Carrie's head shook before her words came out on a sob. "No, he won't. He's going to make me live like he does, like a hermit."

The sadness in Carrie's eyes reminded Brenna of that first night when the girl had showed up on her porch.

"I miss you coming over, Miss Sullivan," Carrie said. "And I miss you sticking up for the things I want to do. Without you, Dad has gone back to all his old-fashioned ideas. No, it's even worse because now he misses you, too."

"I don't know about that," Brenna said.

"Of course he does! Please come out to our house and…"

There being no point in letting Carrie hope for something that was not going to happen, Brenna raised her hand. "I can't, Carrie. You'll have to talk to your father on your own. I can't be a go-between any longer. It's not right, and not what your father wants."

"I'll die out there in that cabin," Carrie moaned. "What happened between you and Dad, anyway? He was so nice when you were around. He was a different person."

"Maybe he was, but I guarantee you, my presence won't help now," Brenna said. "I'm sorry, but again, all I can do is urge you to be patient, to try to understand."

Carrie stood. She drew her lips between her teeth to keep them from trembling.

"Maybe you should talk to Mrs. Granger in counseling about this," Brenna suggested. "I can speak to her first, let her know what's going on."

"Never mind," Carrie said. "Just write me that late pass. I won't bother you again."

Brenna scribbled the note and handed it to Carrie. The girl left the classroom without another word, and Brenna remembered with agonizing clarity the other time she had let down a student.

WEDNESDAY AFTERNOON BRENNA was tired of sitting at her classroom window waiting for the coaches and players to come on the practice field. What good did it do to catch glimpses of Mike with the team? He could have come in the building any of the past three days to talk to her, but he hadn't, and she was staying late at school when she could have been home.

Seeing herself as pathetic and cowardly, Brenna decided that if Mike wouldn't come to her, she would go to him. Perhaps a conversation was all it would take to put this relationship back where it belonged. And someone had to start it.

After school on Thursday she waited in the parking lot for Mike's truck to pull in. When it did, she marched right up to the driver's-side door and knocked on the window.

Mike's face went through a transformation. At first he almost smiled the way he used to whenever he saw her. But then, as if he'd reminded himself that he was still angry and she wasn't worth his time, he scowled at her.

"Unlock the passenger door," she said through the window.

"I'm late, Brenna. I've got to get on the field."

"You're going to be later. I'm not leaving until we talk."

The sound of the automatic locks disengaging told her that at least she'd won this round. She walked around the front of the truck and got in. And nearly forgot her reason for being there. Mike looked so good in shorts and a chest-hugging Ravens T-shirt. His sunglasses shielded those incredible dark eyes, and she resisted the urge to take the smoky lenses off. She wanted to see all of this man who had become so dear to her, so comfortable. And lately, so distant.

"Nice to see you," she said.

He averted his gaze from her by concentrating on his fists around the steering wheel. "What's this about?"

"I'm sure you know. We need to get some facts clear, Mike. What happened to Carrie has driven a wedge between us. I need to know if you blame me for any of it or all of it."

"No, I don't blame you."

The confession was a shock, and she didn't know whether to believe him. "Then why have you stayed away from me?"

He shook his head, glanced at her. "I said I didn't blame you, and I don't. But I sure as heck blame myself. I should have known better."

"Than what?"

"Than to take anyone's advice about how to raise my own daughter."

So that's why he'd cut himself off from her. That sounded just like the old Mike, always blaming himself for what amounted to other people's shortcomings. Carrie misbehaves because he's not doing a good job as a father. His wife didn't disclose her illness because she didn't have faith in him to take care of her. How could Brenna, another of a long list of disappointments, ever help him to rid himself of these terrible feelings of guilt?

"I should have followed my own instincts about Carrie, which were to keep her close, keep her safe."

"Even if she was miserable?"

"She wasn't miserable, not all the time. She was a good kid who was lonely, yeah, but she would have come around. I could have gradually let her make some decisions, small ones. Instead I let her jump into a social life with kids you convinced me were…" He stopped, breathed deeply. "Never mind. I should have been a better parent, more responsible."

"You're very responsible, Mike! You go overboard being responsible. But you can't watch that child every moment of the day. She's bombarded with influences at school and online. She has desires and goals and feelings that she's sorting through. Feelings all teenagers have. Feelings about her mother."

His eyes cut to her. "Don't bring Lori into this."

Brenna started to reach out toward him but drew back her hand. *Stay calm, Brenna,* she said to herself. *You're already violating your latest pledge to yourself.* "But Lori is a major factor in what's going on with Carrie," she said. "I think that promise you made to Lori is tearing you apart and ruining your relationship with your daughter."

That was quite a statement and certainly

not in keeping with Brenna's renewed philosophy of noninterference.

"You just don't get it, Brenna, and you never will," Mike said. His voice was raspy with emotion. "I couldn't do anything to save Lori. I sat by her bed like a stupid lump of clay, trying to say the right things when inside I was dying myself because she hadn't trusted me enough to call me home. She thought I couldn't handle it, that I was so selfish and determined to save the world that I couldn't deal."

Brenna didn't know Lori, but she didn't believe this was true. "Did she say this in so many words?"

"She didn't have to. What other reason could she have had for leaving her husband out of the most shattering event of her life? The truth is, she chose to die alone rather than have her stone-cold husband at her bedside. She didn't believe I could ease her suffering."

Brenna's heart ached at the depth of Mike's emotional wounds. After a moment she said, "I don't think she believed that at all."

He smirked at the idea.

"No, really. It's my view that she trusted

you so completely that she didn't send for you until the end. That she knew you would be the man she needed you to be at the most crucial point of her struggle."

He looked up at the top of the truck's interior. "I guess we'll never know what she was thinking, will we?"

"No, we won't, not for certain."

"All I know is that she made me promise to protect our daughter, and I've got to do that the best way I can. I have to go by my instincts—mine! And after what happened the other night, I felt I was losing control, that somehow I'd let Carrie's life fall into the hands of people who weren't looking out for her the way I know I should."

"People like me?"

"It's not your fault, Brenna. I know that. You were trying to help, but I did listen to you. I adjusted my attitude about Carrie to make you happy. And Carrie, too." He stared out the side window. "Believe it or not, making you happy became very important to me."

She touched his arm. "I sensed that, and it's okay, Mike. It's good."

"Carrie liked you, and…" He paused, turned to stare into her eyes. "I wanted you to like me, so I lost sight of what I was doing, who I was living for at this point in my life. I lost sight of the promise."

They both remained silent while Brenna tried to sort out the pain tearing at this man's heart. She'd come this far, maybe she was breaking through. Maybe one last word… "And what about you, Mike? Are you happy living for Carrie?"

He remained silent for so long she was certain he was carefully constructing his answer. "Honestly? I was happy with you. Happier, more content than I'd ever thought possible after losing Lori. But this isn't about me, and it isn't about you. We're the grown-ups here. I've thought about this a lot. As far as Carrie is concerned, I don't think there is any common ground between you and me, Brenna. And it's got to be Carrie first."

His face blurred in the moisture that gathered in her eyes. "That's it, then? I'm the home ec teacher and you're the new guy, and that's all we'll ever be to each other?"

"That's all we can be now," he said.

She sat a moment longer and then reached

for the door handle. "Good luck at the game this weekend," she said and got out of the truck.

BY FRIDAY AFTERNOON, and the beginning of another long weekend, Brenna had adjusted her attitude the only way she knew how. She wasn't going to cry any more tears for Mike Langston. She'd had a full life before he'd come to Mount Union, and she would build another one. She still had friends and places to meet them. She could be the person she was before Carrie had come onto her porch and her father had screeched to a halt at her curb.

As she drove home from school, she thought about the clothes in her closet and which outfit would be suitable for a night on the town in Athens. She and a friend were going to a concert at the university and then hitting some clubs afterward. This lifestyle had suited her fine just a few weeks ago. She could make it enough now. She wouldn't think about Carrie. She wouldn't think about Mike.

She wouldn't think about anything but having a good time....

Then she pulled into her driveway and

thoughts of her Friday night plans evaporated like snow on a hot chimney. She stopped bumper to bumper behind a familiar sedan. On her porch sat her mother and father, and they had suitcases.

CHAPTER SEVENTEEN

BRENNA STEPPED OUT of her car, and her mother rose from the swing she'd been occupying. "Surprise, Brenna May!" Alma Sullivan called.

Brenna's dad had propped his injured leg on a wicker ottoman. Unable to get up easily, he remained seated and maintained a passive expression.

Oh, boy. Brenna walked onto her porch and accepted her mother's rosewater-scented hug. "Mom, Daddy, what are you doing here?" she said when her mother backed away.

Alma smoothed her floral print blouse over her twill slacks. "We just up and decided to come for a visit." She looked at her husband. "Isn't that right, Carl?"

He winced. "That's about it."

"How's your leg, Daddy?" Brenna asked.

"Can't deny it's slowed me down some, but I'm doing as well as can be expected. I'm off the pain pills at least."

Brenna bent over his chair and brushed a kiss against his cheek. "That's progress," she said. "Did you have any trouble finding my place?"

"Your mother drove. She stopped at a 7-Eleven and got directions to the street."

Brenna went to her front door and slipped her key into the lock. "I see you've brought suitcases. You're planning to stay for a while?"

"We'll talk about that in a bit," Alma said, pushing an errant strand of gray-streaked hair off her damp forehead. "In the meantime, can we get your dad inside? This heat is hard on him with his cast and all. He's been suffering this summer something awful."

"Sure, of course." Brenna turned to her father. "Do you need help, Daddy?"

He reached for a pair of crutches she just noticed leaning against the porch wall. "I can manage with these dang sticks," he said, struggling to rise.

Alma went to his side and lifted him under one arm. When he was stable, she wrapped her fingers into the back waistband of his trousers and nudged him toward the front door. Their actions were well coordinated, as if they'd gotten his movements down to a science. Brenna followed them inside with a suitcase in each hand.

Carl made it to the sofa, where he collapsed against the crocheted white pillows Brenna had selected to accent her prized piece of furniture. He set the crutches on the floor and raised his leg to the mahogany coffee table. He looked around the room. "Nice place, Bren," he said. "You've done real good, kid."

Alma walked to the fireplace and admired a pair of vases on the mantel. "Such pretty things you have, Brenna. Nice pictures and flower arrangements. Even the porch looks like it could be on the cover of one of those decorator magazines."

"Thanks, Mom. I've worked hard to get the house exactly as I want it." Brenna forced a smile to cut the sharp edge of her words. They sounded almost like a warning, as if she wanted to add, "And it had better stay this way."

Her mother didn't seem to notice. She just fussed over her husband, plumping the pillows and removing his baseball cap and one shoe. For as long as Brenna could remember, Alma fussed over Carl, as if her attention could somehow make him become the man she wanted him to be. If only some of the time she had fussed over Brenna, too.

"Have you got iced tea, Brenna?" her mother asked. "I'm sure your father would like a glass."

"I can make some," she said.

"I'll help." Alma followed Brenna into the kitchen. "Oh, my, you've got a fancy glass-top stove. And all stainless-steel appliances. Must have cost a fortune."

I worked a second job one summer to pay for them, Brenna recalled. She filled the teakettle and took three tall glasses from her cupboard. "Dad still likes two sugars, right?"

"And lemon if you have it," Alma said.

"Sit down, Mom," Brenna said. "It will take a few minutes for the water to boil, and you must be tired from driving."

Her mom pulled one of Brenna's buttermilk-colored chairs away from the table and sat. "I'm not tired so much from driving, Brenna, but I am tired. I'm dog-tired."

Brenna sat across from her. "Why don't you tell me what's going on, Mom? Why are you here? You've never come in the four years I've lived here."

She hoped her mother wouldn't mention the lack of invitations. Brenna had asked them to visit a couple of times, but her parents always said they were homebodies and didn't want to travel. Secretly grateful, Brenna quit asking.

Alma nodded toward the living room. "You can see what he's like, darlin'. Can't do anything for himself. I wait on him hand and foot."

"That's only temporary, though, Mom," she said. *And, besides, you always have.*

"Yes, I know, and I'm not complaining. He would do the same for me, but I'm not as young as I used to be. My back aches from helping him up and down. I've got to tend him in the shower, fetch anything he wants to eat." She shook her head. "There's no end to it, and frankly, Brenna, I need a rest!"

Any thoughts Brenna might have had that her parents were just passing through vanished. "That's why you're here?" she said. "To get some rest?"

"I'm hoping. I thought if you helped me out with Daddy some, I could get my strength back. You know I wouldn't ask if I had any other options."

Brenna's stomach muscles clenched when

her mother uttered the familiar phrase. How many times had Brenna heard every favor start out with "You know I wouldn't ask…"? The truth was, her mother didn't hesitate to ask for whatever she wanted. And Brenna always tried to provide. Even when she was a little girl, she'd save up her pennies to get her mom a dime-store cologne or new apron. Anything to bring a rare smile to Alma's lips. Or a word of praise.

The kettle whistled, and Brenna got up to steep the tea bags. Maybe she wasn't all that excited about going to a concert in Athens, but all in the same week she'd lost Mike and gained Mom and Dad. Still, they were here now, and she would make the best of it.

"I guess you could stay a few days," she said. "Until…"

"Oh, thank you, honey," Alma said. "Your place is so nice. It'll be like a real vacation. I promise we won't stay more than a week, maybe two at the most."

Two weeks! She had suggested a few days. Brenna tried unsuccessfully to trap a sigh. "Why don't you get some ice and finish the tea for Daddy?" she said. "I'll take your suitcases into the guest room."

KNOWING THE CHOICES in her freezer wouldn't satisfy either of her parents, Brenna ran to the supermarket and picked up a half-dozen pork chops, her dad's favorite. Her mother's way of fixing the small cuts of meat was to drench each one in milk and flour and fry them in about a half inch of oil. Brenna compromised on the artery-clogging recipe by making her own breading and baking the chops with slices of pineapple. Not Southern, but healthier by far. She also made the macaroni and cheese she'd made for Carrie, knowing that would be a hit.

After dinner and cleanup, she went out on the porch, where her dad had gone to smoke his cigarette. "Would you like some company?" she asked, taking a chair next to him.

"Sure. What's your mother doing?"

"Catching up on her shows."

Her father nodded with familiarity.

"Can I get you anything, more iced tea maybe?" she offered.

He shook his head. "That was a good meal, Brenna. Thank you. And please, Bren, don't think you have to wait on me. I figure your mama told you that I'm practically helpless, but I'm not. And even if I were, you're not responsible for me. You have a full-time job, and Alma can take care of my needs. I won't be laid up like this forever."

She wrapped her palm over his arm and felt strangely soothed by the well-worn flannel of his shirt. "Well, if you do think of something…"

"This whole trip was Alma's idea, Bren. You know I don't like to travel. I'm content to stay home, but your mother seems to think the weight of the world has fallen on her shoulders."

"Once you're better she won't feel that way."

As if he hadn't heard her, he continued, "And I never like when she calls you up and asks for money."

"You need it, don't you?"

"Oh, we always need it, but I figure the bill collectors can wait a few days until I find an odd job or two. 'Course now, with this leg…"

"It's okay, Daddy. When your leg is good again, you'll get jobs."

He smiled at her. "I'm proud of you, Brenna. You've made something of yourself. Got this fine house and a respectable job." He looked away. "No thanks to your parents."

Those five words were more honest than any she'd ever heard from her father, and Brenna felt a rush of fondness for the man who, thirty years ago, at thirty-four years of age, probably hadn't planned to have a kid. Her parents hadn't done a whole lot for her, but she was sure she had cost them money, money they never had enough of. "Thank you, Daddy," she said.

They sat quietly for a minute until he said, "I'm not the smartest man, Brenna," he said. "Your mama, she's got smarts, but me, not so much. I always thought I could make enough money without ever getting my high school diploma, but I was wrong. I didn't have enough skills to compensate for a lack of learning. The jobs I did get didn't last long and didn't pay much."

"You did the best you could," she said, not really knowing if that were true. Her mother always claimed that Carl Sullivan was a disappointment as a provider.

"I'll deny this if you ever tell it," he said, "but your mama, with all her smarts, lacked ambition. Maybe we both did, truth to tell. But she expected me to take care of her and you in a finer fashion than I ever did."

Brenna recalled the advice her mother repeated to her from the time she first learned to walk. "It's just as easy to love a rich man as a poor one." Brenna had grown up thinking that was true. Now she knew it wasn't so. A person can't manipulate love. It just happens.

She leaned over and rested her head against her father's sturdy shoulder. "It's okay, Daddy. Just get better. That's all you need to think about now."

MONDAY AFTERNOON MIKE stood on the sidelines of the high school football field and halfheartedly watched his defensive players run drills. His focus was off. He almost felt guilty about taking the paycheck Bobby Montgomery had negotiated for him to assist in coaching responsibilities. But he didn't help out for the money. He did it for the love of the game.

He couldn't concentrate today. The past week had been torture for Mike. He'd dedicated himself to an exclusive existence of being a father, and that meant giving up everything else. He had to make changes in the way he was parenting because he'd promised Lori. If only he could make Carrie understand that everything he did was for her, to keep her safe, to guide her into making the right decisions. If only he could convince himself that his own decisions for her were the right ones. He didn't enjoy watching his daughter mope around the cabin while he held her future in his hands.

Today, especially, he ached knowing Brenna was teaching only a few hundred yards away in that venerable brick building. Physically she was so close, but emotionally he had pushed her to the limits of his world. He was mad at himself for taking her advice, yet he'd been miserable since giving her up. She'd probably already moved on, and that hurt most of all. Deep down he figured he had been only a temporary diversion for her anyway. Brenna had her priorities, and a garage mechanic wasn't one of them.

Mike had priorities, too, and Carrie had to be number one. So he'd made a decision that he hoped would move his little family forward a step at a time.

Movement at the edge of the field caught Mike's attention. He stared at the man who walked toward him, a familiar middle-aged guy in shirtsleeves, his tie loosened and blow-ing about his neck. What is Bill Kraft doing out here? Mike wondered. The principal didn't generally show up on the field unless it was game night.

Kraft came up to him and extended his hand. "Need to get a chance to talk to you, Mike," he said.

"Sure. What about?"

Kraft pushed a shock of thinning hair off his forehead. "Most important is to tell you how much we appreciate your contribution to the team this year."

"No problem. I've enjoyed it."

"Well, you've made a difference. And Bobby can't say enough about you." He smiled sheepishly. "I'm aware that this gig doesn't pay a whole lot."

"I'm not complaining," Mike said.

"There's one more thing," Kraft said. "It concerns that matter you asked me to investigate for you."

Mike's interest spiked. He hadn't forgotten about the favor he'd asked the principal, but so much time had passed and so much had happened that he wondered if Kraft had. "You have information for me?"

"I do." He took a paper out of his shirt

pocket. "Everything you need is right here including current contact details. If there's anything else I can do, just ask."

"Okay, thanks."

"Thanks again to you. Hope we can count on you next year, too. I'm going to put this position before the school board. Hope to make it a legit paying job."

It was time to fess up. Best to just say it, like pulling a bandage off quickly. "About that, Bill. I won't be here next year."

"What? You're leaving Mount Union?"

"Yes, sir. I'm moving my daughter and me back to California. I think it's the best thing for us right now."

Mike hadn't told Carrie this decision yet, but he knew she'd be delighted. It was what she'd wanted since they arrived in Georgia. He'd be back in her good graces again. As for what he wanted… He'd learn to live with the choice.

"I'm sorry to hear that," Kraft said. "I thought after all your help with the team and the Cultural Arts Center, you'd started to feel like part of this community."

Truthfully Mike hadn't believed he'd fit in anywhere since Afghanistan. Without his wife, his pals from his old days, no place had felt like home. But strangely, this small town, which Brenna seemed to love so much, was beginning to feel comfortable.

"How soon are you moving?" Kraft asked.

"Not sure yet. It'll be a couple of weeks. I have some loose ends to tie up." He stared at the paper in his hand. "Including this information you just gave me. I haven't told anyone about this decision yet, not even my daughter, though I won't have any problem with her approving the plan."

"I won't say anything," Kraft assured him. "I'm just sorry to hear it." He shook Mike's hand again. "Good luck to you. If you change your mind, you know where my office is."

"Yes, sir."

Kraft headed back across the field, and Mike slid the paper into his shorts pocket. He'd make a phone call tonight, do this one last thing for Brenna so maybe they would part on good terms. He hoped so at least. It wasn't Brenna's fault that he'd listened to her advice and let his priorities slip. It wasn't her fault that her goals and ambitions were so very different from his. It wasn't her fault that she had this special smile and way of laughing and prodding him with such a gentle hand. She'd made him come alive again.

"Coach!"

He shook his head and turned toward his players.

"What's next, Coach?" one of the boys asked.

I wish I knew, he thought as he consulted his practice chart. *I wish I knew.*

CHAPTER EIGHTEEN

"YOU SO DON'T CARE!" Carrie said. "How could you think that I want to move back to California?"

Her question defied logic. "It's all you've talked about since we got here," Mike said.

"Maybe at one time, but that was ages ago. Everything's changed since then."

He took a long, steadying breath of fresh air coming in the cabin window and rose from the sofa. "What has changed, Carrie? Can you at least give me a hint here? We still live in this cabin you call a prison. I still insist you call me from wherever you are. You're still grounded for what happened." He could only shake his head. "Why do you all the sudden want to stay in Mount Union?"

"It's just like you to never pay attention, Dad," she said. "I have a boyfriend, a really super boyfriend. Even after all you've done to keep us apart, we still like each other."

She gave him a hard, cold, typically teenage stare. "You tried, but you couldn't ruin everything. Some things are even bigger than your stupid rules."

He couldn't help wondering what his daughter and Charlie were doing to keep this romance alive. Had they played hooky to get time together? Were they sneaking behind the bleachers, an old trick from his day? He wasn't comfortable knowing Carrie could be keeping secrets from him about her time with Charlie. He used to have a spy in the school who would give him updates, but he couldn't very well expect Brenna to clue him in now.

He figured he was walking on thawing ice when he said, "There will be other boys. I understand there are quite a few of them in California."

"Dad! Are you serious? Is that how you thought about Mom?" She tried to mimic his voice and only succeeded in making him sound whiny. "Oh well, she died, and that's too bad, but there are lots of women out there, so I'll be okay."

His face heated along with his temper. "You're crossing a line, Carrie, and you know it."

She had the good sense to look repentant. "I'm sorry. That was an awful thing to say. I know you loved Mom, but you can't keep doing this to me."

"Doing what? Trying to make you happy?"

"No, you can't keep running away and dragging me with you!" Her voice cracked. "Because every time you do, I'm the one who suffers. And just when I'm getting comfortable in a new place, you do it again."

He blinked rapidly several times while he tried to digest what she'd just said. "That's what you think? That I'm running away?" Her words were like a blow. He wasn't running. He left California for Carrie because the memories were too hard for his little girl to bear. He thought starting over in a new place would help her heal. But coming to Georgia had just introduced a new series of problems, and now he thought the best decision was to take her back to the environment she was used to. He was doing this for her!

He stared into her glistening eyes. She was so close to tears. He'd thought his announcement would make her happy, but he'd only made her cry. He couldn't do anything right.

She sniffed, ran a finger under her nose.

"Daddy, I'm sorry. I don't want to go to California but I will if you want, if it will make you happy. But we have to make a decision and let it stick. No more moves."

Make him happy? Lately he had shoved his own happiness so far to the back of his mind that the concept almost seemed alien. Certainly unattainable. His time with Brenna, sparring with her, helping her, kissing her, had been the only happiness he'd known for himself since coming home from the army. And now he'd misjudged his daughter's desires again.

Was Carrie right? Was he running away? Maybe that was what he'd been doing all along, when he left California and now when he planned to leave Georgia. Mike Langston, army elite ranger who'd never run from a fight in all his years in the military, was terrified of facing civilian life, of learning new rules. He was especially terrified of failing to keep a promise to a dead woman.

He opened his arms. "I'm sorry, too, baby." She fell into his arms and cried against his chest. He just held her, smoothing his hand down her hair, whispering nonsense sounds into her ear.

She muffled a laugh. "Daddy, I don't even know what you're saying."

"Me, neither. I guess it's the Langston version of a lullaby. But know that I love you, Carrie-belle, so we'll think this through. You and I will decide what's right for us together, and we don't have to decide tonight."

She nodded. "I love you, too," she said.

Suddenly he knew happiness. Not in the way a man was happy with the right woman, but the way a father could be if he learned to give a little, compromise and forgive.

Maybe, if he and Carrie decided to stay in Mount Union, he could hope for a bit of forgiveness from Brenna. He couldn't think of a reason why she should forgive him. He'd acted like a complete blockhead, but just maybe she would.

IN A TOWN the size of Mount Union, anonymity was practically impossible. A resident could plan on running into every person he knew in the short span of a week. Trusting in that, Mike decided to visit the supermarket each day after work in hopes of bumping into Brenna. Friday night at six o'clock, his persistence finally paid off.

After practically camping out at the store, he didn't need to shop for groceries, but he didn't want to look like a stalker. So with his small basket of milk he didn't need and vegetables he knew Carrie wouldn't want, he turned a corner and spied Brenna in the salad-dressing aisle. His heart quickened at the sight of her. She looked so darn good. She looked up immediately, saw him and locked onto his eyes with her intense gaze. He couldn't have looked away if he'd wanted to. And he didn't.

Until he saw that she wasn't alone.

He continued down the aisle, trying to figure out what stupid thing he could pretend to look for on the shelves. Inside he wanted to crawl artillery-fire style to the storeroom and escape out the back way.

"Mike." Her voice was soft and breathy, maybe even a little embarrassed.

"Oh, Brenna." He picked a bottle of soy sauce off the shelf and turned it slowly in his hand. "Good to see you. How have you been?"

"Fine." She nodded to the guy at her side. "You remember Alex, don't you?"

"Oh, sure," Alex said. "We've met a few

times. Once at the Riverview Tavern and again at the center Bren's been working on." Alex stuck his hand out. "Say, why weren't you at the opening of that place on Sunday? Bren told me you were a major contributor to the rehab project."

"I helped a little," Mike said. "I heard the opening went well."

"It did," Brenna said. "We missed you. People wanted to thank you for all your hard work. Everyone talked about how wonderful the building looked."

"Glad to hear it." He stood like a statue, hoping sparkling dialogue would come to him. He wanted to ask her if the teens were using the facility, if enrichment classes were starting to fill, if social activities were being planned. He wanted to be a part of the center's future, a part of Brenna's life. But he just stood there studying the ingredients in soy sauce as if he were going to go home and create a chef's masterpiece.

After a moment, Alex rescued the situation. "So how's it going?"

Better in some respects, miserable in others and right now really crummy. He said, "Great."

"I heard you might be moving back to California," Brenna said.

He tried to judge her reaction to the news by her tone of voice, but she didn't give anything away. "Carrie and I are looking at our options," he said. "We haven't decided anything for sure yet."

She smiled politely. "I see. Well, the football team and Bobby will feel the loss if you go."

Sure, but how about you? Will you feel any loss at all?

Mike forced himself to look somewhere other than Brenna's beautiful green eyes. That was when he noticed that her shopping cart was crammed full of food. Cans, frozen dinners, desserts, soda, beer. And more carbohydrates than Brenna would eat in a year. Did this mean Alex had moved into her place? Surely not. Only a few weeks had passed since Brenna had told him that the relationship had "fizzled." Besides, the golden-boy Alex wouldn't mar his perfectly fit body with all the stuff Brenna was buying.

"That's a lot of food," he said.

"Oh, I know. Most of this I don't even eat."

She pointed to the few items in the child seat of the cart. "The salad ingredients are for me."

"Then who…" He stared at Alex.

"Don't look at me. I'm strictly proteins. Steak and eggs."

"Are you supplying a homeless shelter?" Mike asked.

"No. Actually, I have houseguests."

Mike exhaled a long breath. Her guest couldn't be protein Alex, then. But who?

She cleared up the mystery. "Remember I told you about my parents, who live in South Carolina?"

"Sure, I remember." He also remembered the day she asked him to drive her home from the Riverview so she could raid her savings account to pay her father's hospital bill. "They're staying with you?"

"That's right. Going on two weeks now." She looked away briefly, probably recalling that Mike was aware of her parents' dependence on her. "It's okay," she said. "They ran into a bit of misfortune. There was my dad's leg, and my mom was tired. She needed help."

"How long are they staying?" he asked.

"I'm not sure. I suppose at least until they eat up this food."

Alex laughed. "That could take a year! You can appreciate my problem, Mike. I'm trying to get back on track with Bren, and her mom and dad are always hanging around. Tends to cramp a fella's style."

Brenna's face flushed. "We've got to go, Alex. I have ice cream in here."

Alex raised his hands in a gesture of mockery. "That's me, Alex the bag boy." He clapped Mike on the shoulder. "You take care, big guy."

"Yeah. You, too."

"Nice to see you, Mike," she said.

He watched them head to the checkout line and couldn't stop the smile that spread across his face. Brenna and Alex weren't back together, at least not officially. The plan he'd put in motion after Kraft gave him the information on the football field could move forward. Sunday. Mike would go over to her house in just two days and hopefully present her with something that would tell her how much he cared about her. Or maybe she'd end up never speaking to him again. Either way, he had to try.

CHAPTER NINETEEN

SUNDAY MORNING WAS quiet in Brenna's house, at least it would be until church let out and Alma returned. She had gotten up early, eaten a quick breakfast and left to realign with the Lord in her new environment. Brenna was fixing what her dad always wanted on Sundays—pancakes and bacon.

"Can you eat a couple more, Dad?" she asked him. "I still have batter left."

"Always room for another pancake," he said, patting his belly.

She heated more oil on the stove and gave the batter a quick stir.

"So what's with the guy who was here on Friday?" Carl asked. "Are you two serious?"

Brenna was still recovering from the double bombshell of opening her door to Alex on Friday afternoon. First, he hadn't called to tell her he was coming and, even after knowing him for months, she couldn't think of a thing to say to him. Second, since their split, she hadn't considered dating him again, and his suggestion that they try again was a surprise she didn't need. Her life was in turmoil already with Mike breaking up with her and her parents showing up. Brenna routinely enjoyed solitude, a comfortable daily schedule, and her normal existence had been blown to bits lately.

She poured mix into the heated oil. "No, Alex and I aren't serious, Dad. We used to date, but as far as I'm concerned, it ended weeks ago."

"I hope your mom and I didn't spoil a reunion," Carl said. "I heard that fella offer to get us a motel room, so I can only conclude that he wasn't happy to see us bunking with you."

There had been a time when Brenna would have appreciated Alex's offer to pay for her parents' accommodations at the nearby inn, but not anymore. She'd come to realize that her dysfunctional relationship with Carl and Alma wasn't just her parents' fault. The family's problems couldn't be solved by avoiding them. Oddly, she was getting used to having them around. She could almost say they were different people when away from the despair of their day-to-day lives.

She flipped the pancakes. "It doesn't matter, Dad. I don't think he'll be back."

"I'm sorry, Brenna May. He seemed like a nice enough sort."

Right. In the span of sixty seconds, Alex and her father had demonstrated that they had nothing in common. Even more significant to Brenna, Mike and Alex were opposites as well, and despite her former priorities, she much preferred Mike's qualities over Alex's. She'd had time to think about the awkward meeting at the supermarket. Did Mike think she and Alex had become a couple again? Did he even care?

She brought the skillet to the table and slid the last pancakes onto her father's plate. This situation with her parents would have to be resolved somehow. They couldn't stay with her indefinitely. They would have to go home, or start over, or find their own way without viewing their daughter as a financial safety net. But for now, they had inadvertently helped Brenna by being a buffer between her and Alex.

Brenna believed Alex was gone for good.

Once he'd seen her background firsthand, he'd been content to run off into the world he was accustomed to. She smiled thinking of the consequences of a meeting between her parents and Alex's parents. Although such an event would have provided a few chuckles, basically it would have been a disaster. Thank goodness the two families weren't ever likely to meet, not now.

She'd always hoped that Alex's success, his admirable bank account, would be the solution she needed to cut herself off from those pitiful beginnings in South Carolina. She'd wanted a husband who could guarantee that she'd never have to go back to that life again. Now, as she sipped her coffee and watched her father devour the simple meal she'd prepared for him, she knew that South Carolina was part of who she was and arguably the main reason she'd accomplished what she had in her life. And it was her accomplishments that would continue to guarantee her freedom from her South Carolina past.

You don't need a man to make your way on your own terms, Brenna. But then she thought of Mike, and she knew there was one man she needed for entirely different reasons, ones that warmed her heart, not strengthened her security net. Unfortunately, she would have to learn to live without the man who'd taught her that.

For now she had to look to the future as a single woman and a teacher. She couldn't live with her parents; that would never work, not for any of them. But finally, after all this time, she could accept them for the people they were. Flawed but loving in their way. She would continue to help them financially when she was able, learn to say no and commiserate with their problems when she couldn't help.

"Yoo-hoo! I'm home."

Brenna automatically put the teakettle on again. Her mother liked a caffeine pick-me-up in the middle of the morning. "In here, Mom."

Alma, wearing her best black pants and a silk print blouse, her hair pulled back in a neat bun, strode into the kitchen. "Oh, thank you, darlin', for making Dad his breakfast."

Brenna put a mug on the table. "No problem."

Her mother got a tea bag from the cupboard and sat down. "I swear, Brenna, you are spoiling us. We'll never go home if you keep treating us like this!" She stared at Brenna's expression and burst into laughter. "I'm kidding, right, Carl? We won't overstay our welcome. But what a treat this has been for me especially."

Brenna poured hot water into the mug. "So have you made plans to go home, Mom?"

"I said two weeks, didn't I? That means we'll get on the road by Friday." She passed a sorrowful glance at her husband. "Can't leave that trailer too long. Who knows how many leaks we'll find in the roof after being gone all this time. The weather girl said we've had some powerful storms up our way, and I've got to get someone to fix the front steps."

"I'll fix 'em, Alma," Carl said. "I get this dang cast off on Monday next."

Alma took a sip of tea. "It'll be nice to have my man back around the house."

And nice to have my house back, Brenna thought. She would survive a few more days with her uninvited guests—and she would even be left with a few good memories of their two-week stay—but peace and quiet and a chance to reflect over the changes in her life lately couldn't be overrated.

Brenna sighed and fixed a mug of tea for herself. Truthfully, sometimes her perfect little house felt lonely. Not that she wanted to fill spare rooms with her parents, but she could think of two people who would bring a special warmth and comfort into her world. But Mike would probably never forgive her for interfering or forgive himself for listening to her advice. Besides, if he and his daughter were going back to California anyway, then all the forgiveness in the world wouldn't result in a future she wanted.

By midafternoon, Brenna had put a pot roast in the oven. Her father was snoring on the sofa and her mother was watching a rerun of an eighties sitcom. Brenna decided to take a book into her backyard, sit by the river and lose herself in someone else's problems.

She'd just opened the back door when her mother called from the front room, "You got company, Brenna!"

Certain the visitor wasn't Alex but unable to guess who would be stopping by on Sunday afternoon, Brenna set the book on the kitchen counter and went into the living room. It was a nice day, so her front door was open, letting in a fresh fall breeze and an image that made Brenna's heart pound. Mike Langston, wearing jeans that hugged those muscular long legs and a short-sleeved tan sweater, stood on her porch, an uncertain expression on his face.

He raised his hand. "Hey."

"Hi." She hurried to the door. "Is something wrong? Is Carrie okay?"

"She's fine. Show her you're fine, Carrie."

The girl stepped into Brenna's view. "Hi, Miss Sullivan."

"Hello. Well, then why…" She paused when she saw another person behind Mike, someone she didn't recognize. He was a big young man, his curly black hair close-cropped to his head, and his deep bronze skin glowing with health. He was built like a football player, but Brenna couldn't place him on the Ravens team.

"What's going on, Mike?" she asked.

He stepped aside so the young man could get closer to the door. The man grinned, nodded at her and said, "How you doing, Miss Sullivan?"

"I'm fine. Do I know…" She paused. Her heart thumped against her rib cage as she fought to draw a breath. Those eyes, those deep-set, soulful, dark brown eyes that once belonged to a child in need now grounded the face of a sturdy man.

His grin widened and she knew without a doubt. She covered her mouth to trap a sob. Her eyes stung. She was totally helpless and completely in awe, as if a miracle had just entered her life. And maybe it had. "Marcus, is it you?"

"Yes, ma'am, it's me, all right."

She pushed open her screen door and stepped outside. "Oh, wow. Marcus, you look wonderful! I never thought I would see you again. I came to the hospital, but..." Her voice hitched. She swallowed hard and finally managed to say, "Can I hug you?"

"Yes, ma'am, that's what I came for."

She had to stand on her toes to wrap her arms around the shoulders of the young man whose life she thought she had ruined. He was solid and strong and healthy, and her heart soared. "How are you? Are you well?"

He backed away a few feet so she could look him over and proudly spread his arms. "You can see I am. And it's all thanks to you."

"Me? No, I didn't..." There was a story here, one she was dying to hear. She held the door open wide. "Come in, all of you. We have to catch up."

Mike, Carrie and Marcus traipsed inside and stopped short when they saw she had company. Alma had lowered the volume on the TV, and Carl was rubbing his eyes.

"Are we interrupting?" Mike asked.

"No, not at all. These are my parents, Alma and Carl. Mom, Dad, I want you to meet…" She stopped. How would she introduce Mike? Clearing her throat, she said, "Carrie is one of my students. And this is her father, one of our football coaches. And this…" She still couldn't believe what she was seeing. This sweet little boy whom she'd last seen struggling to heal in a hospital bed was in her living room. "This is Marcus Johnson, a former student."

Alma smiled and nodded. Carl reached for his crutches.

"Don't get up," Mike said, and Brenna's dad settled back against the couch cushions with obvious relief.

"Have a seat, everyone," Brenna said, her gaze darting between the two faces of the men who had most affected her life, one so long ago, one so recently. "Tell me how this happened. Marcus, how did you know where I lived? And do you know I've thought about you every day since…"

The young man chuckled, took a seat in one of the chairs flanking Brenna's fireplace and glanced at Mike. "Coach here found me, Miss Sullivan."

"He did?"

"And I'm glad of it. I've wanted to thank you."

"Thank me?" She drew an ottoman close to his chair so she could be near him. "Whatever for?"

"I expect you saved my life. If you hadn't called in Child Protective Services on my dad, I doubt I would be here today."

"But that phone call," she said. "It didn't accomplish what I wanted it to. In fact, all I did was anger your father so much that you ended up in the hospital."

"If that hadn't angered him, something else would have," Marcus said. "What you really did, Miss Sullivan, is you showed you cared enough about me to take a stand."

"Oh, Marcus, but you were so hurt."

"Physical pain heals, ma'am," he said. "And because some good doctors and nurses helped me, mine did. Eventually I would have out-weighed and outpunched my dad, but if I'd stayed with him, I would have suffered other kinds of pain that would have stayed with me forever. You stopped that from happening. You brought attention to what was going on in our house. Because of you, my brother and I got out of that situation. No one else had ever done anything before. No one else had even noticed."

She looked from Marcus to Mike and felt a slow, curling heat spread outward from her core. Mike's brown eyes practically twinkled. He was happy for her. She smiled back at him, mouthed the words *Thank you* and took Marcus's hand. "Is this really how you see what happened to you? As almost a blessing?"

"Not *almost,* Miss Sullivan. A true blessing. I wish I had known you'd come to the hospital that day, but I didn't know much about anything for a while. I would have told you thanks then. Even lying in that bed, I knew I was facing a way out, and I was glad. Just had to take some time and patience."

Tears tore at the back of her throat and burned in her eyes, but she couldn't dissolve now. Not without hearing it all. "What happened to you after you were released?" she asked. "Did you go back to the same school?"

"No. Social Services found me a foster home in another district. My brother went to a home in the same area so we got to see each other every day on the bus." He pulled his wallet out of his back pocket and flipped it open. "This is Darius, my little brother."

The sound that came from Brenna's throat was half laughter, half sob. "*Little?* He's almost as big as you, Marcus."

Marcus chuckled. "Yeah, he's on the junior varsity football team. Might end up at college like I'm going to."

"Really? You're going to college?"

"I've got a few colleges scouting me out," he said with pride. "I'll be playing defensive end."

"And your foster parents? Have you stayed with them?"

"The whole way through school. Still there now for my senior year. Mr. and Mrs. B. are good people." His smile seemed to light up the room as he grinned at Brenna. "But none of it would have happened if you hadn't stepped in."

These past four years she'd moved, changed jobs, avoided going back to her hometown just as she'd avoided getting involved in her students' lives. She'd opted for a complete change and adjusted to a life of noninterference, telling herself that was best, the safest way to protect her fragile emotions. But always something had been missing. A connection, a caring, as she forced herself to see her students as young learning machines and nothing more.

But today a huge weight had been lifted from her shoulders. She hadn't been wrong when she reached out to Marcus and reported his father's abuse. True, his story could have turned out differently, but he convinced her today that her actions had been brave and life-altering. So often in life we take chances with our decisions. Sometimes we overanalyze. Is this the right thing to do? What could be the negative consequences of this action? When, in truth, most people have a built-in compass that keeps them on the right track. And now she knew that she had followed the right track with regard to Marcus.

She placed her hand over her heart, where the beat was strong and sure. She'd followed the instincts of her heart that day. She'd followed them with regard to Carrie, too. Even if she'd lost Mike, she had no regrets.

Her tears swelled. She sniffed and said, "I'll get us some lemonade. You all just relax…" She couldn't say any more without blubbering all over herself. She turned and walked briskly to the kitchen.

She heard her mother's voice. "I should go be with her."

"I'll go," Mike said. "I think I know what she needs right now."

She heard his soft footfalls as he came up behind her. Then his strong, gentle hands were on her shoulders, where she'd so often imagined them these past lonely weeks.

"Brenna." His lips were against her ear, and the sweet tremor of her name resonated through her body. "Are you okay? I hope I didn't do something wrong in bringing Marcus here."

Something wrong? He'd done exactly the most perfect, the most *right* thing anyone had ever done for her in her life. "H-how did you find him? I never gave you his full name."

"No, but you gave me enough, and I called

in a favor from Bill Kraft. All those low-paying coaching hours he got from me paid off."

She turned and he lowered his hands to her arms. "What exactly did you ask Bill to do?"

"I told him I was looking for a former student of yours, a kid who'd been in the hospital. I made him swear not to tell anyone, and I don't think he did, but he got the info."

"He talked to Marcus himself?"

"No. I didn't give him permission to go that far. Once I got the kid's name and foster parents' address I contacted him and the rest is history." He smiled down at her. "And for what it's worth, Brenna, the boy is telling you the truth. He was over the moon to hear about you. He'd been thinking of you, but didn't even know till much later that you'd visited him in the hospital. After that, he just thought he'd disappointed you."

A sob burned in her throat. "Oh, how could he think that?"

Mike chuckled. "Kids, huh? There's no figuring them out."

She wanted to laugh and cry at the same time. Mostly she wanted to reach out and hold on to Mike Langston with all her strength.

But did he want her to do that? Was he reaching out to her as a friend only as she'd reached out to him so many times? Was this a last gesture of kindness before he left town? Or was he knocking down the walls that had separated them since the auto accident?

She swallowed, stared hard into his eyes. "Why did you do this for me?"

His hands cupped her face. "Don't you know I would do anything for you? Granted, it takes a symbolic chunk of concrete to fall on my head to make me realize it, but I would."

She smiled. "And what was that chunk of concrete?"

"Two things, really. You won't believe this, but my daughter pointed out a few flaws in my character, which got me to thinking, both about those flaws and about the good qualities that you seem to have in abundance. And seeing you with Alex again. That tore me up, Brenna."

Her cheeks flushed with heat under his palms. "You were jealous?"

"I guess I was."

"Oh, I like that," she said. Could this mean…

She had to ask. "So you chose this way to say goodbye before you move to California?"

"Well, maybe it would have been...if I were moving. But since I'm not, I won't be saying goodbye at all."

"You're staying?" All at once, none of the rest of it mattered. Her parents could stay as long as they wanted. Her possessions could be swept away in a tornado. She could sit through every football game like a die-hard fan.

His grin warmed her deep inside where happiness grew. "I am. There are people here I just can't bear to leave. Pretty teachers, one nosy woman in particular who opened my eyes to a lot of things I'd been blind to." She absolutely adored this side of Mike. The humorous light in his eyes, the odd quirk to his lips. This was teasing Mike, a man who had learned to look forward with confidence and hope.

"Of course, I can't make a decision like this without clearing up a few details.

"What exactly are those details?" she asked.

"Let's see now." He released her long enough to count on his fingers. "Got to raise a kid amid all these solid Georgia values. Got to help get that football team in shape for another year. Got to get a college education so I can teach down the hall from you and smell all those delicious recipes your students make. And last—" he held up his little finger for emphasis "—got to make some major improvements in Granny's old place."

"I thought you liked simple and homey," she said.

"I do, but I have a couple of women in my life who require a bit more fanciness than an old log cabin provides."

"A *couple* of women?"

"That's right. The younger one, she has to live in that cabin, no matter what it looks like. But the other one, now she's got options."

Brenna smiled. "You mean there's an old, opinionated, stuck-up one?"

"I'd call her intelligent, determined, ambitious and beautiful."

Brenna hadn't played coy in many years but she did so now. She actually tried batting her eyelashes. "I like the sound of her. Would you repeat those words one more time?"

He leaned over and kissed her. "Intelligent, determined, ambitious and beautiful. And I plan on repeating them for a long time to come. But I need you to add 'forgiving' to the list. Will you forgive me for general lunk-headedness, Brenna? And will you say that you won't quit trying to find the soft spots in this rock-hard brain of mine?"

She settled in next to his firm, comfortable body and relished the feel of his arms around her. "It will be my pleasure to keep trying because I've long suspected that you have just as many soft spots as you do hard ones."

"Brenna, you okay in there?" Her mother's voice penetrated the closed door, and Mike stepped back.

"I'm fine, Mama. Coming out with that lemonade."

"Oh, right," Mike said. "I'd forgotten your parents were here. How's that working out for you?"

"Not too bad, really. I think I've come to understand them better in my house than I ever did in theirs."

"Glad to hear it. But if you need a break from family matters, I know where there's this soon-to-be improved cabin outside of town. The people and dog who live in it would love to have you come by and stay a few decades."

"Brenna? Do you need any help?"

"No, Mama. I'm coming." She stroked her finger down the side of Mike's face. "I'd be delighted. But for now I guess we're done here."

The smile he gave her seemed to have been made for this moment. "Honey, I'm just getting started.

EPILOGUE

Two months later, on December 24, in the Mount Union Cultural Arts Center, Brenna and Mike walked down a satin-draped aisle bordered with hundreds of twinkling white lights. Poinsettias in large baskets decorated each row of chairs. The classroom partitions had been removed so a pair of Christmas trees would be the singular focus of the holiday event, not counting the true stars of the show, the bride and groom.

When the students of Mount Union High volunteered to pull off this ceremony on Christmas Eve, Brenna and Mike were only too happy to let them take charge. All they asked was that the wedding be kept to a minimum number of guests. In attendance were the staff of the high school, some members of the Ravens football team, students from Brenna's classes and the mechanics from Alvin's Garage. Bobby Montgomery was best man with his son, Charlie, acting as usher. Diana Montgomery was matron of honor, and Carrie and Sandy were bridesmaids.

Brenna, wearing a flowing white gown and carrying a bouquet of red and white chrysanthemums, was walked down the aisle by her father. Carl Sullivan's recovery had gone very well, and his stride was sure and proud as he gave his daughter to the man she loved with all her heart.

Alma cried softly as the vows were repeated, though inside her head she was probably wondering if all her preparations were complete for the reception she had planned at Brenna's cottage immediately following the ceremony. Alma and Carl had a special pride in the cottage because they had been living there full-time for two weeks to help with wedding preparations. Knowing they would never be content in the single-wide trailer again, and spurred on by a practical yet optimistic belief in their future, they'd decided to sell the old place and move to Mount Union.

They insisted on paying a modest rent to their daughter for her house and began furnishing the bungalow with practical, durable pieces they purchased secondhand with Carl's salary from his part-time job as maintenance engineer for the center. The couple enjoyed a comfortable existence living on Carl's paycheck and his Social Security benefits. Alma even promised to run the air conditioner when it got hot outside again.

At the end of the ceremony, Mike couldn't wait to get his bride alone, so he accepted the congratulations of his new friends, waited until the two of them weren't surrounded by well-wishers and grabbed his wife's hand. With his finger to his lips to keep Brenna from squealing her surprise, he ushered her into the room where she'd dressed for the wedding.

"What are we doing in here?" she said when they were alone in the soft light of a single lamp.

The cool December air coming in a partially open window washed over her bare arms and flirted with the auburn waves brushing her shoulders. She looked up into his dear face and laughed out loud. "Do you want your wife to catch cold? That's a great way to start a honeymoon."

"I promise to keep you warm. Today and always." He proved his intent by putting his arm around her and pulling her to his chest. Her waist-length veil fluttered around them like a halo. Brenna had never felt more protected, more loved. How could this man have ever thought that he wasn't protector enough?

"The new dining room set arrived today, and you're right. It looks nice with the things you moved in from your place. And I put the tree up," he said. "I found the perfect one in the woods and planted it in a galvanized tub like you wanted me to. We can dig a hole for it in front of the house after New Year's and watch it grow for years to come."

"I can't wait to see it…tonight," she said. "Did you decorate it?"

"Mostly Carrie and Charlie did, but I supervised."

"We'll have the tree all to ourselves," Brenna said. "Thank goodness Carrie is excited about staying with my parents for the evening."

"We'll be completely and utterly alone in Grandma's old cabin tonight," Mike said. "We can do whatever we want. Watch grown-up movies, play Scrabble, you name it."

She grinned. "Yeah, that's exactly what I

want to do." He lowered his head and kissed her thoroughly.

"We'd better go back with our guests," she said. "They'll be sending out a search party."

"Okay. But before we go in…"

"Yes?"

"I want to clear something up. In case you think I'm a man who has a hard time keeping his promises, I want to set the record straight."

"Okay."

"From now on, Brenna Langston, I promise to keep you warm and safe. And I promise to love you and thank fate every day that you came into my life when you did."

He smiled the full, satisfied smile of a happy man. "And if we do have a baby in the future, I promise I won't interfere with your parenting skills—much."

* * * * *

LARGER-PRINT BOOKS!

GET 2 FREE
LARGER-PRINT NOVELS
PLUS 2 FREE
MYSTERY GIFTS

Love Inspired®

Larger-print novels are now available...

LILPDIR13R

Reader Service.com

Manage your account online!

- Review your order history
- Manage your payments
- Update your address

> *We've designed
> the Harlequin® Reader Service
> website just for you.*

Enjoy all the features!

- Reader excerpts from any series
- Respond to mailings and
  special monthly offers
- Discover new series available to you
- Browse the Bonus Bucks catalog
- Share your feedback

Visit us at:

ReaderService.com